FRED II

Timeless Tenant Tales
Buffalo West Side Stories

A Novel by

Frances R. Schmidt

and

James A. Costa

CCB Publishing
British Columbia, Canada

FRED II Timeless Tenant Tales: Buffalo West Side Stories

Copyright ©2025 by Frances R. Schmidt
ISBN-13 978-1-77143-627-4
First Edition

Library and Archives Canada Cataloguing in Publication
Title: Fred II timeless tenant tales: Buffalo west side stories /
by Frances R. Schmidt and James A. Costa.
Names: Schmidt, Frances R., Costa, James A., 1931-,
ISBN 978-1-77143-627-4 (pbk) – ISBN 978-1-77143-628-1 (PDF)
Additional cataloguing data available from Library and Archives Canada

Cover artwork: Cover design and illustration by Emily Starkweather.

Publisher: CCB Publishing
             British Columbia, Canada
             www.ccbpublishing.com

This novel is dedicated to
my daughter, Jennifer; my son, Dennis, Jr.;
my late husband, Dennis;
and to my special Schmidt family.

Introduction

Some of you may remember me from my previous book, *FRED: Buffalo Building of Dreams.* Others should know I am a four-story building over a century old, located on the corner of Niagara Street and Potomac Avenue on Buffalo's West Side.

Although I'm an inanimate object, I've been personified in a manner I can't explain. As you may already know, I'm aware of all that happens within my weathered brick-and-mortar exterior. The windows are my eyes and the walls my ears. Over the years I have acquired most of the emotions humans possess. I can even identify the ethnicity of my tenants, not only by their names and accents, but by the odors of cabbage, garlic and various sauces wafting from their kitchens into my halls. I lack only the power of locomotion and audible speech.

My first book was an historical novel dealing with families newly arrived in our country. They were difficult times for virtually everyone. Jobs were scarce and government assistance almost nonexistent. Those who had families sponsoring them were most fortunate. Many others, however, had to depend upon their own resourcefulness to survive. Those tales were centered primarily on the history and struggle of families occupying my premises shortly before and into the early years of the Twentieth Century.

Now I'd like to relate several stories of families who lived here about the time of the outbreak of WWII in 1941. Over the intervening decades since the end of WWI in 1918, many things changed. Fueled by the passage of the Prohibition amendment in 1919, the 1920s ushered in a decade of crime and corruption, as well as prosperity and technological progress. It ended with the crash of the stock market in 1929, and marked the beginning of the Great Depression of the 1930s. Only the creation of Social Security and Public Welfare programs helped people through those dark years. The onset of WWII, however, put the Depression behind us and brought a measure of prosperity to most people willing and able to work. As the saying goes, 'Times, they were a changing.'

As I intimated earlier, I've seen and heard thousands of conversations within my skin of bricks. Over those first forty years I have learned that humans are a complex and unpredictable species, and because my tenants come from all walks of life, I've observed the best and worst in them. I've marveled at the generosity and kindness of some, and despaired at the depths of cruelty and wickedness of others. Because of this dichotomy in human nature, I've been glad I wasn't one of them as often as I've wished I were.

I try to stay uninvolved in their petty squabbles and everyday lives, but when I hear something that especially upsets me, I can make myself heard by rattling my plumbing, squeaking my floorboards and popping my internal timbers like old bones. My tenants attribute the sounds to changing temperatures and my old age. Those with more active imaginations swear they're hearing ghosts haunting my passageways.

No one has ever guessed I'm a living being of sorts. I may not have a soul, but in an inexplicable way, I do have a heart. I suppose it happened over time from hearing and seeing so many sad stories. To the casual observer, I may be only a pile of bricks and mortar, wood and glass. But those who think deeply recognize I have character and have stood proudly for well over a century protecting my tenants from the ravages of frigid Buffalo winters and occasional scorching summer days.

In a sense my tenants have become my children. Together we're a family. I've been there for them through the best and worst of times. Like all families, each has experienced its joys and sorrows, and each has a story to tell. If you would indulge me, I'd like to relate several to you. In most cases, I will let you hear them in their own words, exactly as I heard them. Sometimes I make assumptions based on my experiences over the years and what I hope are intelligent guesses. Occasionally, I may be wrong, but I will always admit it when I am.

I've chosen the years right before and after WWII because of the rapid economic and cultural upheavals taking place in our country during that time. Heaven knows, the glittering Flapper Age of the 1920s and the quiet despair of the Great Depression that followed provided me with enough stories to last a lifetime. However, despite the horrors of war, a new dawn was breaking. Jobs were being created overnight and money started flowing into people's pockets. A sense of optimism and hope pervaded the country. Great changes were underway, but prosperity for most people still lay ahead.

I should mention here that by the time WWII broke out, I had learned a great deal about the English language. At first it was difficult because so many of my tenants were immigrants— most of them from Europe— who spoke broken, if any, English. Not until the 1920s, when Miss Alice Wagman and her widowed sister Agnes moved in together, did I begin to learn proper English. A long-time librarian at the Buffalo Public Library, Alice Wagman was constantly correcting her sister Agnes's speech. She called her sister an embarrassment and took every opportunity to correct her whenever she made a grammatical error. Although Agnes resented this treatment, I profited greatly from it. The first thing I learned was to never say 'ain't.' I also learned the difference between 'who' and 'whom' and 'lie' and 'lay.' I even developed a sizable vocabulary. Miss Wagman hated the word 'maybe.' She said it was a word used by the uneducated, and insisted Agnes say 'perhaps,' instead. I have never forgotten that.

Wander through my passageways with me today, and you will feel the haunting grip of nostalgia, and whiff the scent of past decades metabolized in my wooden floors, doors, and the laths buried behind my plaster walls.

Join me now as I relate the first of my tales.

Chapter 1

You may recall from my earlier book that, in 1938, Anna and Bianca, two of my tenants, moved in at the same time and became close friends. Anna was forty-one, and Bianca, born in 1917, was twenty years her junior. Originally from New London, Connecticut, Anna moved to Potsdam, N.Y., where she worked as a waitress for years before enrolling in college, ultimately graduating with a B.A. degree. Weary of finding only part-time teaching positions there, she decided to move here to Buffalo, New York, where she hoped to land a permanent job and to be near an ailing aunt, who, unfortunately, died shortly after Anna arrived. Anna and Bianca became quite close, eventually forming almost a mother-daughter relationship. Bianca had already fallen in love with Benedict, a young man who lived across the street.

When Bianca and Anna were better acquainted, Anna confided to her that more than twenty years earlier, her husband, Jack, had been killed in WWI a year after they'd been married. Six months later, she said she suffered a miscarriage.

Sitting at Anna's kitchen table, Bianca listened sympathetically. "I'm so sorry, Anna. It must have been terrible."

Anna reached across and covered Bianca's hand with her own. "It was a long time ago, Bianca. Time heals. It doesn't

1

hurt so much anymore." She rose to pour another cup of tea. "So, tell me…" she said, cheerfully as she could, "…how are you and your boyfriend, Benedict, getting on. I haven't seen him in a while."

Bianca brightened at the mention of his name. "Oh, Benny? He's been busy working overtime. We're trying to save as much money as possible before we get married. We'll need furniture and other things."

"Have you set a date?"

"Not yet, Anna, but you'll be the first to know."

After Bianca left, Anna picked up her cup of tea and padded over a thick, shag carpet into her small living room. I liked the way she decorated it with table lamps, stained-glass shades, a maroon-cushioned couch with colorful throw pillows and a large, print Afghan she often used to cover and warm her legs when she felt a chill in the air. The walls reflected a soft, pink glow around the room, creating a cozy atmosphere.

I watched her sip her tea, then put her head back and close her eyes. She stayed that way a long while before setting her cup aside and getting up. She opened her closet door, took a Thom McAn shoe box from the shelf and sat down again with it on her lap. When she lifted the cover, I could see the box was filled with photographs. She took one out and spoke to it:

"Jack. Jack, can you hear my voice, my darling? It's been more than twenty years since I heard yours. I told Bianca that being without you doesn't hurt as much anymore. But it does, my darling. It never stops hurting. It never will. I told Bianca we were married and that you died in the war. It wasn't true. Nothing I told her was true. They were all lies. I was ashamed of the truth. Please forgive me, Jack." She kissed his picture.

From my windowed vantage point, I could see a smiling young man with deep dimples framing his mouth. His eyes looked very much alive and seemed to smile. I noticed Anna's eyes glisten as she kissed his picture again.

"It seems like yesterday, a hundred years ago, since you held me in your arms, comforting me, telling me you still loved me, despite what you found out. You had every right to leave me, but you didn't. I betrayed you and you forgave me." She picked out another picture.

"Remember this one, Jack? You took me ice skating down on Brimmer's Pond shortly after we met. My ankles kept turning in and I had to cling to you to keep from falling. Later you said you brought me there on purpose because you knew it would happen. That was pretty sneaky, Jack. Remember how we both laughed about it afterwards?"

She picked out another picture. "How about this one, Jack? See your arm hugging me and your cheek next to mine? I can still smell your aftershave lotion, Jack, a fresh, clean pine smell. Whenever I sniffed that fragrance, I knew you were near. Oh, Jack, there's so much to remember and so much to regret."

She dropped the picture on her lap and laid her head back again, whispering to herself as she relived moments of her life, but I could hear every word falling from her barely moving lips.

Her brow wrinkled. "I hurt you, Jack, so cruelly, yet you were willing to forgive me. I still suffer the pain I inflicted on you. It never goes away, Jack. Never. I've been to church and prayed to God. I've spoken to Father O'Brien at St. Lucy's church. I remember him asking me, "Ahna..." (He always pronounced my name that way) "...Ahna," he said, "if you truly loved Jack, how could you hurt him so?"

I couldn't answer because of my shame. Father said we're mysterious creatures who often do things to ourselves that we know will hurt us. Yet we persist. He said the ancient Greeks understood personal guilt and personified it as the Furies, mythological divinities who punish us. He said forgiving ourselves is harder than forgiving our enemies and that Holy Confession may be God's solution to my problem. I did confess, but it didn't help. After all these years I still don't understand it, Jack. I probably never will.

I watched Anna as she lay gazing up to the ceiling. She was silent for a while, then seemed to slowly brighten. She spoke aloud.

"That article in the newspaper last week, I remember now… the psychologist who said some studies show that people who are depressed often find relief in writing down their experiences and feelings. He said many of them find writing poetry to be helpful, and that such activities occasionally lead to a catharsis, a big word meaning a 'sudden release of tension and anxiety.'"

Anna rose and crossed over to her writing desk by the window. It was perfect for me. The strong light streaming in made it possible for me to read every word she began putting on paper.

Dear Diary,

I was 15 years old when I first met Jack Newcomb. He was a senior at our high school, and it flattered me to think that a senior, a handsome football hero, no less, could possibly be interested in a lowly sophomore like me. It was a bright spring day. I was sitting in the bleachers beside the athletic field and remember looking away from our track team up into the blue sky, watching a flock of quacking ducks flying overhead, their flapping wings winking at me as they caught the light.

"Is this yours?"

Startled, I looked to the side and there he was—I'll never forget it—my first ever image of Jack, standing there looking so muscular in his football uniform, and handsome, with a big smile and deep voice.

"It was on the ground near you," he said, handing me my compact.

Flustered, I thanked him as I took it. "It must have slipped out of my pocket."

"It's OK," he said, looking into my eyes so intensely I had to turn away. "I just happened to spot it here on my way into the building to clean up and change. We just finished scrimmaging."

"I know, I was watching for a while," I lied, trying to sound interested.

He slapped some dust off his uniform. "My name's Jack, Jack Newcomb. What's yours?"

"I'm Anna Good."

"Anna Good. That's not a bad name. Get it?" He laughed. "Pleased to meetcha, Anna Good," he said, taking my hand and shaking it vigorously.

"Same here," I said, pulling my hand out of his tight grip.

He began turning away then stopped. "Say, Anna, do you like milk shakes?"

He caught me off guard. "I s'pose so. Doesn't everybody?" I mumbled.

"Yeah, dumb question. Well, look, after I'm freshened up I'm stopping for one at Scheck's drug store. Maybe two or three. I'm pretty thirsty. You want to join me? My treat."

I hardly knew what to say.

"If the answer's no, it's OK." He started to turn away again.

"No, no, I was just wondering if I have enough time. I told my friend, Molly…" I looked at my watch. "How long before you're finished?"

"Twenty minutes, tops."

"All right. Where should I meet you?"

"The front of the building. I'll be out in a flash," he said, breaking into a jog.

And that's how it began. A short time later we started dating regularly. Jack was warm and considerate in every way, what they call a true gentleman. I had been warned to be wary of senior boys, especially those who were 'fast' and who 'ran the school,' as they say. Jack never tried anything with me, though, not ever. Once, his hand accidentally slipped near my breast. He almost fell over himself, apologizing. Actually, it was all I could do to keep from laughing, seeing his face all red and sweating for almost an hour.

About a month later, right after seeing a Mack Sennett comedy that put us in a good mood, we took a long, slow walk along the street, holding hands, laughing and enjoying each other's company. Afterwards we stopped at Avery's candy and soda shop for a Coke and a chocolate milkshake (Jack loved his chocolate milkshakes). When he slurped the last of his down, we wandered over to Brook's farm and plopped ourselves on one of his haystacks. It was a warm, sunny day and the air smelled fresh and clean. After a few minutes Jack reached into his pocket.

"Anna," he said, looking straight into my eyes, "will you be my steady?"

At first I was stunned and could hardly speak. When I found my voice, I said, "Yes, Jack, I will."

Of course, I was thrilled to death as I watched him take my

hand gently and slip the ring on my pinky finger. Then he pulled me into in his arms and pressed his lips to mine. Breathless, I squeezed him close to me. Slowly, he eased me back, kissing me in a way I had never been kissed. I never wanted to let go. Although no one was around, we spoke in whispers, making promises we meant to keep forever.

We were inseparable after that and went everywhere together, like to the ballpark and the movies. Everyone called me 'Jack's girl,' and I loved hearing it. Some girls, mostly seniors, were jealous. I could tell by their narrow eyes and fake smiles they didn't like me. Whenever we ran into them, I made the situation worse by snuggling up to Jack's arm and looking innocent as can be. That made them hate me even more, but I don't think Jack ever realized the drama taking place before his very eyes.

I don't know exactly when it happened, but I know it wasn't sudden. It had to be over a period of months. Jack seemed to change. He was less and less inclined to go places anymore.

"Anna, I'm tired. Why don't we just sit on the porch swing and relax."

"Jack, there's a concert in the town park. Can't we go there for a while?"

"If you want to go, Anna, go 'head. I want to take it easy for a bit."

And such is the way it was, with Jack gradually turning into a stick in the mud. I wanted to do things, like go to the beach or the movies or for a hike in the hills, but he was always too tired, or not interested. All he wanted to do was sit around and talk, mostly about sports. Half the time, though, he didn't even want to talk about that.

Jack was acting like an old man. Although I was disappointed, I still loved him. We talked about getting engaged soon. I only hoped he'd get his old spirit back and show some enthusiasm for life. I was beginning to think he wasn't interested in me anymore and wished we would break up, but didn't have the heart to do it himself. He was still his sweet self and always treated me with respect.

I finally figured out that Jack wasn't really the outgoing type I thought he was. When I brought it up to him, he admitted I was right. His cheerfulness in front of others was all an act. He said he was comfortable only with me, not with other people. Of course, I was flattered to hear it; nevertheless, I wasn't happy. I wanted us to go places, to be with other couples, do things and have fun together. But Jack didn't want any part of that. We went on that way for quite a while, with me entreating him, and him going along with me occasionally, but always reluctantly. Frankly, Jack was becoming boring. Very boring. And I was becoming restless. Very restless.

I had recently turned seventeen and, as if things weren't bad enough, our lives took a turn for the worse. I was just sitting down for lunch one afternoon when his mother called:

"Anna? Anna, I have some bad news," she said, her voice cracking.

"Not too serious," I said, hoping she'd say it wasn't.

"Jack's in the hospital? I'm here with him now."

Alarmed, afraid to hear what was coming, I asked, "Why? What happened?"

"He broke his neck."

"Oh, my God!"

"Don't panic, Anna. The doctors said he'll be immobilized for several weeks, possibly a couple of months, but the good news is that they don't think he'll be permanently paralyzed."

"Where is he, Mrs. Newcomb. Where are you now?"

"I'm at the Emergency Hospital."

Jack's mother said Jack had gone to a local gymnasium called the Turnverein for his daily workout. Afterwards he went for a swim in the pool, as he usually did, only this time when trying a new dive, he hit his head on the bottom.

Feeling sick to my stomach, I rushed to the hospital as quickly as I could and took the elevator up to Jack's floor. Mrs. Newcomb was sitting in a chair next to his bed with her handkerchief pressed to her nose. She started to cry openly when she saw me coming into the room.

"How is he?" I asked, stepping in close to his bed.

She shook her head.

Jack looked pathetic, with his sad eyes gazing up to me. I reached down and touched his hand.

"Your mother told me what happened, Jack. You had a freak accident, that's all, but the good news is you're going to come out of this a new man. It'll take a little while, Jack, but that's OK. We just have to be patient."

The gentle way he squeezed my hand and smiled at me broke my heart. I felt guilty for the thoughts I'd been having about him. I didn't like myself very much at that moment.

After the first two days Jack's mother no longer came by herself in the morning because her knee pain made walking difficult. Instead, she waited until Jack's brother, Norman, came home from work to bring her later in the afternoon.

Several days passed, with both of us professing our love and discussing plans for our engagement and future marriage. Our conversations lifted our spirits and made the time pass more quickly.

About a week later I was sitting in the waiting room while the nurse gave Jack his morning sponge bath, when a young, handsome guy about my age came in, slipped out of his jacket and sat across from me. He crossed his legs and opened a magazine he picked from the end table. Neither of us said anything at first. I pretended to be interested in the watercolor paintings on the wall, while surreptitiously taking in his polished leather shoes, tan gabardine pants and white, open-collared shirt. He browsed through the magazine, looking casually interested in the pages he was turning slowly one after the other.

After a few minutes he set his magazine aside, flashed a bright smile and said, "Pretty monotonous, having to sit around waiting like this, isn't it?"

Naturally I agreed.

One comment followed another and after a few minutes of exchanging small talk, we introduced ourselves. Before we parted he told me his brother had been stricken with a heart attack and might not make it. I said I was sorry to hear it; then I briefly told him about Jack's accident. A wan smile crossed his face as he listened and nodded in sympathy to my words.

The next day and for several days thereafter, we met in the waiting room, and before I fully realized it, we were becoming ever friendlier, even sharing information and thoughts we ordinarily reserve only for family and close friends. He dazzled me with his quick smile and contagious laugh.

I can't honestly say how we got around to it, but before long we were having coffee and sometimes, while Jack napped, we had lunch together in the hospital cafeteria. I found him so attractive with his cleft chin and charming manner that it scared me, but not so much that I stopped seeing him. He made me feel beautiful, the way his eyes wandered over my hair, my face. He exuded a sense of excitement that was sorely missing in my life with Jack. I soon found myself thinking about him more than I wanted to when he wasn't around. I couldn't help feeling drawn closer to him every time we met, until one day as we were about to leave the waiting room, he pulled me into his arms and kissed me. It was sudden and shocking. Afterwards, of course, I felt terribly guilty, but at that moment, I didn't let it stop me. I couldn't have resisted if I wanted to. My lips clung to his as he held me in his hungry embrace.

"Anna," he said, "I want to see you, I have to see you, to see more of you, more and more of you."

I made a weak attempt to break away. "Please. This isn't right."

He pulled me tighter. "It is right, Anna. I can't help what I feel, what we both feel. Don't deny it."

All I could do was picture Jack right down the hall laid up in his hospital bed, helpless. "No, don't you see? I'm committed. I can't do this to Jack."

"Anna, this is life. Sometimes people get hurt. But is it fair to us to deny what we're feeling? Is it fair to Jack if you stay with him, knowing your feelings are stronger for somebody else?"

I looked into his blue eyes. "Can't you see how this will hurt him if I leave him?"

"It doesn't have to be right away, Anna. Besides, you can't let sympathy stand in the way of our happiness. It isn't fair to you, and it isn't fair to him."

And there it began, the many meetings and secret trysts that eventually led to my pregnancy and abandonment by the boy who deceived my foolish heart. I told Bianca that Jack and I had been married, that he had been killed in the war, but those were all lies. I also told her I had a miscarriage. Well, that wasn't exactly a lie. Rather than disgrace my family with an out-of-wedlock child, I helped the miscarriage along by mixing and ingesting aspirin and several different drugs. By then Jack had been discharged from the hospital and was working to get his body back to normal, or as normal as possible.

I might have left it there, I suppose, if not for my conscience beginning to haunt me, even in my dreams, until one day I couldn't stand it anymore and was forced to confess to Jack what happened, the whole sordid story, from beginning to end, about how lonely I felt, how I had been charmed by someone who said he loved me, pretended to understand my feelings and wanted to comfort me, how I was enamored of him, attracted to him, dazzled by him with his wit and the magnetism that enveloped him like electricity.

My words pierced Jack's heart like daggers. I'll never forget his reaction when I revealed all this to him. The blood drained from his face and he literally turned white. Initially, I thought he'd pass out; then I thought he might explode and hit me or even kill me. But he did neither. In fact, he sagged in his chair and squeezed his face in his cupped hands. He remained that way a long while, gulping his breaths. When he finally looked up, his eyes were puffy and damp.

"I can forgive you, Anna," he said softly. "I know you'd never intentionally hurt me; you're much too good for that. You didn't have to tell me this. Besides, who am I to judge? I'm not perfect, either."

I burst into tears hearing his words, so soothing, so understanding. I felt more horrible than I did before I confessed. I didn't deserve such kindness, especially not after such a terrible betrayal.

Jack rose and pulled me toward him. "We can start fresh,

Anna. We can forget the past."

I cried in his arms, then leaned back to see his comforting smile. "All right, Jack," I said. "If you mean it. If you really can—"

"I can, Anna, and I will."

But I knew, even in that moment of forgiveness with a chance to start again, I could never do it. How long would it take before my betrayal began eating at him and the accusations start. Besides, my sin was too great for me to forgive myself. I had betrayed Jack and destroyed a life within my womb. Not having the courage to face him, or perhaps fearing that I would give in and live a life of guilt and regret, I left Jack a note, telling him I was leaving New London forever and begged him not to try finding me. I apologized as sincerely as possible and wished him all the happiness he deserved. I believed that by going away, I could leave my painful past behind.

Several years later, I heard through a cousin that Jack married a pretty widow with two children. Apparently, he found happiness after all, and for that I'm thankful to God. I realize now how much I loved Jack and will always love him. I was young, foolish and gullible. I learned my lesson, but too late for us to ever find happiness together.

So here I am today, dear diary, a spinster schoolteacher who has chosen to live out her life in a perpetual self-imposed penance. In so doing, I've found a measure of peace, but I'm still haunted by regrets. I admit to being depressed whenever I think about my past and all that has transpired. However, I've found happiness in teaching children and helping others less fortunate than I whenever I can. It's partial atonement for what I've done, and it will have to do. Whether writing my story here will make a difference in my attitude and feelings toward myself, only time will tell.

As for the boy who blinded me with words and attention, I've heard several stories over the years about him, not all of them bad. Jeffrey, his brother, passed away in the hospital shortly before Jack was released, and Brad inherited the grocery store they ran together. Several years later, rumors reached me, saying Brad was involved in a scandal over a girl everyone called Crazy Annie. They say he drove her insane, but who really knows if such gossip is true. I also heard that, since then, he's become successful, even philanthropic. I guess even a Romeo like Bradley Beit can be converted and saved from himself.

The school year's over and I have the whole summer to myself. I'll be taking a bus trip to visit the Grand Canyon in Arizona. It's not only something I've always longed to see, but I need to get away for a while to restore my spirits and energy. With a little luck I'll meet someone interesting along the way. Life is full of unexpected twists, turns and surprises. Maybe a pleasant one will be waiting for me.

Chapter 2

One of the saddest stories I ever heard took place in the early 1940's. It involves the Rosellini family, and the misfortune that struck them about five years after they moved into my building. Vito Rosellini was a wiry little man with a high, thin voice and a thick black mustache which he proudly kept neatly trimmed. His wife, Josephina, a heavy-breasted woman with shiny black hair, always made sure her Vito had a hot meal when he returned home from work at the Hecker's flour mill on Seneca Street.

When Vito walked in the door after work, looking very much like a ghost with his lined face and clothes powdered with white flour, the first thing he said was, 'How much longer to we eat?' And Josephina would say, 'When it is ready it will be ready, but first you go wash up.' She never failed to say it with a broad smile on her round face and a twinkle in her large, brown eyes. It was obvious to me that Josephina loved her husband very much, especially the way she catered to him. But she never said she loved him out loud. Neither did he say it to her, though it was obvious he did in the way he treated her and looked at her with adoring eyes. In fact, the word 'love' never fell from anyone's lips in that home. It didn't need to be spoken aloud because it always showed in their faces, words and actions.

I liked the way Vito's eyes brightened when he saw his steaming plate of pasta fazool on the table. It was his favorite.

He'd sit down, lift his wine glass in a silent salute and take a drink. Josephina sat at the opposite end of the table and on each side sat their two children, Dorothy, fifteen years old, and her ten-year-old brother, Anthony, nicknamed Sonny. They would carry on small talk.

Sonny usually said something to rile them up. For instance, one day he said:

"Did anybody get killed or a leg cut off at the factory today, Papa?"

"Shut uppa you mouth," Josephina hollered. "Thisa no place to talk about such things."

"That'sa OK, Josephina," Vito said, making a circular motion with his hand. "He'sa just a boy. That'sa way boys talk."

"Maybe so, but not a my table. Now say you're sorry."

Sonny dropped his head, with his mop of black hair drooping over his eyes. "I'm sorry, Mama."

"That's a better. Now mangia. Eat."

After eating, Vito would sit in his old leather chair they brought with them when they moved in. It was so old that the leather was cracked like dry skin and torn in a few places, but it was comfortable. Then Vito would pick up his newspaper and read as best he could, while Josephina and Dorothy cleaned up the kitchen and washed the dishes. Afterwards, Josephina would come up behind Vito and massage his neck. He would moan his satisfaction. He never thanked her, but she knew he appreciated it. Soon after, he would fall asleep. And then Josephina would put her fingers to her lips and squint a warning for her children to keep quiet.

On Sundays the family would dress up in their best clothes and go to Holy Cross church. If they went straight home after Mass they always talked about what they had seen and heard.

Sometimes, if the weather was good, they would walk together in Front Park. As often as not, Vito would dig into his pocket and say, 'Anybody want ice a cream?' They laughed because, of course, Sonny, jumping up and down, was always the first to shout out his 'yes yes yes!'

Up to the time Dorothy was almost twelve years old, she used to sit on Vito's lap and he would read the comics to her. The 'Katzenjammer Kids' strip was her favorite. She liked the comforting smell of his chair and her father's pipe tobacco that clung to his clothes. But more than that, she felt safe and secure in his arms, especially after she fell on the sidewalk a year earlier while playing hopscotch. The fall wasn't bad, but Dorothy's face landed on a piece of broken glass and cut her face, leaving a red scar more than an inch long. When she talked to people, Dorothy always propped her cheek against her hand, as if she was listening intently, but she was really hiding the scar.

"I'm ugly, Papa."

"What kind of talk you talk? Who say you ugly?"

Tears wet her cheeks. "Other kids. They make fun of me. They call me scar face."

"Scar face! They have eyes but like the bat, they cannot see. You pay no attention to them, my bambina. You are beautiful girl." Then he would hug her tight against his chest.

And so their lives went on, a peaceful, loving family, despite living near the poverty line. It went on that way until one fateful day when a knock came on their door. When Josephina answered, a man stood there, floppy cap in hand and hangdog face. It was Marco, one of Vito's best friends who also worked at the mill. His rheumy eyes couldn't meet hers. He didn't have to say anything; the news he had was obvious. He barely spoke a few words before Josephina dropped to the floor, wailing hysterically. Neighbors rushed in and lifted her onto the couch, comforting her as best they could, fanning her with newspapers and trying to force her to drink black coffee. Fortunately, the children were in school, but when they arrived home that afternoon, they found a house full of people. Then, they too were soon crying and hugging their mother for comfort, while Josephina kept repeating, 'Goombye, Papa, goombye Papa.'

Two days later Vito's body was laid out in the parlor, with chairs provided by the Lombardo Funeral Home surrounding the casket and filling up the room. Josephina never knew Vito had so many friends. For three days mourners came, bringing food and offering condolences and help if she needed it. Dressed all in black, with a rosary wrapped around her hands, Josephina told anyone who would listen how Vito had taken a younger worker's place on a dangerous machine that crushed him.

'They killa my husband,' she repeated over and over. 'They killa my Vito.'

I heard the church was crowded after the funeral and many people shed tears for Vito and the family, now deprived of its breadwinner. Some wondered how they could endure, not least of all, Josephina herself. Each sleepless night she worried herself thinking about how she and the children would survive. Sonny understood their plight and said he would get a shoeshine box and bring home some money.

Aware of her plight, Father Dominick of Holy Angels church made it his business to see her. He was an ascetic man with a bald crown and benign smile that lent him a saintly St. Joseph look. Beloved by all who knew him, he had visited me many times over the years, primarily to give last rites to several of my dying tenants and comfort to their families.

Josephina gratefully welcomed him into her apartment and

clasped his hands as he prayed more than an hour with her for her and her children and the soul of her late husband, Vito, whom he assured her was now peacefully and happily in heaven with Jesus Christ. Consoled, Josephina thanked him profusely as she led him out and promised to attend Mass on Sunday, regardless of her weakened condition.

Not long after the funeral, two men came to her door. They were dressed in shiny, blue gabardine suits, white shirts and dark bow ties. The taller one with a pocked face and square jaw led the way inside. Both men carried dark, leather briefcases at their sides. They told her they had business regarding Vito to discuss with her. Frightened by their imposing presence and the intimidating briefcases they swung and brandished like weapons, Josephina politely invited them in.

Sitting on each side of her at the kitchen table, the tall one opened his briefcase and drew out a sheaf of papers, but it was the other man, a flabby-faced man with thick, black eyebrows who spoke.

"Mrs. Rosellini," he said, handing her his business card, "we are Attorneys Livingston and Sanborn, here to extend our deepest sympathy on behalf of the Hecker's Corporation. We're also here as representatives to specifically discuss our company's terms for settlement of the unfortunate accident which claimed your husband's life. Are you open to a discussion now?"

Nervous and unsure of herself, Josephina bowed her head uncertainly. "I think yes, OK."

"Good, very good. Now," he said, taking the papers from Sanborn and speaking sternly, "we have a proposal for you to consider. However, I should warn you in advance, Mrs. Rosellini, that if you should refuse our terms and choose to reject our offer— which we believe to be more than fair— we will be forced to take up this matter in court. That could be a costly and messy business, something I don't think either of us want."

"No," Josephina said, shaking her head vigorously, "no, no court."

She remembered, and I remembered, too, what Vito used to say about the law: 'Josephina, the law is not for us. We are not the Irish or the English. Those people, the bigga shots, they run the government, the city, everything. To them, we are just the donkeys who digga the mud in the ditches, and who sweat in the filthy coal mines. For us, there is no justice.'

While Livingston was arranging his papers and drawing out his fountain pen, I watched Josephina tighten her shoulders and stiffen in her chair.

"Mr. Lawyer, I—"

"Livingston."

"Yes, Mr. Livingston. My husband's friends, they say the machine whicha killa my husband was a broke. Lots of times they say they complain to the boss, but the boss say itsa not broke, so go to work or get fired. So I don' think itsa my husband's fault he die."

A mirthless grin passed over Livingston's face. "Of course they would say that, Mrs. Rosellini. Workers always try to blame their problems on the company. And maybe they were just trying to make you feel better by blaming the machine." He sorted through the papers. "Mrs. Rosellini, Hecker's maintains that your husband, Vito Rosellini, failed to operate the machine in question in a safe and prescribed manner. Furthermore, our records indicate the machine was inspected two days earlier and found to be in perfect working condition. Our legal team has concluded that Vito Rosellini's death was the result of his own negligence." He looked at her sharply. "Do you understand what

I'm saying?"

"I'm a sorry, but maybe, like somebody told me, maybe I should get a lawyer who knows—"

Livingston stood up abruptly, scraping his chair back, and began slapping the papers into his briefcase. "If that is your wish, Mrs. Roselllini, I withdraw our offer to—"

Shocked by his sudden action, Josephina panicked. "No, no, it'sa all right. I'm a listen to what you say. It'sa all right."

"A wise decision, Mrs. Rosellini, a wise decision, indeed," he said, slowly sitting again. He removed the cap from his fountain pen. "As I was about to say— without admitting liability and in the interest of good will as well as to clear our books of this matter— the Hecker's Corporation has decided to offer you the sum of one thousand, eight hundred dollars. Do you find this offer acceptable?"

Josephina hesitated.

"I assure you, Mrs. Rosellini, this is more than a fair offer. In view of the facts, it is quite generous."

"OK." She nodded. "Yes, OK. I sign."

"Fine." He shuffled the papers and straightened a couple of long forms before her. "Now," he said, handing over his pen, "if you'll just sign by the X on each page, we are prepared to issue you a check here and now for said amount."

Josephina realized it was more money than she and Vito ever had at one time, but she also realized that it wouldn't last forever. Nevertheless, she felt she had no choice. Tears welled in her eyes and her hand trembled as she took the pen and signed the papers.

He blotted the ink. "Very good, Mrs. Rosellini. I think that about wraps up our business here," he said, signing the check

21

and sliding it over to her. He rose from his chair and handed the papers to Sanborn, who placed them in his briefcase. "We wish you well," Livingston said as the two men shuffled out of the apartment and down the hall to the stairs.

Before they left the building, I heard the tall one snicker.

"Well, that's another feather in our cap, Bernie. A few more of those and we should get a raise. A well deserved one, I might add. Too bad we don't get a commission on the money we save the company. Let's bring it up at the next corporate meeting."

Livingston laughed. "She was easy. Did you see the panic in her eyes when I mentioned we could take her to court? And the way her hand shook when she signed the release? Scared to death.... Yeah, she was an easy mark."

Sanborn nodded. "But not as easy as the Martinez case. That one took the cake. You got that old lady to sign the release on her husband's coffin lid."

I heard them chuckling together as they left my building.

The next morning Josephina guarded the check with her life as she hurried to the bank to deposit it. She knew the check was crucial to her existence. What neither she nor I could foresee was the trouble that lay ahead for her.

Chapter 3

One day I heard Miss Wagman, the librarian, complaining to her sister Agnes that, if Mrs. Chapman, the landlady, didn't get the police to disperse those boys always crowding the sidewalk and blocking her way when she came home, she would move to another neighborhood.

"Bad enough I have to move around them," she said, breathless, "but their sneering faces and coarse language are simply atrocious. Where in heaven's name are their parents, anyway!" She laid her groceries on the kitchen table. "They have no respect for their elders, absolutely none." She slipped a loaf of bread into the breadbox. "What is this country coming to these days, when a person can't walk home from the store without being harassed by a bunch of hooligans?"

Agnes took the quart of milk and put it in the ice box. "I've seen them hanging around the corner; they think they own the street. And they're so loud Mrs. Banner downstairs says she sometimes has to shut her windows to get some peace and quiet."

"And how is it the police are never around when you need them? That's what I'd like to know!"

"Goodness gracious, Alice, your arms must be tired from carrying all these groceries. It's a wonder you didn't drop anything."

"Well, we have to eat, don't we, Agnes? Who else is going to do this for us?"

"It would be good if those boys were decent enough to offer their services. It would keep them off the streets and put a little money in their pockets at the same time."

"They don't want to work, Agnes. Just troublemakers, that's all they are," Alice said, still breathing hard from her long walk from the store. "Nothing but troublemakers. If I had my way I'd give them a what-for."

Chapter 4

Now I would like to introduce you to Timothy Huggins, who lives in my cellar, rent free, courtesy of my landlady, Mrs. Bernice Chapman, a portly woman with sloped shoulders, soft hands and a kind heart. Timothy's the twenty-eight-year-old son of Mrs. Chapman's best friend, Cecelia Huggins. People around here who meet Timothy for the first time often tap their heads and consider him 'touched.' It may be true, but he's harmless. Despite that, and what's more important, he's the most cheerful, helpful person anyone could ever hope to meet. Everyone who knows him likes him. He has a crooked smile always on display, bulging green eyes, and an unruly mop of reddish hair that doesn't seem to know which way to grow.

Whenever Timothy encounters a new tenant, man or woman, the first thing he says is, 'Welcome friend.' Then he throws his arms around them and gives them a big hug. That's how he got his nickname. You see, Timothy believes he was named Huggins by God, and that his mission in life is to hug everyone he meets to show love. Anyway, that's what I heard Mrs. Chapman tell one of her new tenants who was shocked and offended by Timothy's sudden embrace.

Although Timothy lives free, he earns his keep by feeding my coal furnace in the winter, scooping out the ashes and lugging the filled barrels outside. He also does small jobs like changing light bulbs, mopping floors, carrying out garbage and keeping an eye out for anything suspicious going on. When he has time, he cleans up tables and straightens out the furniture around the restaurant on my first floor. It's a fair-sized place called Joe's, where people stop for a hearty breakfast or just coffee and doughnuts, and usually a hamburger or hot dog for lunch. Fish frys are very popular on Friday nights and attract a good crowd.

But Timothy also loves to play pranks on people. For instance, a few days ago I heard a shriek coming from the librarian's apartment:

"Agnes, quickly, quickly, the broom, get the broom!"

"What's wrong, Alice, what's wrong?" Agnes shouted back, scurrying across the kitchen.

"A rat, Agnes! A rat, right by the door. A big, gray one and it's staring at me with its beady eyes! Quick, Agnes, I think it's going to jump!"

Alice snatched the broom from Agnes's hands and began swatting and pounding the rat furiously, over and over, shrieking threats until she realized it wasn't a real rat after all. It was a toy rat she'd been batting around the floor.

"It's that darn Huggs," she said, fanning herself and trying to catch her breath. "Up to his old tricks again." She handed the broom back to Agnes and wiped her brow. "Well, he's not funny. Someday he's going to give someone a heart attack."

It was a week before that when I heard cursing echoing in the hall. It was Lizzie Shanahan's voice.

"Huggs or no Huggs, one o' these days I'm going to give that boy a good old-fashioned, Irish wallop in the snoot he'll never forget." Delicately, she picked up a plaster imitation of coiled brown dog poop Huggs had placed in front of her door. "Good thing my little Rosie didn't step on it," she said, carrying it by her fingertips and dropping it into a paper bag. "She could've tripped over it and hurt herself."

Anxiously waiting in the basement to hear such a cry, Huggs would pace the floor, puffing on his cigarette and nervously flicking away his ashes until he heard the outrage echoing in the halls above. Then, after bouncing on his toes and giggling with great glee, he would plop himself on his narrow cot between my coal furnace and his card table, stretch out with his legs crossed at the ankles, all the while chuckling with a broad smile on his face and giving himself a satisfying bear hug before curling up into a ball and falling peacefully asleep.

On the card table beside his cot stood his radio, a pack of Chesterfield cigarettes, a few sticks of Juicy Fruit chewing gum and a jar of itching powder. Every Saturday afternoon, like clockwork, Huggs went downtown to see a cowboy movie at the Keith's or the Little Hippodrome on lower Main Street, two theaters I've heard others call 'rat holes.' Afterwards, he'd treat himself to an ice cream sucker and head up the street to a novelties store next to the Shea's Buffalo Theater, where he bought his toys. I wondered how he was going to use the itching powder he had saved on the table and who'd be his next victim.

As if I didn't hear enough complaining and yelling because of Huggs's antics, I was startled one quiet morning, when it sounded like a riot breaking out. Slamming doors shook my walls, wailing babies and screaming voices filled the air and echoed through the halls. Pandemonium was breaking out everywhere:

"Hey, you up there! Quit that ga-damn racket or I'm calling the cops!"

"How can I get any sleep with you idiots making all that noise? I work nights!"

"Can't you have some consideration for other people? We

27

live here, too, you know!"

"Now see what you've gone and done? You woke up my babies!"

"I'm sick of you guys arguing all the time. And now this! In a minute I'm coming up there with a baseball bat and break your heads!"

"Mrs. Chapman's gonna hear about this. You're gonna get your asses evicted. Both of you!"

It took me a while to realize what happened. Apparently, Bob Sherman, a balding car salesman with a fat gut, got so angry with Willy Dee disturbing him with his loud drum playing, that he went out and got himself an accordion. I saw him lugging a box up to his apartment the day before, but I didn't know what was in it until the commotion broke out.

Later, I heard the others say that when Willy Dee started drumming, Bob began playing his accordion. The faster Willy Dee hit those drums with his skinny, tattooed arms, the more furiously Bob pumped out a cacophony of musical noise. Then it really escalated, and that's when I saw it all for myself. Before long, they flung their apartment doors open, with Bob standing in his doorway, squeezing the life out of that music box that was even bigger than his belly, while Willy Dee dragged his drums almost into the hallway and began beating them to death, his rainbow- colored arms a blur.

By then, dogs were howling and the whole building was in an uproar. A bunch of my tenants stampeded to the fourth floor and threatened to throw both them and their instruments out the window if they didn't stop right then and there. Reluctantly, Bob and Willy Dee withdrew into their respective apartments, dragging their instruments inside with them, all while hurling insults at each other:

"I'm not through with you, Willy, you freaky jerk, not by a

long shot."

"Go on, you fat, big-mouth tub of lard!"

"Keep up your crummy drumming like you been and you'd better have eyes in the back of your head!"

Willy Dee turned to the angry crowd, breaking up and trampling down the stairs. "Did you hear him threaten me? Did you?"

Someone shot back, "Did you hear us!"

Three days later Bob Sherman moved out, lugging his accordion along with everything else he could carry. The next day Mrs. Chapman confronted Willy Dee:

"But it wasn't my fault, Mrs. Chapman," he argued. "That fat idiot started it."

"You broke the house rules with your noise and you were warned before about disturbing others. You're just as guilty as Mr. Sherman. You have to go. Huggs will help with your things."

Willy Dee's shouting and Huggs's griping added to the racket Willy Dee's stomping feet made on the stairs, along with crashing cymbals and drums thumping behind them every step of the way down.

I now had two empty apartments waiting to be filled again. To the relief of all my other tenants, peace was restored, but who could predict what drama my new tenants would bring with them.

Chapter 5

Willy Dee, the mad drummer who drove everyone crazy pounding his drums, was quite a contrast to Desi Torres, a quiet, slender, unusually pale fourteen-year-old Hispanic boy with shiny black hair and black circles under his eyes. He lived with his mother, a fairly young woman, with thin shoulders, long straight hair and slanted, dark eyes.

Mrs. Torres worked six days a week at Martino's vegetable stall at the Washington Street market. She was fortunate enough to have a neighbor who also worked at the market and had a car to drive them there. When Desi wasn't in school, he stayed home quietly playing his clarinet, and that's where the difference between the Desi Torres and Willy Dee begins and ends.

Unlike Willy and his nerve-wracking drums, Desi played the clarinet pleasingly, not like a beginner student, but very much like a professional. There were never any ear-piercing squeaks, so commonly heard from an amateur clarinetist. Desi's playing was soft, smooth and pleasant to the ear. At any time of the day you might hear his subtle rendition of popular tunes, like 'Love Walked In,' or 'Amapola.' On occasion, if you were lucky, you could hear him play Gershwin's 'Rhapsody in Blue.' When Desi's clarinet hit the high-pitched note that opened the piece, everyone in the building stopped to listen. No matter where they were or what they were doing, they were transfixed by the ethereal music swirling around them. It was soothing to the mind and soul. Regardless of what he was playing, his dulcet notes floated through the corridors, filling them with sweet sounds that warmed the atmosphere and the hearts of everyone who heard them.

I won't go further into the Torres' background, except to mention the day I saw a heavily- breathing doctor with a rounded belly and shoulders slowly carrying his bag up the stairs and go into their apartment. Mrs. Torres led him into Desi's bedroom, where Desi's limp body lay stretched out on his bed, his breathing shallow and quiet. Standing beside his bed was his clarinet, its silver keys glistening in the light falling in from the window. After running his stethoscope over Desi's frail chest and examining him further, the doctor asked a few questions, then beckoned with his head to Mrs. Torres. In the outer room he whispered that he wanted Desi brought into General Hospital for testing as soon as possible.

The following week the diagnosis was in. Mrs. Torres broke down in tears when told the kind of illness leukemia was and what she could expect. A few more weeks passed before mother and son packed up and left my premises. I overheard someone say they were returning to her family in Cuba, but it might have been only a rumor. After they were gone I felt a deep sense of emptiness. Nothing was quite the same without the comforting music that once filled the air and pleased so many people.

It was two months later when one of my Hispanic tenants, having just finished a late breakfast in Joe's restaurant, lit a cigarette and opened one of the local ethnic newsletters that bring items of interest to the various immigrant groups living in the neighborhood.

"Ah, Dios mio , no!"

The loud exclamation turned the heads of two city sanitation workers sitting nearby on their morning coffee break. "Ah, Dios, no, what, Pedro? What?"

"Muerta!"

"Muerta? Who, Pedro? Who died, Pedro?"

"El nino. The kid, you know?" He poked his finger in the air. "Upstairs. Make the nice musica."

News of the Desi Torres' death traveled fast and saddened everyone, but none more so than Jennifer Page, a precocious fifteen-year-old girl who lived with her soon-to-be divorced mother in the apartment across the hall from Desi. Jennifer was an energetic young lady, with neat bangs, eyeglasses and dimples so deep in her cheeks she looked as if she was smiling, even when she wasn't.

Jennifer already had her life planned—or had it planned for her. Her goal was to become an architectural engineer. A brilliant student, she studied hard and rarely, if ever, received a grade below an 'A.' However, her real interest was writing stories, which she practiced every evening after finishing her homework. Often she would stop writing to listen to the music emanating from across the hall. Intrigued, she decided one day while her mother was out, to go over and formally introduce herself.

She knocked once, then twice. The music behind the door stopped and a soft voice called, "Who is it?"

"My name is Jennifer. I live across the hall from you."

There was a moment's silence, then, "Come in, it's open."

When she stepped inside, she saw Desi sitting in a chair with a music stand in front of him. His clarinet lay across his lap.

"I hope I'm not interrupting," she said, "but I've been

wanting to tell you how much I enjoy your playing."

"Thanks," he said, shifting uncomfortably and brushing a lock of black hair from his pale forehead. "I was just practicing my scales," he added, pointing to the music book on his stand. "I've seen you around, Jennifer."

"I've seen you, too, Desi, but I never had a chance to talk to you." Her eyes passed over the room.

"I'm alone. My mother's working.... Can I get you a glass of water or something?"

"No, thank you." She nodded toward his clarinet. "Have you been playing long?"

"About four years. I started taking lessons at Wurlitzer's downtown. My teacher was Mr. Buffalino, but he died a year ago, so I'm not taking lessons anymore."

"You play beautifully. Everyone who hears you says so."

Desi's face flushed pink. He stumbled for a moment, then said, "Do you play anything?"

"Only the radio." She laughed. "Actually, no I don't, but if I did I wish I could play like you. I like to write stories."

Desi perked up. "You do? What kind of stories?"

She put her finger to her cheek. "Mostly uplifting stories, which I think is the right word, 'uplifting.' Something that makes people feel good about themselves or about other people."

"That's how I feel about music. I like to make people happy in their heart, like I do inside when I play."

Jennifer beamed. "Then we have something in common." She looked over to a stack of records on a small table next to a phonograph. "I see you like to listen to music, too."

Desi lifted himself from his chair and retrieved a couple of records, still in their paper sleeves. He handed one to her. "I like this Benny Goodman record a lot. He plays the clarinet, you know. "

"I know. They play his music all the time on the radio. Is he your favorite?"

"I like Woody Herman, too, but Artie Shaw, even more, I think. I guess it depends on what tune they're playing." He sat down again and cradled his clarinet in the crook of his arm. "I don't just listen, though. I memorize the clarinet part of the music, and then I play along with the record until I do it perfectly."

"Without reading the music? I never heard of anyone doing that. It must be awfully hard."

"Well, it does take a little practice." Desi suddenly brightened. "Would you like to hear me do it? Play along with one of them, I mean."

"Yes, I'd love it."

"OK. Oh, excuse me, Jennifer. Why don't you sit there in that chair?" He rose again, went over to the phonograph and wound it up with the handle. "Would you like to hear Artie Shaw's 'Concerto for Clarinet' or 'Moonglow'?

"I love 'Moonglow.'"

Desi set the record on the turntable, placed the needle on the edge, brought his clarinet to his lips and played along. After the record finished, he said, "See what I mean?"

Jennifer clasped her hands together. "It was wonderful, Desi. You blended right in with the clarinet in the orchestra. It was perfect. If I didn't actually see your fingers moving I would've thought it was only the record playing."

"Thanks," he said, blushing again as he sat down.

"Sometime I'd like to read one of my stories to you. Do you think you'd like that?"

"I know I would, Jennifer. I never met a writer before."

"I don't know if you can call me a writer yet, but I'm trying. I send in my stories, but they keep coming back to me like homing pigeons. I have a drawer full of rejection slips. The editors tell me they like my stories, but then they say 'no thanks' and say I should try again. Maybe someday I'll get lucky. If I—" She stopped suddenly when she heard the echoing slam of a door. "Oh, that must be Mother. I don't want to upset her wondering where I'm at. I'd better be getting back."

"I'm glad you came over, Jennifer. Whenever you want to come and talk again will be OK, even if my ma's here. I know she'll like you."

"Thanks, Desi," she said, bouncing up and heading for the door, laughing. "And thanks for the musical performance. I really enjoyed it."

When Jennifer came back into her apartment, her mother was standing at the kitchen table, sorting out papers she had taken from her large purse. She was a tall, sophisticated woman, neatly groomed with a perfectly *permed head of auburn hair. Her rimless eyeglasses reflected the same kind of cold light that showed in her face.*

"And just where have you been?"

Jennifer hesitated, then said, "I was across the hall, visiting."

Her mother gave her an icy look. "Across the hall?"

"Yes, Mother, at the Torres'. I was talking with Desi, you know, the boy who plays the clarinet?"

Her mother peeled off her gloves, put them in her coat pocket and, along with her hat, hung them on a hook behind the door. "You have no business over there."

"Well, we can't help hearing how pretty he plays. I just wanted to meet him and let him know how much we enjoy it. Desi's really nice. He's quiet and kind of shy."

"Desi? What kind of name is that, Mexican? Puerto Rican...? Whatever it is it makes no difference; I don't care one way or the other. One thing's certain; he's not our kind, so I'm ordering you to have nothing more to do with him or any of his family."

"But Mother—"

"Don't 'but Mother' me. You heard what I said. We're not in this building by choice with all these... these foreigners and other strange types. They give me the willies, especially that one— what's his name? ...that redhead who tried hugging me when we first came." She shuddered. "The sooner we get out of this...this tenement— if you can even call it that— the better off we'll be. The place even smells bad with all those cooking odors and that greasy-spoon restaurant downstairs making it worse."

She pulled a chair from under the table and sat down. "I'm tired. It's a long trip back and forth to the Brisbane Building."

"Did you see your lawyer again?"

"Yes. He said everything will be settled very soon and we can be in our own place— near decent human beings where we belong. Far from here, that's for sure. If it wasn't for that good-for-nothing father of yours, we wouldn't be in this predicament."

Jennifer sulked. "Mother, I don't see what it hurts if I talk to him, to Desi. In a way we're a lot alike. I like writing and he likes music. In our own way we like to make the world better with what we do."

"Oh, stop your foolish daydreaming, Jennifer, and be sensible. I can see we've already been here too long. It's affecting your mind."

"Mother—"

"That's enough," she snapped. "Did you do your homework?"

"Not yet."

"'Not yet.' I see. Well, get on with it now."

After that episode in the kitchen, Jennifer saw Desi only when her mother was out of the house. They spent many hours together exchanging their thoughts and ideas. Most of the time Desi would play a tune for her and she in turn would read parts of her stories to him. They even considered the idea of him writing a song someday, and her putting the words to it. They obviously developed not only a real friendship, but a deep fondness for each other, as well. I might even call it young love.

Although Jennifer saw how Desi seemed to struggle just to get off his chair, and noticed his shortness of breath, she didn't really think too much about it except that maybe he ought to get out in the sunshine and exercise more. She was too wrapped up in their conversations and dreams for the future to give it any more thought.

When Jennifer heard the news of Desi's passing, she was, of course, devastated and cried the whole day. Throughout the week, despite her mother insistence she get out of her bedroom and stop brooding, Jennifer stubbornly refused, stayed at her desk and continued writing, often with flowing tears. This time, however, she sensed a lyricism in her words, conveying not only interest in the narrative, but also an emotional spirituality capable of capturing the imagination and heart of anyone reading them. A week later she mailed out her short story titled, 'A Boy and His Music.'

It wasn't long after that when Jennifer's anxious fingers tore open the envelope addressed to her and drew out a congratulatory letter and a check from a popular magazine for twenty-five dollars. Tears welled in her eyes remembering Desi, the shy, sensitive neighbor who confided in her and with whom she shared her deepest thoughts. She remembered his gift for music, the light in his eyes when he played and how his love for music transcended his illness and all the bad things he'd ever heard about in this world.

It was a blustery January day when Mrs. Page and her daughter, Jennifer, moved away, leaving behind all the furniture they brought with them, including a refrigerator. Although I've often wondered whatever happened to them, especially Jennifer, I never saw or heard from them again.

Chapter 6

It must have been a couple of months after Mr. Rosellini was killed in an industrial accident that I happened to overhear Alice talking to her sister Agnes at the supper table. Trouble lines crossed her forehead.

"Agnes, I'm worried."

Agnes dabbed her napkin to her mouth. "Did something happen at the library, Alice?"

"No, it's what I observed outside when I came home."

"Don't keep me in suspense, Alice," she asked, pushing her thick eyeglasses up from the tip of her nose. "What did you see?"

"Agnes, what's the name of that young girl, the one whose father was killed in a factory accident?"

"You mean that nice Italian family? The Rosellinis?"

"Yes, that one. What's the daughter's name, do you remember?"

"I do, Alice, I do. She's the sweetest thing. If I happen to be in the hall cleaning the floor, she always gives me a 'good morning' on her way to school. In fact, one time when I accidentally knocked over my bucket, she scurried right back to help me clean up the mess. I told her, I said—"

"Her name, Agnes, her name!"

Agnes pressed her finger to her cheek. "She has a younger brother and I've heard him call her 'Dolly,' but that's not her actual name. Her actual name is...let me see now... She told it to me one morning... it's on the tip of my tongue..." She tapped her head, thinking. "Oh, dear, ... something like—"

"Agnes, for heaven's sake!"

"Don't rush me, Alice, don't rush me. You know that makes me nervous and, besides, my memory isn't what it used to be... let's see... Oh, yes, I remember now. Such an easy name. I don't know how I could have forgotten it, even for a moment. It's the same as—"

"Agnes!"

"Dorothy! It's Dorothy. I'm, sure of it. Her name is Dorothy."

Alice sat back in her chair and brushed a lock of gray hair from her forehead. "That's odd. That's not a typical name in Italian families. They usually have names like Mary or Antoinette or Theresa. Like the saints, you know."

Agnes smiled. "Maybe they saw the 'Wizard of Oz.' It was Judy Garland's name in the movie. Maybe they took it from that."

Alice scowled. "The girl's a teen and the movie came out... when, Agnes, a year or two ago?"

"Oh, my, Alice, you're right. You see now how my mind is playing tricks on me these days?"

"Well, it makes no difference what her name is. That girl is headed for trouble."

"Really, Alice? How do you mean?"

Alice lowered her voice. "Well, this isn't the first time I've seen those juvenile delinquents swarming around her like flies around honey. But today, one had her cornered against the wall, hemming her in with his arms, like two bars of a cage. When they saw me coming, she ducked her head down and he backed off, but as soon as I passed, he had her pinned again. I saw it when I glanced over my shoulder just before I turned the corner."

"It appears like she's asking for trouble, doesn't it?"

"Agnes, avoid saying 'like.' Say 'as if.' Even when like is correct it sounds—"

"Mercy me, Alice, there you go again," Agnes snapped, picking up her plate and teacup and carrying them to the sink. "Take a good look at me, Alice. I'm a fifty-five-year-old widow, a former seamstress with weak, baggy eyes, sagging breast and thinning gray hair that used to be blond. Now, I ask you Alice, is anyone ever going to say to me, 'Shame on you, Agnes, don't you know you should never say like?'"

"Well, we should never stop trying to improve ourselves, Agnes, if for no other reason than self-satisfaction. Besides, you're not that old. You're younger than I am."

"Except not as healthy, especially with my sugar, but all right, Alice, you win again. Anyway, I made my point." She cleared the dishes from the table. "So why don't you finish what you were getting at with Dorothy."

"It's not hard to see she's quite developed for a young girl. Not more than fourteen or fifteen, I'd say, and already attracting the boys like bees to flowers."

"Do you think something bad is going on, Alice?"

"Of course, I can't say for sure, Agnes, but if it isn't, I think something soon will."

"If you're that concerned, maybe we should say something to her mother about it."

Alice laid her tea bag aside and shook her head doubtfully. "I don't know, Agnes. People can be funny how they take things. We don't really know the lady. She could think we're being overly suspicious, or that we're just two, old busybodies trying to stir up trouble. She's certainly not going to want to hear us put her daughter in a bad light. Or even hint at it."

"I suppose you could be right, Alice, but if we don't speak up and something does happen to that poor girl, how are we going to feel?"

Alice sipped the last of her tea, sat back in her chair and breathed a weary sigh. "I don't have a good feeling about this, Agnes, but at the same time I don't want to chance a confrontation with the woman. She's not a shrinking violet, from the little I've seen and heard of her. Who knows what she's like or how she'd react. Those Italians are hot-tempered, you know, most of them, anyway. I guess keeping quiet is our wisest choice. We can only hope our fears are unfounded."

"Let's pray we're not making the wrong decision, Alice."

"Amen to that."

Chapter 7

It was a dark gloomy day, so much like the strange man who rented my furnished apartment on the second floor just before the outbreak of WWII. He had a full head of black hair, feathered gray around the edges, although he didn't look more than thirty or thirty-five years old. His eyes, sunken as if in dark wells of worry, avoided the eyes of anyone he happened to encounter in passing. He seemed friendly enough in a subdued sort of way; nevertheless, others always gave him wide berth whenever he approached.

When he moved into one of my furnished apartments, he brought only two pieces of luggage: a cumbersome, black suitcase, and a leather briefcase. The first peculiar thing I noticed on some mornings was his habit of tucking his briefcase under his arm and putting his ear to the door before opening it and leaving for an hour or so. I wondered what he was listening for and where he was going. Was he afraid someone was coming after him? Was he a criminal hiding from the law? Could he possibly be a German spy? After all, the name he signed on the lease for my owner, Mrs. Bernice Chapman, was Gustav Schwartz.

Occasionally, when I wasn't occupied watching or listening to other tenants, I'd spy on him. Purely out of idle curiosity, of course. I noticed that, for quite a while, no one ever visited him or called him on the phone. When he received mail, he always opened it anxiously, as if waiting for important news. He was predictable in his habits.

Upon awakening at 7:00 o'clock sharp in the morning, he made breakfast, usually just coffee and toast, retrieved his Courier Express newspaper from outside his door, then plopped himself on the couch, where he faithfully pored over the pages. During the day, while listening to the radio, he made a small lunch for himself, washed his clothes in the bathtub, and his handkerchiefs and socks in the kitchen sink, wrung them out by hand and hung them to dry on a rope strung across the living room. He always grunted and slapped at them angrily when ducking under them as he moved from one place to another.

He seemed forever exhausted, especially late every night after returning from work, when he'd eat a light supper, and scour the Buffalo Evening News newspaper he'd pick up at a Deco restaurant on his way home. Afterwards, he usually fell into a restless sleep in his easy chair, with his newspaper crumpled on his chest. Only when he began snoring loud enough to wake himself did he get up and stagger into his bed for the rest of the night.

At least once a week during the late morning he would sit at the small desk against the wall, spread open the Courier Express again and write in a notebook he drew from his briefcase. Hunched forward, he blocked my view. I could only tell that he was in deep concentration. Sometimes he'd mumble words I couldn't make out, throw down his pencil, sit back in his chair, squeeze his forehead and expel a long breath.

Late one afternoon on one of those days when all is particularly quiet, I happened to observe Gustav don his blue suit jacket, pick up his briefcase and check his pocket watch. Again, as always before leaving for work, he put his ear to the door, listened a moment, switched off his light, set his lock and slipped out into the hallway.

"Oopsie daisy."

Startled, Gustav recoiled and stared at the young girl with blond braids, looking straight ahead and smiling.

She took hold of his sleeve. "Oh, I'm sorry, Mister. I didn't hear you come out of your apartment."

"That's OK. I hope I didn't step on your toe."

She giggled. "No you didn't, but it was my fault, anyway. I'm really sorry if I surprised you. I'll try to be more careful from now on."

As Gustav hurried toward the staircase and started down, he glanced back at the sound of the little girl humming a tune. He was about to continue down but stopped when he saw her dragging her hand along the wall.

"Is something wrong, mister? I don't hear you walking. Did I leave one of my toys on the step? Mama says I have to be careful about that because someone could trip and fall. Mama says... oopsie daisy." She dropped the doll she was carrying under her arm.

Gustav was about to start down again, when he saw her feeling around the floor for it. He didn't realize until then that Rosie was blind. He watched a moment, saw her retrieve her doll and brush it off.

"I'm sorry, Shirley," she cooed. "Did you hurt yourself? Mommy's sorry, Shirley."

Gustav shook his head as if clearing it and continued down.

I wasn't paying attention when Gustav came home late that evening after work, but I was the next morning when I heard a knocking at his door. Gustav opened it a crack and peered out. Standing there was Rosie's mother, a slatternly woman with stringy hair and a sharp voice. She had a dish in one hand and a cigarette in the corner of her mouth.

"Top o' the morning to you, Mr. Schwartz," she said, taking a puff of her cigarette and blowing the smoke off to the side. "It is Mr. Schwartz, isn't it? Gustav Schwartz? That's the name on your mailbox downstairs."

"Yes."

"I hope I'm not interrupting anything important," she said, stifling a cough.

"What is it?" he asked.

Misunderstanding, she answered, "This? Well, sir," she said, holding out a plate, "this is my own special dish of corned beef and cabbage I'm bringing you, as a kind of compensation, if you gather my meaning."

Gustav looked at her quizzically.

Her voice came raspy but strong. "For the run-in you had with my little Rosie yesterday out in the hallway, don't you know. She told me how she wasn't paying attention— that's the trouble with my Rosie sometimes, daydreaming instead of paying attention to where she's goin'. Maybe you noticed and maybe you didn't, but Rosie can't see. Damaged something with a fancy name in her eyes that only doctors in Boston might fix. Still, that's no excuse, because carelessness calls for no sympathy. She's almost eight and her hearing's good and sharp."

"Nothing, it was nothing."

"Don't say 'nothing,' because it *was* something, so here you are," she said, pushing against the door with her bony elbow and handing him the dish.

Looking a little mystified, Gustav reached his hand out tentatively and took it.

46

"My name's Elizabeth, but seeing as how we're friendly neighbors now, you can call me Lizzie," she said, taking a puff on her cigarette, "Lizzie Shanahan."

Gustav nodded. "Lizzie."

"Lizzie Shanahan. Right you are, and if you have a need for something, anything at all, Mr. Schwartz, you just rap on my door." She pointed back with her cigarette. "Right down the hall, same side." She backed away, coughing. "And don't you be worryin' about returning the plate. I got plenty and there's only Rosie and me. But if you want, you can give it back anytime it suits you."

Gustav nodded and closed the door. He set the dish on the table and went to his desk against the wall. He closed his eyes where he sat, propped his head in his hands and let out a low moan.

Chapter 8

It was Saturday afternoon on an early fall day when I saw Gustav place the clean plate on the floor outside Lizzie's apartment. He stuck what I assumed to be a 'thank you' note on it, knocked on the door and moved as quickly and quietly as he could down the stairs. As he always did on his way out to do an errand or to go to his afternoon job, he paused briefly at my partially open front door and peered out to the street.

At that same moment a blue Ford convertible pulled around the corner of Potomac Avenue and parked at the curb. An attractive young woman with long, dark hair primped in her rear-view mirror before slipping her purse strap over her shoulder and getting out. She pulled up the collar of her jacket, smoothed her yellow skirt and walked around to the front door of the building. Gustav bumped her shoulder as he rushed past her.

"Well, excuse me!" she said, watching Gustav hurry down the street.

Still annoyed by the rudeness of the stranger, she hesitated a moment, then stepped inside, blinking her eyes in the relative darkness of the hall. Spotting the numbered mailboxes on the wall next to the telephone, she came closer to read the names and apartment numbers. Gathering herself up, she headed upstairs. She bit her lip, as if gathering her courage, then

48

rapped softly and waited. A few moments later the door sprang open.

"Sarah!"

"Aunt Lilly!"

They embraced each other, kissing and hugging and swaying until Lilly stepped back, holding Sarah out at arm's length.

"Just look at you," Lilly said, her admiring eyes combing over Sarah. "My, Sarah, how you've grown! You're hardly the sweet little thing I remember, sitting on my lap and singing songs with me."

"Oh, Aunt Lilly, it's been such a long time. It seems like forever."

"Forever and a year, my dear."

"You look just the same, Aunt Lilly. You're still as beautiful as I remember."

A smile crossed Lilly's small, wrinkled face. "Well, I should be," she tittered. "After all, I'm still sweet sixteen," she joked, taking Sarah's jacket. "Tell me, dear, how was your trip from Oregon? No problems, I hope."

"Smooth as can be, Aunt Lilly. And I'm getting here just in time to see the trees changing color."

"It's a beautiful time of the year and will get better yet."

"Aunt Lilly, do you mind if I freshen up a bit. It's been a very long ride. My bags are in the trunk of my car, but I can get them later."

"Of course, dear, of course. You must be absolutely exhausted."

When Sarah came back, Lilly hooked her arm into Sarah's

and led her to a wicker couch near the window. I listened to them laugh together and make small talk.

"I know you're thirsty and you must be getting hungry, so sit there, Sarah. We'll be eating shortly. In the meantime relax while I bring us some lemonade. I'll be back in a minute."

Sarah sat with her hands placed primly on her lap and gazed around while she waited. She leaned over, looking very interested in the variety of potted plants lining the window sill.

Lilly returned carrying a pitcher of lemonade. She bent over and filled the glasses, already in place on the white wicker table. In its center stood a sturdy, green glass vase, filled with fresh yellow roses draped randomly over the edges.

"The flowers are beautiful, Aunt Lilly, just like these others on your window sill. They remind me so much of the cottage you lived in when I was little." Sarah sipped her lemonade. "And your beautiful garden! Remember how the metal gate squeaked when you opened it?"

"It was like a little voice welcoming us in," Lilly said, picking up her glass and sitting beside Sarah.

"I loved relaxing in the lawn chair in the middle of all the flowers, Aunt Lilly. I can see it all in my mind. I can even smell the fresh greenery. So beautiful! It was a Garden of Eden, with its collage of clay pots and hanging plants. I remember them all blooming with pink pansies, fire-red geraniums— so colorful, all of them— strawberry-colored petunias and sweet- smelling lavender. I can still picture them like a painting on the wall."

Lilly shook her head, pensively. "I loved my climbing rose bushes, Sarah. They were like a rainbow waterfall of yellow, white and pink."

Sarah turned to Lilly. "Do you know what used to fascinate me in the garden, Aunt Lilly?" she asked without waiting for an answer. "It was the insects, the way the spiders would spin their webs between the leaves to capture and harvest bugs. I was so fascinated by everything. I wasn't even afraid of the bumble bees buzzing around gathering honey."

Sarah reached over and laid her hand on Lilly's arm. "And nothing was more beautiful than watching the butterflies fluttering every which way or sitting on leaves, twitching their colorful wings. The birds, too, especially the cardinals whistling and sailing across the yard like little fireballs. It was really a magical place, Aunt Lilly."

Lilly reached over to pour more lemonade into their glasses. "That's all in the past, Sarah. I couldn't take the garden with me. But you'll notice I've kept what I could and my tastes haven't changed much. I still have my oval maple table with its four matching chairs. You see, I still have the red-checkered cushions on them, too."

"I notice you've also kept your antiques, there on the shelves, just the way you did in your cottage. I always loved them, especially the dish with the flower designs embedded in the colored glass."

"Ah, yes, Sarah, my dish."

Sarah looked at her aunt quizzically. "The way you said that, Aunt Lilly, 'my dish.' Is there something different about it? Or special?"

"Let's not talk about that now. First, tell me, do you play cards?"

"Not since I was in grade school. I used to play with Joey. He always beat me."

"How is your brother these days, Sarah?"

"I haven't heard from him in quite a while, not since his last letter from New Zealand. I think he's running away from any possible permanent relationship. But that's Joey. Ever since he was a kid he was a little wild and unpredictable. And how about you, Aunt Lilly? We've been out of touch for so long, with my living in Oregon with my parents, and you here. Why did you give up the cottage and that beautiful garden?"

Lilly sat back, crossed her legs and pulled her black skirt over her knees. "I had to move, Sarah. Living out there in the sticks was hard, especially when my husband went senile. Worse when he died."

"Uncle Henry died of a heart attack, didn't he?"

"He did, but his whole body gave up the ghost after his mind went haywire. The clincher was my health. After finding out I have the beginning of kidney disease, I had to move to be near the doctors and a hospital."

Sarah took her aunt's hand in hers. "That had to be so hard on you, Aunt Lilly."

Lilly brightened. "At first, yes, but I got over it. There comes a time in everyone's life, Sarah, when serious problems have to be overcome. Sometimes it seems almost hopeless, but it can be done."

Sarah looked doubtful. "I don't know, Aunt Lilly."

"You're obviously facing a problem, Sarah... Now, you did say you played cards as a child."

"Yes, but I was never lucky."

"Luck is one thing. I'm talking about something else."

"You mean playing for fun?"

Lilly looked into Sarah's eyes. "That, too, of course, but I'm saying playing cards reveals a lot about ourselves. Figuratively speaking."

"Figuratively?"

Lilly took a deep breath. "Yes, you see, it depends on the hand we're dealt. We can bluff our way through each game, lose by the rules or win in spite of them."

Sarah looked skeptical. "I'm not sure what that means, Aunt Lilly, but to me, life is a roller coaster and being happy is an illusion."

"I can see you're rather depressed, Sarah. You must try to remember, though, happiness comes in degrees. Life is like a game of bridge. It takes time to get good at it. If you lose, you can always play again another day. If you keep losing you'll still survive. Life isn't like a roller coaster where you don't get a second chance when it goes off the rails or breaks down. Then it's game's over."

Sarah shook her head, her lips frozen into a pout. "Why do bad things happen in the first place, Aunt Lilly? Sometimes I wonder if it's fate. Do you believe in fate?"

"Sooner or later, bad things happen to everyone. We never know exactly why. I've never really made friends with fate. It's the deck of cards I trust. We win or we lose. Life is 'living the deck.' We never know for sure what or when anything will happen."

"I know you went through a lot, even before Uncle Henry's sickness. I remember hearing bits and pieces. If it's not too painful, will you tell me what happened, Aunt Lilly, and how you managed to survive?"

"Well, Sarah, if you really want to hear it, it's faded far enough into the past and you're old enough now, so I can tell you. As you know, Uncle Henry came into my life in our later years. We weren't together long, really. I had been alone a long time before I met him, and yes, I was angry, very angry. My family was dead, all of them, my mother, father, two sisters and baby brother. Drowned when their boat capsized in a squall that burst over the lake without warning. The boat was captained by Jesse Pordum, my fiancé at the time. The ride was a surprise for my Dad's fiftieth birthday. I had come down with the flu and being too sick to go, I urged them to go without me. Insisting on it was the worst mistake of my life. I couldn't forgive myself.

"I felt cheated. On one terrible afternoon, in one terrible moment, I lost everything I ever loved. The cards were stacked against me then. It took many years to pick up the pieces and rebuild my life and that didn't happen until I decided to shuffle a new deck of cards for myself and let go of the past. I had to start over."

Sarah listened sympathetically. "I never knew the full story, Aunt Lilly."

Lilly was silent for a few moments, then said, "Loss always brings change, Sarah."

"Loss makes me bitter and afraid, Aunt Lilly."

Lilly smiled knowingly. "I understand, Sarah. I was the lead character in my own tragedy. It was a play I didn't write, but one day, almost on cue, a gust of wind blew the newspaper across the patio near my garden. When I bent down to pick it up I noticed a black ant scurrying along carrying a crumb larger than itself toward a secret destination. I watched it climb over stones, twigs and leaves in its path. Once or twice it dropped its load, but gathered it up again and continued until it was out of sight. Suddenly, I didn't feel alone. I realized how much that insignificant insect and I had in common: we were both struggling with the burden we carried." Lilly took Sarah's hand and stroked it. "Are you following me, Sarah?"

"I know what you're saying, Aunt Lilly, but still…life seems so ugly to me. I feel like a ping pong ball just bouncing around and looking for a table to land on."

Lilly laughed. "I know the feeling. But keep in mind, Sarah, happiness can come at any time. You have a choice. You can waste your life wallowing in despair or capture that moment in life that's waiting to be appreciated. Seize the moment while you can, Sarah."

Sarah's eyes were damp when she looked to her aunt. "Aunt Lilly, my fiancé left me a month ago. It came as a shock. I was looking forward to marriage, to having children. As an only child I always wanted siblings. I love children. I've been teaching Sunday school for the past year and it's so fulfilling. They're such a joy to me. If—"

"Sarah, my dear girl, you needn't say anything more. It's obviously over. You can't rewind the past. Don't waste precious time with regrets, and never ever allow hurtful people to live in your brain."

"But Aunt Lilly—"

Lilly stood up. "Hush. Come." She reached for Sarah's hand and pulled her along. "I have something to show you," she said, walking slowly over to her old wooden ice box on the far side of the kitchen. She reached up and took the glass dish sitting on top of it. Moving across to the window, she held the dish up to the light. The early afternoon sun cast a soft glow over it.

"That's the pretty dish I remember and admired so much."

Lilly held it higher to catch more light. "Come close. What do you see?"

"All I see, Aunt Lilly, is a candy dish. A dusty candy dish. An old one, to be sure, but still a beautiful one."

"What else do you see?"

"Nothing."

"It's a clue to my secret, Sarah. It holds truth without

55

words." To Sarah's puzzled look, Lilly said, "Beauty inspires us to survive."

"What do you mean?"

"When I begin to feel sorry for myself and think about what could have been or should have been, I pick up my dish. It reminds me that, despite adversity, I must endure, just as this dish has endured the ravages of time. If this little dish, this colorful little object covered in dust can survive the packing, moving and handling over the years and still remain intact and beautiful, whatever life throws its way, why can't I?"

"This dish did all that for you, Aunt Lilly?"

"Yes, Sarah, the ant that wouldn't be deterred by hardship, and this beautiful dusty dish, which I regard as symbols of the human spirit and the everlasting beauty of life. Life is a precious gift not to be wasted." She handed the dish over to Sarah. "When you leave, Sarah, it's yours to take and keep."

Sarah looked down to the dish balanced on her hands. "Along with your dusty dish philosophy."

Aunt Lilly smiled. "A nice way to think of it."

"Aunt Lilly—"

"Say nothing more, Sarah. Believe."

It wasn't long after Sarah left for Oregon that I saw her Aunt Lilly sit down and write a letter to her. I could only read part of it, but that's all I needed to get the gist of it. This is what I saw:

'Dear Sarah,

You've been gone less than a week and I already miss you terribly. Being together and reliving those wonderful days of picnics and gatherings with our whole family thrilled me more than you can know. Above all, seeing you again after all those years filled a need in me that desperately needed filling. Sarah, do you think you could make an ailing, old lady happy again and pay me a visit next summer or sooner, if possible? There is so much yet to talk about and so much to see. Even if it's only a week or two, we'd have time to visit Niagara Falls and see a few of the wonderful shows always playing here in Buffalo....'

Lilly wrote more, I'm sure, but that was all I could read. I didn't know if or when Sarah replied until summer arrived.

Chapter 9

There's was always some kind of noisy activity taking place within my brick walls. Aside from my tenants constantly coming and going, with a recently evicted one banging his drums at all hours— not to mention barking dogs, slamming doors, shouting tenants, and blaring radios— customers and delivery men tramped in every day to Joe's restaurant: the Bond Bread man with his loaves of fresh bread and rolls; the Freddie's man with his doughnuts customers loved to dunk in their coffee before eating; the Sahlen's man with his franks, hamburger and ham; the Weckerle man with the milk, butter and cream; and the many other vendors bringing necessary supplies needed to run a restaurant, such as napkins, pickles, mustard and various condiments.

Then, of course, there are others: the iceman lugging chunks of ice upstairs for the iceboxes and dripping water on my wood floors, which always sent Huggs grumbling to find a mop; the repairmen who make frequent visits to fix plugged toilets or blown electric fuses; and the carpenters fixing broken door hinges and such. Huggs often escorted the meter readers into the cellar and held their flashlight for them while they jotted down the numbers in their pads.

It was the day before Gustav was visited by his friend, Wilhelm, when a repairman toting his toolbox up the stairs caught my attention. Usually, these tradesmen wore grungy dungarees and soiled shirts, but this one was exceptionally neat, with his gray slacks and clean, blue sport shirt. Suspicious that he might be a burglar in disguise, I was about to give him more attention, when I was distracted by yelling:

"Hey, what the hell do you think you're doing!" the man barked, shoving Huggs back.

"You just moved in, so I only wanted to welcome you here with a hug," Huggs said, hurt in his voice.

"What are you, nuts?" The man waved his cocked fist. "Back off! I said back off!"

Hearing the commotion, Joe rushed out of his restaurant and stepped between the two, his short, hairy arms outstretched between their chests.

"Hold on there, hold on. I'm sorry, mister, but you see, Huggs here is our unofficial greeter. Whenever a new party moves into the building, Huggs always welcomes them that way."

His face flushed an angry red, the big man unclenched his fist and dropped his arm. "Well, hell's bells, man, somebody shoulda told me or give me a warning. I ain't used to no guys wrapping their arms around me like they want to wrassel or dance or something worse."

Huggs piped up. "I'm sorry, mister. I didn't mean no harm. It's just what I do."

The man thumbed his chest. "Yeah, well, it ain't what I do!"

"OK, everybody's got the story now, right?" Joe said, giving Huggs a little nudge. "Don't you have a job inside?"

"Oh, yeah, I almost forgot, Joe, I gotta take the garbage out of the kitchen," Huggs said, moving quickly away and into the restaurant.

The man picked up his suitcase and started for the stairs. He looked back at Joe and rolled his eyes. "Is he…" he tapped his head "…you know…?"

"He's OK," Joe said, "just overfriendly. By the way, if you need any chores taken care of, Huggs is the guy to call. He's not only our unofficial greeter, he's our all-around helper, too."

The next morning while *I was watching and trying to figure out what Gustav was jotting in his black ledger, a soft rapping at the door interrupted him. Gustav closed the book quickly, shoved it in the table drawer and hurried across the kitchen.*

"Who's there?" he asked, his voice hushed.

A quiet voice answered. "It is me, Wilhelm."

Gustav opened the door a crack and peeked out before opening it wide and stepping back. "Wilhelm Brenner. Come in, my friend, come in."

Although the day was quite warm, the man wore a dark overcoat with a gray scarf wrapped around his neck. He carried with him the cold fragrance of fresh air.

"Here, Wilhelm, sit here by the light of the window and away from the door." He pulled the chairs up. "Would you like something to drink? A glass of wine to warm you? Coffee?"

"Nothing. I cannot stay long."

Wilhelm sat down at the table and set his black fedora on the chair next to him. Gustav sat across from him and leaned forward anxiously on his elbows.

"Tell me," Gustav whispered, "what news do you have for me?"

"Not good, my friend," Wilhelm said, taking his eyeglasses from his pocket and curling the arms carefully over his ears, "not good."

"But the money I gave you, the three thousand dollars, it was delivered, yes?"

"As far as we know, yes, they received it."

"Then what's the holdup? My Greta and the little ones, Inga and Hans, they should be on their way here by now."

Wilhelm let out a weary sigh. "Gustav, our contact has told me that conditions are getting worse all the time. They are combing the city streets and even the villages for Jews. All of them. Men, women and children. Even the old and crippled ones are being corralled and shipped out on trains every day."

Gustav reached across the table and grabbed Wilhelm's sleeve. "Have they taken Greta and the children? Tell me, Wilhelm, have they taken my family?"

"I don't know, Gustav. I'm sorry," Wilhelm said, peeling Gustav's hand away. "I am still waiting to hear something definite from our contact in Stuttgart."

"Where, Wilhelm, where are they taking our people?"

"Work camps, Gustav. To be used as slave labor. That much we know for sure."

"But there are rumors, are there not, Wilhelm? We've all heard these are not only work camps; they must be death camps, otherwise why would also they take the old and sick."

"I don't wish to believe they're death camps, Gustav. I don't think we have yet become barbarians."

"Nevertheless, it may be true. Don't you remember a few years ago, Kristallnacht, how they smashed the windows of the synagogues and Jewish businesses? That was only the beginning. In any case, we can't take a chance. We must get my family here. Quickly, Wilhelm, quickly!"

"Patience, my friend," Wilhelm said, patting his hand. "We

have not given up. Our problem now is the border. It has been sealed against any Jews trying to leave Germany. But we have an underground working for us."

"What would it take to insure their escape? Money? More money?"

"Money always helps."

"How much, Wilhelm? What do you think?"

"Perhaps another two or three thousand dollars. But, Gustav, there still is no guarantee. As you know, the regime is very efficient at everything it undertakes. It is ruthless. America may be at war with Germany any day now because of their aggression."

The sound of voices in the hall stopped their conversation. Gustav put his fingers to his lips and motioned Wilhelm to stay put. He rose quickly and padded to the door, opened it a crack and saw Rosie standing there.

"Rosie, what is it? Were you calling me?"

"No, Mr. Gustav. A man was standing by your door a minute ago and I asked if I could help him, but he ran away down the stairs. I know he went out because I heard the downstairs door slam shut."

"A man, Rosie? How do you know it was a man?"

Rosie smiled. "Because he was wearing the same kind of shaving perfume Willy Dee used to use, only not so strong."

"Willy Dee?"

"Yes, he's the man who used to live upstairs. That's what he called himself, Willy Dee. My mother says he was a creepy boy with pictures of snakes and things on his arms, and greasy blond hair growing over his ears. Mommy said he used that perfume because he was smelly. His neighbor— Mr. Sherman I think his name was— he always complained because Willie Dee made so much noise playing his drums. Mr. Sherman reported him to Mrs. Chapman. Lots of times. Mrs. Chapman told Willy Dee to cut it out. He always said he would, and he did for a while, but then he started up again."

"Tell me, Rosie, did you notice anything else about the man by my door?"

Rosie put her pinky finger against her dimpled cheek. "Well, when I first smelled him…." She giggled. "Smelled him. That's funny isn't it, Mr. Gustav, to say that?"

"Yes, yes, it is, Rosie, very funny. Go on. Then what?"

"I reached out and touched his jacket sleeve. I was going to ask him if he was looking for you, but as soon as I touched him I felt him spin around and dash down the stairs."

"What did you notice, Rosie?"

"Well, his sleeve was very smooth, like a silk handkerchief I touched once. My mother said worms make it, that's why they call them silkworms, and it comes from China and costs a lot of money. That's how I know he was somebody important, maybe even rich."

"Did he say anything, Rosie?"

"No, but when I touched him I knew he shouldn't be there because I heard him choke on his air."

"You mean he gasped."

"Yes, I surprised him, I guess. Or maybe I scared him, but I didn't mean to, honest, I didn't."

"You startled him and that made him run away."

"I think so. That's how I know he was young, too, because nobody old can run down the stairs so fast that their feet sound like bam bam bam bam bam all the way down. But one more thing, Mr. Gustav. I think he dropped something running because I heard a klunk."

"A klunk?"

"Something heavy. Maybe a can of something, like a can of beans I heard Mommy drop one time."

I watched Gustav walk slowly down the hall to the stairs, where he stooped and picked up a gun. He came back.

"You were right, Rosie, it was a can. A heavy one," he said, slipping the gun in his pocket. "I'll take it down to the restaurant later. It probably came from there."

Gustav bent over and whispered something in her ear, but I don't know what it was. Just then, Rosie's mother, Lizzie Shanahan appeared in the hall, a cigarette burning between her nicotine-stained fingers.

"Is my Rosie pestering you again, Gustav?" she asked, coming out and taking Rosie's hand. She jerked her back. "Are you bothering Mr. Schwartz again, Rosie?" she chided, her voice raspy. "How many times do—"

"Please, Mrs. Shanahan, don't scold her. She told me someone was standing outside my door. She did me a big favor."

"Oh, she did, did she? Well, you come along, Miss Goody-Two-Shoes, inside where you belong." She took a long drag on her cigarette and waved the smoke away. "As to whether she did you a favor or not, Gustav, she couldn't know it beforehand. And that's why she's to mind her own business." She opened her apartment door and pulled Rosie inside. "Good afternoon to you, sir," she said, slamming the door behind her.

Gustav backed into his apartment and returned to the table.

"You heard?"

"Everything. Gustav, this shows what we are up against."

"Do you think he overheard us? Whoever it was?"

"No, Gustav, we were speaking quietly and we are far from the door."

"But the fact that someone was here at all tells us something." He pulled the revolver from his pocket and laid it on the table between them. "The gun Rosie thought was a can. I picked it up on the stairs just now. Look, Wilhelm, the barrel, see? It's loaded, too. My assassin, if that was what he was, dropped it in his rush to get away."

"Not necessarily an assassin, Gustav, but can you see the possible danger you're in? No doubt the danger both of us are in. We cannot meet here anymore. It's too risky. We will have to set up a new location. Someone could have followed me. Gustav, keep the gun for protection. You may need it if someone intends to do you harm."

"Why me, Wilhelm? Why me?"

"They may think you are too untrustworthy and want to dispose of you. We spoke of it before."

Gustav nodded his head, pondering. "Wilhelm, is it possible to smuggle me back into Germany? Perhaps from the inside I could be of more help. I would find a way to get my family out."

"Gustav, first let us see what the circumstances are. We have heard nothing in over two weeks. Perhaps your Greta and the children are stranded refugees at the moment. They could even be in England. It would take time to get them here, or to even to get word to us. Communications are difficult these days. There are thousands like them trying to escape Germany. Because of it, there is much confusion across the continent. Let us not think the worst."

Gustav sagged in his chair. "You're right, Wilhelm. I must not panic."

"There is no doubt of it now, Gustav; you are under surveillance by enemies. This place is being watched. It's not safe. They have their eyes on both of us now, I'm sure."

"Because I belong to the Bund. That is how the government has traced me, Wilhelm. But I had to join the German organization. It is the only way I could get my family here more easily and quickly. That was my thinking at the time, my hope."

"The FBI doesn't know that. As a member of the Bund, you are to them a probable spy. You've aroused their interest. And to make it worse, you are not trusted by the Germans, either, because you were born in America. What happened here this day is proof of that. Who knows who is really after you. And," he added, "who knows how safe I am. After all, I am a member of the Bund, as well. When I joined, I thought it was a club where we meet and drink beer with German friends, like the Knights of Columbus for the Italians. Now I cannot get out. I know too much."

"Couldn't it have been an FBI agent? That seems most likely, Wilhelm."

"It's possible, but I don't think one of them would be so careless as to lose his weapon, Gustav. From what I've heard, they are quite efficient."

"But, Wilhelm, why would the Germans fear me. I've lived in Germany for—"

Wilhelm waved him off. "I know, because your father took a professorship at Bonn University, you spent many years in Germany, that's true. That's where you attended school, met Greta and started a family. Still, you are not German born, so you are suspect. By now, to make it worse, they must also know you are a Jew."

"Then I'm in limbo."

"Not necessarily. As an engineer working at the Curtiss Aircraft plant, you are considered valuable and still useful to them."

"But they are growing impatient with me, Wilhelm. Last week Otto Kreuger jumped on me, saying that since I began working there, I've brought no worthwhile information to pass on to the Fatherland. And that aide of his, Bruno, in his silk suit and shiny shoes, the way he looks at me with narrowed eyes... I know he doesn't trust me."

"Stall them. Make them believe you are doing your best." Wilhelm picked up his hat and rose from his chair. "As for another payment, let us try again, but you know, Gustav, you are taking a chance of losing it and getting nothing in return."

"For my family, Wilhelm, I'll gamble anything. My very life, gladly, if it would help."

"All right, Gustav, talk no more about it. Be patient until we are sure of where we stand."

"Wait while I get the money." Gustav returned with a thick envelope. "Here, Wilhelm, two thousand dollars may not be enough. Give them another three thousand. I pray it will bring my family to me."

Curiously, Wilhelm eyed the envelope in his hand. "This is a great deal of money to come by," he said, looking Gustav in the eye. "Gustav...."

"It's my only hope to free my family," Gustav said, moving around and helping him on with his coat and scarf. "Don't keep me waiting so long next time, Wilhelm." He led him to the door. "We can't meet here again, of course, now that we know we are being watched. Santasiero's restaurant nearby might work."

"No, it is too close and not crowded enough," he said, stuffing the envelope in his pocket. "In one week from today meet me at the Buffalo City Hall. Inside, we can each occupy a telephone booth and speak to each other that way. Twelve o'clock sharp."

"Wilhelm, can't you telephone me here if something develops before that time?"

"No, we could be overheard. However, if I believe I can come here without being followed or detected before then, Gustav, I will take the chance. We must be extremely careful now that we are certain we're both under surveillance."

"Wilhelm, do you think I should move away from here?"

"I think not. That would arouse even more suspicion. Besides, they would have no trouble tracking you down. Stick to your usual routine and go to work at four o'clock every day. Come straight home after your shift at midnight. Stop at no bars. Attract no attention."

"Of course, of course, you are right. But my nerves can't take much more, Wilhelm. I must know something definite about my family."

"I understand, Gustav," he said quietly as he stepped out of the apartment into the hallway. "Believe me, I do understand."

After Wilhelm left, Gustav went directly to his closet. Fondling the gun, he spun the bullet-filled chamber with his thumb and eyed the barrel before hiding the gun under a hat on the shelf. "Let someone come for me now," he muttered, "I dare them."

After listening to Gustav's conversation with Wilhelm, I began to pay attention to a man who came into Joe's restaurant on my first floor. Middle-aged, with a swarthy complexion, he was clean-shaven and neatly dressed in a dark suit and hat. He always sat where he could see through the side window to the foyer. No one could enter or exit the building without being observed by him. His order was always the same: two hamburgers with onion and catsup, and a Coca Cola. Because he appeared standoffish, with his head and eyes averted, no one attempted to engage him in a conversation, not even Sylvia, the friendly waitress. I thought of him as a mysterious stranger and determined to keep an eye on him.

Chapter 10

"No, no!" Mrs. Rosellini cried, storming from one side of the room to the other, wringing her hands, clasping them together and raising them and her eyes to heaven. "Oh, Gezu Cristo, why, why, why?"

Dorothy sat curled with her legs tucked under her in their parlor chair, her face buried in her hands, crying. "Mama...."

"No mama me, you...you disgrazia. Disgrace!"

"Good thing your father, he's dead. If he was a here he would kill you. But first he would kill him who do this to his bambina. He always call you his beautiful bambina."

"I'm sorry, Mama. I'm sorry."

"Sorry. Sure you sorry. Me, too, I'm sorry. What good to say that now. Too late! Too late!" She paced the floor. "Whata we gonna do? What? Gezu Cristo, what?"

Dorothy moaned. "I don't know, Mama."

"Who is he, this boy? This ah-ni-mahl. Who?"

Dorothy wiped her tears with the hem of her skirt. She shook her head. "I already talked to him, Mama. He says it's not his baby. He's lying, Mama, he's lying. He said his friends will back him up."

"Is he Italiano?"

"No. He's American."

She scowled. "How old this…this American pig?"

"Sixteen, I think." She looked up with pleading eyes. "Mama, he said he loved me. I believed him. I wanted to believe him. Papa wasn't here anymore. I wanted him to love me. I believed him when he said my scar didn't matter and I was beautiful to his eyes."

"How long? How many months you miss?"

"Three, I think, Mama." Her face looked red and tortured. "Mama, will you send me away? Will they take me away to that home for bad girls, Mama?"

"Nobody take a you no place. You no belong there with them. We gotta time." She looked hard at her daughter. "Anybody else know? You tell anybody?"

"No, Mama, only him."

"OK, then still you go to school. Tell nobody nothing. Mama think of something." She tapped her head with her fingertips. "I think of something. I still gotta money from you papa."

"Oh, Mama."

Mrs. Rossellini suddenly pulled her daughter to her feet and hugged her. "My little baby, my little bambina," she said, tears filling her eyes. "Don'tchu worry. Mama make it all right."

Just then Sonny burst into the room from the hall and slammed the door.

"How many times I tell you," Josephina said, wagging her finger at him, "close a the door easy. You wanna wake a the dead?"

Sonny stopped and glanced from his sister to his mother.

"What's the matter with Dolly? Why's she crying? Your eyes, too, Mama. Were you crying?"

"None of your business. Go washa your hands. We eat pretty soon."

"For your information, I live here, too. I got a right to know what's going on."

"You got a right to I slap your face! You hear me good. Now, go washa you hands and scrubba good. I don' want to see black dirt on my clean towel."

"I'm not a stranger here, you know. This is my house as much as yours. I'm an American and we the people got rights," he growled, skipping over to the bathroom. "I learned it in school last week about the Constitution which says those very words." He yelled out the bathroom door, "Well, I'm people, too!"

When they sat down to eat, Sonny kept badgering them.

"Something funny's going on here. What happened, Dolly?" he mocked in a musical voice, "your boyfriend break your heart?"

Josephina raised her hand as if to slap him. "Shutta you mouth and eat."

Sonny ducked away, grinning. "You can't fool me, Dolly. I seen you talking to him outside. Lots of times. It's that curly-haired guy with the big muscles he likes to show off, ain't it? Thinks he's a hotshot with those cowboy boots he always wears." He snickered. "And you sneaking around reading them love notes when you think nobody's looking." He smirked. "I sure would like to see that diary you write in all the time."

Dorothy turned teary-eyed to her mother. "Mama, make him shut up!"

"For the lasta time, I said shutta you mouth. You talk too much. Eat!"

Sonny shoveled macaroni into his mouth. "If Papa was here, he'd tell me what's going on. He told me someday I'm gonna be the man of the house."

"Some a day is not now."

"Well, then, why the big secret? Are we moving or something? We better not be."

"Not a your business. In time you find out."

Sonny sulked. "Well, I just hope we ain't moving again. I got good friends here."

Josephina leaned back and nodded. "OK, when a you finish, Sonny, you go outside and play for another hour, then you come back. You gotta homework, right?"

"I already did it."

"Sure, in a your dreams. You come back one hour. And stay away the street."

After Sonny left, Josephina and Dorothy stood at the sink washing and drying dishes.

"Sonny, he give me an idea. I donna think we got a choice."

"What is it, Mama?"

"Later. I tell you later. Now, you go finish your homework and go take a nap. Sleep. You needa to rest."

Mrs. Rosellini watched her daughter leave, then went into her own bedroom, where she lit a candle standing on the dresser behind a picture of the Virgin Mary. She put her hands together and bowed her head.

"Madre mia in heaven, helpa my Dorothy. Helpa me.

Please." She said three 'Hail Marys,' made the sign of the cross on her forehead with her thumb and sat on the edge of her bed.

"Vito, my husband, ifa you can hear me, please you helpa us. Your bambina, she's got bad trouble. Tell me whata my idea I'm thinking about is right to do. I pray you gonna say it'sa OK. I'm a tired. I'm a lay down and think some more and sleep a while."

When Josephina woke up, she took a pad and pencil from her dresser drawer and sat on the edge of her bed. She opened to a clean page and began to write. Because it was in Italian, I couldn't read it. When she finished, she folded the paper neatly and placed it in an envelope, ready to mail.

Chapter 11

About three weeks later I heard Sonny grumbling aloud as he jumped down the stairs two at a time.

"'Go outside and play. Go outside and play.' That's all she ever says when she don't want me to hear what's going on. Always secrets, secrets, secrets. Either I'm too young to hear or I gotta shut up because it's not a boy's business." He stopped at the bottom of the stairs, cupped his hands around his mouth, and yelled. "In case you don't know, this is a free country. Didn't you ever hear of freedom of speech? Anyway, who cares! It's only dumb girl talk, anyway! If Papa was alive he'd lay down the law and tell you a thing or two!" He left the building, stomping his feet and slamming the door behind him.

When I looked inside the apartment, Josephina was sitting on the couch with Dorothy.

"I gotta news for you, my little one." She took a letter from her apron pocket. "It'sa from your Cousin Annamarie Gotti."

"Annamarie?"

"In Italy. My brother Nino's daughter. You don' know nothing about her, right?"

"I did hear you and Papa mention her name a couple of times, I think. And Uncle Nino's other kids. You never said anything about her, though, not that I remember."

"OK, I tella you now. Nino, my older brother, he's gotta eight children, maybe you remember that, but Annamarie, she's a different."

"How different, Mama. Is she crippled or something?"

"Nothing like a that. You see, one a day late at night, my brother Nino, he's a come home from the cheese factory where he's a work and he pass a the church. It'sa dark, but he can see a bundle on the step by the church door. He thinks a package, maybe clothes or something somebody give for the poor and he's a walk away, when he hear a cat cry. Anyway, he thinks a cat, but when he hear again same cry, he knows this a no cat. It'sa bambino."

"A baby?"

"In a blanket. A note, too, that say, 'Please take a care my baby.' So he take a home the baby."

"Lena, his a wife, at first she say, 'Take a back the baby. Give to the church. How can we feed another mouth witha no money. Besides, I got 'nough a work take a care five bambini already.'

"But Nino, he say, 'No. This,' he say, 'is gift from a God.' He say, 'God, he want this baby here with us.'"

"And Aunt Lena agreed?"

"Whatta could she say. Nino, he's a the boss."

"That's interesting, Mama, but why are you telling me all this now? And why did you send Sonny away? This is no big secret, is it? Why can't Sonny hear this, too?"

Josephina flounced on her cushion. "Let a me finish my story first, then you aska your questions. OK?"

"I'm sorry, Mama."

Josephina patted her daughter's knee. "No be sorry, justa listen. Annamarie, her husband, Pietro Gotti, he worka the railroad. He die last year when a train run him over. They married only two years, long enough to have baby, but they don' have no baby. This I already know from my brother Nino's letter.

"After you tell me what happened you, I'm thinking about what we gonna do? I ask God, I ask Papa, help me think what to do? Sonny, he give me idea about we move away. I sleep. When I wake up, I see Annamarie's face, and I remember her story. So I write to Annamarie."

"Mama! You told her about me?"

"It'sa OK. I ask if it'sa all a right we come live with her until....you know. I tell her we got insurance money, so not to worry about that."

"Mama!"

"Annamarie write me. Here, this letter," she said waving the envelope in front of her. "Two days ago it come." She unfolded the letter, smoothed it on her lap and read parts of it. "You see, she's a understand. She say she grateful your Uncle Nino Cadenza, my brother, took her in like his own bambina. She say she's a glad to pay back an' we can come anytime."

"Mama, Italy!"

"Only maybe for a year, maybe not so long. Then we come back."

"Mama, I can't. I won't go to Italy."

"So then whatta you gonna do? Hah? What? You gonna parade a down the street with a big belly so everybody can talk?"

Dorothy eyes flooded. She began rocking back and forth.

77

She stroked her hair. "My baby, we got a no choice. No way we can stay here. Pretty soon you show. Then everybody know."

"Sonny's going to go crazy. He won't go, Mama. He loves it here. He loves his friends."

"Too bad. First thing, I take a care the passa-port business. After that I go buy the boat tickets to Palermo. Already I told Mrs. Chapman. I tella her we moving back to Italy to helpa my sick brother Nino."

"Mama, don't we have any relatives here in America? Anybody at all?" she asked, trembling. "Or another place we can go to here in America?"

"Nobody. No place. It'sa gonna be OK. You will like it there, Misilmeri, a nice little town Papa and me we come from near Palermo in Sicily. Thanka God for Annamarie."

Sobbing, Dorothy threw her arms around her mother. "Mama, I'm sorry. It's all my fault. I ruined our lives."

"No say that," Josephina said, hugging her back. "I believe God knows a what he's doing. We don' understand, but he got reason for this, like for when he give a Annamarie to your Uncle Nino, and when he take a your Papa, and for everything else, good and bad. Do not be afraid. Be strong." She made the sign of the cross and kissed the crucifix hanging from a strand of black beads circling neck. "It'sa gonna be OK, my baby," she said, bending over and kissing her daughter's forehead. "You wait and see. Everything gonna be OK."

The time to leave eventually arrived. By the way Sonny was carrying on that morning, everyone within a city block would think someone was being murdered as Josephina prodded and poked him ahead down the stairs with her suitcase. Dorothy trailed behind, half- dragging two bags.

"I don't want to go to no Italy!" Sonny wailed. "I'm not Italian, I'm American!"

"Shut uppa you mouth and a move. You are what I say you are."

With as many suitcases as they could carry banging the walls, they stumbled down the stairs, Dorothy tucking in her chin to hide her tears, while Sonny kept yelling:

"Why? Why do you wanna go there? All my friends are here. What's so good about Italy, anyway?" He stopped moving. "I ain't going! Besides, I heard somebody say there's going to be a war."

Josephina shoved him. "War or no war, that's a not our business. We gotta no choice. Now move!"

"Why?" He broke into tears and pleaded. "Why, Mama? Why?"

"In time you find out. Now, shut up and a be careful how you walk and don' fall. We late already."

The last time I saw Mrs. Rosellini, Dorothy was sobbing openly and her mother was stuffing Sonny into the back seat of a taxi. As the cab drove away, I could hear Sonny shouting 'I'm an American!'

Only time would tell whether I'd ever see the Rosellinis again.

In their hurry to leave, they almost knocked over a couple— a most unusual couple— who had signed an Agreement with Mrs. Chapman the day before to rent one of my furnished apartments for a month.

Chapter 12

The unusual couple I mentioned stood transfixed hearing the ruckus and watching Mrs. Rosellini shoving and cuffing her son to the taxi. When they were gone, the lady picked up their suitcase and carried it inside.

I was as surprised as anyone else when the two came into Joe's restaurant. Everyone seated around having lunch saw them and their names printed in big yellow letters across the sides of their luggage: 'Queenie and Little Fritz.'

Queenie stood about six feet tall, and Little Fritz was probably less than four feet tall. They were the oddest couple I'd ever seen. When I first spotted them, I thought he was her child. They sat together, ignoring all the faces staring at them as they gave Sylvia their order.

"Anything on the cheeseburger?" Sylvia asked, taking in at a glance his little-boy face and tiny hands.

"Onions and ketchup," Little Fritz answered in a high-pitched voice.

"And you, ma'am, would you like your tuna salad on white, rye or whole wheat?"

"Whole wheat, if you please."

Queenie and Little Fritz spoke in whispers as they ate their sandwiches, while people stole sidelong glances at them. When they finished their food, Queenie turned to the others seated at their tables and in a rather deep voice announced, "Ladies and gentlemen, I see we have piqued your interest and you are no doubt wondering who we are."

Everyone stopped eating and turned their full attention to this woman with her heavily powdered face, long, curly blond hair, blue eyelids, long, black eyelashes and red lips.

"This is Little Fritz, my husband and my partner." She turned to him. "Stand up Fritzi and take a bow."

Little Fritz stood up on his chair, his over-sized yellow bow tie hiding his chin, and bowed in several directions.

Queenie continued. "You may have heard of us—"

"Then again, you may not have heard of us," Fritz interjected, sweeping his floppy red pompadour off his forehead.

Everyone laughed.

"Little Fritz and I have been in show business for a long time, haven't we Fritz? Ever since our vaudeville days."

"You're giving away our age, Cutie."

"Well, didn't we start as babies?"

"Oh, right-o."

"Right-o? Why are you saying right-o, Fritz?"

"Because you're standing on me right toe."

Everyone laughed again.

"You see," Queenie said, "that's the kind of cornball stuff you'll get from us if you catch our act at the Palace Burlesque next week."

Little Fritz piped up. "That's right, folks," he said, smiling.

"But don't be put off by that corny bit you just heard. Actually, we're a ventriloquist act, and I'm the dummy."

"Oh, you got that right," Queenie said.

"Yeah, well, you married me, didn't you?" Fritz shot back. "So who's the dummy?"

The other customers clapped and whooped at that.

Queenie smiled. "Isn't he adorable, folks? That's why I love him so much."

"Anyway, folks," Fritz went on in his falsetto voice, "we'll be in town for at least two weeks, depending on popular demand. Right, love?"

"Right-o," Queenie said, planting a quick kiss on his lips and turning back to the people. "And that's it folks, the long and short of it."

"Get it, folks?" Fritz said, "The long and short of it?" He flipped them a salute. "We hope to see you all at the Palace."

Queenie picked Fritz up like a child and placed him on the floor, grabbed their suitcase with one hand and took his hand with the other and out the door they went, doing a 'Shuffle off to Buffalo' dance step.

Chapter 13

Not long after Mrs. Rosellini and her children moved away, a colored couple moved into the empty apartment. It was the same one occupied by my first colored family so many years earlier. My new tenants' names were Jeb and Rosalie Morrison, a young couple no more than twenty years old. He called her 'Cotton,' I suppose because she looked almost Caucasian with her off-white skin color and crystal-blue eyes. In fact, some people who passed them did a double-take and were ready to scowl their disapproval, until they realized she was probably a mulatto. Jeb told Mrs. Chapman, Bernice Chapman, the landlady, they had just moved up from the Atlanta area to be near relatives and would be looking for work. He said they didn't have much in the way of possessions, but he assured her they had enough money for rent until he could land a job. Fortunately for everyone, the burgeoning war was opening factories and making jobs plentiful.

When Mrs. Chapman learned they had almost nothing and were sleeping on old blankets on the hard floor, she managed to get them a second-hand bed from a used-furniture store nearby. From the basement, she also gave them a couch, a few chairs, a table, a scarred icebox and incidentals left behind by former tenants and stored away.

"We sure do appreciate the boss lady gibbin' us these things," Jeb said, his muscular arms glistening with sweat as he jockeyed the couch up to his second floor apartment, with Huggs holding up the lower end.

"Mrs. Chapman, she's got a good heart, that's for sure," Huggs answered. "She does lots of favors for lots of people, lots of people. That's what she does, gives favors to lots of people. Some people around here call her Saint Bernice, but I don't think she really is one. They just call her that."

"Like I said, we sure do appreciate it, Cotton and me. We never did see so much kindness from anybody before."

"Cotton? What's that?"

"Cotton ain't a 'what.' Cotton's a 'she.' My wife. In a minute you be seeing her, soon's we get this heavy, ol' couch inside." He strained to tilt his end through the doorway. "Huggs is a funny name. I never heared it said anywhere before."

Huggs grunted, lifting his end. "My real name's Huggins, but people call me Huggs because it's my nickname and because I always like to hug new people I meet. That's why they call me Huggs, too, because I'm a hugger. I didn't get a chance to hug you because Mrs. Chapman said to hurry up and help you move this couch."

Jeb laughed. "No offense, Mr. Huggs, but don't you be huggin' me. Where I come from, we ain't the huggin' kind, less'n it's yo' mama or yo' dawg."

They set the couch on the dining room floor and stepped back, panting hard.

"Sure would help if'n this building had a elly-vator... Oh, this here's my wife, Cotton." He gestured with his hand. "Cotton, this is Huggs."

Standing there turned slightly sideways, her hands clasped in front of her and smiling shyly, Cotton said, "My pleasure, I'm sure."

Jeb laughed again. "Cotton's like me, she don't much take to huggin', neither, least not by strangers."

The corners of Huggs' mouth turned down. "Well, I didn't mind helping, especially since Mrs. Chapman said to do it, but I sure wish I could've gave you a hug. And Cotton, too."

"Maybe someday, Huggs. Jes' maybe. Much obliged for your help. Now don' forget, gib my thanks to the boss lady."

That was my first acquaintance with the Morrisons. When I looked in a month or a little later, they were sitting at the table.

"Now, Jeb, you jes' stop your broodin' like a child and eat. I fixed your grits and eggs and bacon jes the way you likes them. And I knows you's hungry. So go ahead and dig in and get off'n your chest what's makin' you frown the way you been lately."

Jeb picked up his fork and slumped in his chair. "Tell you the truth, Cotton, I jes' ain't happy with my job."

"Well, it's a job, ain't it? And it pays reg'lar every week. It's more'n we ever had where we come from, dirt poor like we was."

"I know, I know, but still...."

"Still what, Jeb? Still what? You was OK wid it before. You was happy to get it, you 'member that? We had our own little ice cream and pie celebration, we was both so happy. Compared to where we was, this is like we died and went to heaven."

"Well, it ain't heaven to me now, Cotton, and I know it ain't never gonna be. The pay at the warehouse is good, thass true, but I ain't goin' nowhere."

"Where do you wanna go, Jeb? Whatchu wanna do? What else can you do?"

Jeb slammed his fork down hard. "Cotton, I wanna be somebody, not jes' some mule pushing around a two-wheeler on the docks loadin' up and emptyin' trucks. There ain't no future in it for me."

"We're eatin' reg'lar', ain't we, Jeb? And paying our bills widout worryin' where the money's comin' from better'n we ever did b'fore, ain't we? We're even puttin' somethin' away for…" She looked down to the swell of her stomach and smiled. "…for our baby."

"I know all that, Cotton, I know," he said, shaking his head miserably, "but it still ain't enough." He dug into his eggs and chewed a piece of bacon.

Cotton rolled her eyes, her fingertip tapping the side of her button nose. "'It ain't enough,' he says, 'it still ain't enough.'" She looked hard at him. "Well, what *is* enough, Jeb? Kin'ly tell me so's I know, too." She got up to set her ironing board in place.

"Cotton, when I'm working, I look at them who's around me, and I listen good. I pays 'tention how they talk to each other. They's respect in their voice, even when the other'n's not the boss. I don't get a whiff o' that treatment, Cotton. And some of the things they say hurt me. Hurt a lot, Cotton. Or when they don't say nothin' to me and make me feel invisible. And I always got to shut my mouf and keep it shut or else get canned." He slammed his fist on the table. "And that ain't right!"

"So what you gonna do about it, Jeb, break somebody's head open like you did back home when that ol' foreman slapped your face and called you a common nigga laborer jes' because you complained the sammich meat he gave you all for lunch was spoiled green?" She turned gloomy. "He landed in the hospital, Jeb, and sure as shootin' you was gonna land in jail. Caused us a lot o' hurt, too, havin' to split fast and leave our famblies behind like we did."

"No, you right, Cotton, punchin' don' work. It jes' gets a man in more trouble. But maybe it's a good thing we hustled outta there, anyways. We din't have no chance in a court 'o law, no more'n others like us scratchin' a living out o' the dirt till we die and they covers us up wid it along wid their lies." He shook his head. "Cotton, I been thinkin' lately."

"Thinkin' like what, Jeb?"

"What I think I needs is to get an eji-cation." He shoveled a lump of grits into his mouth.

Cotton faced him with her fist on a saucy hip. "Jeb, you cain't hardly speak English. And what schoolin' you had don' add up to a hill o' beans. Bein' all growed up already like you is, you cain't hardly start with the li'l chill'un, so how you gonna get an eji-cation? Tell me that if'n you can."

"Thass true enough, Cotton, you're right, but I hear tell they's got night school for immy-grant folks who come here from other countries and don' know no English. So, they's got to start from scratch, don't they? But I already knows the words, mos' o' them, anyway. I just got to learn how to say 'em right and put 'em together so's they makes sense to people."

"Oh, honey, they makes sense to me."

"I'm glad, Cotton, still, that ain't enough. But if'n you believe in me, I can do it."

"I do believe in you Jeb. I always did, you know that, and I always will."

"Then, by God, I can and I will do it!"

Her voice came sultry and warm. "If'n you can really do it, Jeb, which I don' hones'ly know how, then maybe you can teach me."

"I surely will, Cotton, I surely will."

Cotton turned serious. "So what're you gonna do, Jeb?" she asked, laying his work shirt over the ironing board.

He picked up his fork. "Honey, tomorrow I'm gonna check out that school." He took another mouthful of grits. "If'n all them whiteys can learn and be somebody, so can I! They's no better than me."

Cotton looked askance. "Jeb, if'n you do get all that schoolin', what're you gonna do wid it?"

Jeb set his fork aside and had a faraway look in his eyes. "Cotton, do you 'member when we rode that big ol' bus to Atlanta when your granny died?"

"How could I forget? The holes in that one muddy road sure did bump us around and keep us awake so we couldn't hardly get no sleep."

"Not that so much, Cotton. You 'member that park we went strollin' in after the funeral?"

"I cain't never forget that, neither, Jeb. It was so pretty with all them colored flowers everywhere and the air smellin' so clean and fresh."

"And you 'member that airo-plane that flew over our heads when we was lollin' along?"

"I sure do, Jeb? We hardly never seen even one o' them where we hailed from."

"Well, Cotton, seeing that airo-plane sailing around so pretty up there, well, it got me to thinkin'."

"I 'member you was quiet a long time, looking up at it, Jeb."

"That I was, Cotton. I was thinkin', first, how nice and clean the worl' mus' look from way up there, flying near the clouds, away from all the bad stuff happenin' alla time around us on the ground. Then I was thinkin', it mus' make a man feel mighty good, too, all by hisself, wid nobody bossin' him around and orderin' him to do dis or do dat— or else! Cotton, thass bein' free, somethin' we never can feel walkin' aroun' down here. Feel free." He took a final mouthful of grits, some spilling over his chin.

"I 'member we both said it looked like a big ol' bird floating around up there."

"Thass when I got the idea, Cotton."

"What idea you talkin' about, Jeb?"

He looked hard at her. "Cotton, I never spoke it to you before, but I would like to be a airo-plane pilot."

"Oh, Jeb, a airo-plane pilot? Sometimes a dream can be too big for a man's head to hold."

"Maybe so, Cotton, but still I'm saying it. That's what I want to be, a airo-plane pilot."

Cotton stepped over and cradled her arm around his neck, rubbed her cheek against his and planted a kiss on his lips. "I loves you, Jeb. More than anything in the world. I loves you because you's my man an' I'm proud o' you no matter what you do."

"I loves you, too, Cotton." He leaned back with a gleaming white smile on his face. "Now, 'stead o' standing there looking down at me, all silly like, you best go wipe some o' them grits off'n your mouth that you took off'n mine from kissin' jes' now."

After listening to Jeb talk about what he hoped to do, I remembered Alice, my librarian tenant, talking to her sister Agnes about a book:

"Oh, my," Alice said, setting her book aside and removing her eyeglasses. She leaned her head back in her chair and sighed.

"What are you 'oh, my-ing' about?" Agnes called from the kitchen.

"This novel. It's so sad."

"What is it, Alice?"

"It's a John Steinbeck book titled 'Of Mice and Men.' It's about two migrant ranch hands who travel from farm to farm, but one of them keeps getting them into trouble."

"One of those troublemakers you always hear about?"

"Not really, Agnes. He's just a big, powerful man with the mind of a child. Lennie— that's his name— he causes problems everywhere they go."

"Well, if he's mental, who can blame him?"

"There's more to it than that, Agnes. Anyway, Lennie and his friend, George, work hard and struggle to save enough money to buy a little farm of their own, but...I'd better not tell you what happens. You may want to read it. It's a very short book, a novella. It says something about the vicissitudes of life."

"There you go again, Alice, another one of your big words."

Alice ignored the comment. "'Of Mice and Men.' If you understand the poem that title comes from, you'll have the key to the story."

"How am I supposed to know that, Alice? You're the educated one with the books, not me."

Alice and Agnes got into a word tussle after that and I never got to hear an explanation. Maybe I'd figure out the connection between the book and Jeb and Cotton someday, but at the moment, I was as confused as Agnes was.

Chapter 14

One of the saddest and darkest moments I remember began the day a wisp of a girl no more than eighteen moved into one of my few available furnished apartments on the second floor. She was quite pale, with light blue eyes and long, brown hair. Her gray coat was almost threadbare. In fact, she had a pathetic, mousy look, as if she had just been released from an orphanage. Or a prison.

When she entered the apartment she gazed around a moment, set her bag down and untied her yellow *bonnet and stripped it off with her coat. She sat in the big chair in the corner of the room, put her head back, closed her eyes and breathed out a long sigh. She seemed a forlorn creature to me, a lost soul momentarily at peace with the world, or perhaps with herself. Maybe both.*

The next morning I saw her enter Joe's restaurant, where a few people who wandered in off the street were already sitting. She took a seat by the window. Sylvia, a slatternly waitress with a long face and slightly buck toothed, approached her.

"Whatcha having, honey?" she asked, pad and pencil in hand.

"Coffee and toast, please."

"Rye, white or wheat?"

"Wheat, please."

Sylvia jotted down her order. "You're new here, ain'tcha, honey?"

"I came in yesterday."

"Well, welcome to Fred."

"Fred?"

"Fred's the name of our building. I don't know who named him, though. What's your name, honey?"

"Catherine."

She smiled. "I'm Sylvia, your cheerful morning waitress. Every day except Sundays, that is. I refuse to work on the Sabbath. Not because I'm so holy, which I'm not, but it's my day to be totally free and nobody giving me orders. Sunday's Mable's day. She's Joe's wife. He owns the joint. Or leases it. I don't know which. Same thing, anyway."

Sylvia returned a few minutes later with Catherine's order. "If you need anything else, honey, let me know," she said, laying the check on the table.

Shortly after that, Mrs. Sheila Graham, a morning regular, came in and sat at a small table opposite Catherine. When she caught Catherine's eye, she nodded. Catherine, smiling wanly, nodded back.

Sylvia approached her, pad in hand. "The usual, Mrs. Graham?"

"Two soft-boiled eggs, yes, and tea, but would you please tell your cook to be more careful. Yesterday the eggs were almost hard-boiled."

"The cook will be sure to hear about that, Mrs. Graham, I guarantee it!"

Mrs. Graham was a long-time tenant who kept mostly to herself. She was a dignified woman past middle age with neatly coiffed gray hair and eyeglasses that roosted half way down her nose. Her gray eyes peering over the top of the rims had a shrewd cast to them. I saw her watching Catherine, who was sipping the last of her coffee and gazing out the window.

"Excuse me," she said, "but aren't you the young lady who moved into the apartment next to mine?"

Catherine turned to her. "If you mean on the second floor, then yes, I am."

They introduced themselves and carried on for a few minutes with small talk.

"Are you local, Catherine?"

Catherine nodded. "Yes."

Mrs. Graham studied her for a moment, and seemed about to say something, when Sylvia returned with her order.

She picked up her spoon and said, "Well, my dear, if there is anything I can do for you, please don't hesitate to ask. Or we can simply chat. I have a great deal of time on my hands that I can well afford to fill."

"Thank you," Catherine said, sliding a few coins out of her change purse and laying them on the table.

Mrs. Graham watched Catherine closely as she walked past her and out the door.

Except for the occasional echo of slamming doors in my hallways, things had been quiet since the drummer and the accordion player moved out. I suppose it was early afternoon three days after Catherine arrived when I heard sobbing coming from her apartment. When I looked inside I saw her reclining on the couch with her arm folded over her eyes. The lights were low and the radio was playing soft music. Of course I couldn't know what her trouble was and could only wait until circumstances changed.

I didn't have long to wait. About an hour later Sheila Graham emerged from her apartment, shopping bag in hand and headed for the stairs. Suddenly she stopped and turned her head, listening. She moved to the side and put her ear close to Catherine's door. She paused a moment, her lips pursed tightly, and rapped softly. She waited then rapped again. After a few moments the door opened a fraction.

"Oh, Mrs...."

"Graham."

"Mrs. Graham, of course," Catherine said, opening the door wider.

"Please excuse my boldness, my dear, but I couldn't help hearing. Can I be of any help?"

"No, I'm all right," Catherine said, pulling her housecoat tight around her and tucking under her sleeve the handkerchief she'd been using to dry her swollen eyes.

"Really, dear, forgive me, but I know distress when I hear it. I would appreciate if you would let me spend a little time talking with you. Being a lonely widow, friendless really, I could use a little company myself." A weak smile crossed her lips when she said it.

Catherine looked down at the shopping bag. "No, Mrs. Graham, I—"

"Sheila. Please call me Sheila."

"Thank you, Sheila," she said, slowly closing the door, "but I see you're on your way to—"

"Oh, tush," she said, waving her hand. "That can wait till

tomorrow."

Catherine opened the door again and stood aside. "All right, Sheila, if really want to."

"Thank you, Catherine," she said, stepping in and glancing around.

"Can I offer you coffee? Or tea?"

"No, thank you, dear. But I would appreciate sitting, if you wouldn't mind. My legs are not meant for standing very long and need all the rest they can get. They say they're the first things time steals from us."

They sat facing each other in front of a fake fireplace. Catherine looked uncomfortable. Sheila spoke first.

"Now, my lovely young lady, although we've just met, if you would trust me enough to confide in me, I would consider it a great privilege. I've had great deal of experience over the years." She paused. "You've been weeping."

Her head bowed, Catherine nodded.

"Tears wash away sadness, my dear. Though it may not seem so now, eventually they dry."

Catherine shook her head doubtfully.

"You don't think so? All right, then, try to think of me as an aunt or confidant and tell me, if you will, what's troubling you so deeply."

Catherine raised her head, her voice subdued. "I wouldn't know where to begin, Mrs. Gra—Sheila."

"Why not at the beginning, dear. Where you were born. Who your parents are."

Catherine touched the corner of her eye. "I was adopted."

"Many are."

"Yes, I didn't know, but…."

"Go on, dear, it's all right."

"Oh, Sheila, I can't—"

"Please, go on. Don't be afraid. Please."

Hesitating, Catherine gathered herself up. "Well, I guess when I was about ten years old, I was home alone and bored after doing my homework and –oh, Sheila, this isn't right. You just met me. It's not fair of me to burden you with my problems."

"Catherine, believe me, trust me, you aren't burdening me. Please go on."

Catherine sighed. "All right, Sheila. If you insist. I've been holding it in a long time, but I trust you…." She paused a long moment, as if gathering her thoughts. "Well, for no particular reason I can think of now, except for childish curiosity, one day I decided to explore my mother's bedroom dresser. Making sure I left nothing out of place, I rummaged carefully through one drawer after the other. Seeing nothing of interest, I was about to close the last drawer, the bottom drawer, when I saw sticking out from under some old pajamas a brown folder with the inscription 'Buffalo City Court.' My curiosity thoroughly aroused, I peeked inside and found a smaller folder containing legal papers. The first words I saw in bold, black letters were 'Family Court,' followed by the name of a judge. Looking farther down the page, I saw my parents' names and mine. Needless to say, I was shocked to see they were adoption papers. My adoption papers."

"I can understand your shock. Did you say anything to your parents?"

"No, I was afraid to. But I thought about it every day. Who

were my real parents? Why did they…or maybe it was just 'she'… give me up?"

"Natural questions to ask."

"Yes, but it got me thinking, Sheila."

Sheila looked at her curiously.

"You see, Sheila, when my parents adopted me, they had no children. Four years later they had a child, a girl. The next year they had another girl."

Sitting with her hands clasped over her lap, Sheila listened intently, her eyes pinned on Catherine as she spoke almost in a whisper.

"Up until the time Mary was born—she's my first sister— I was treated all right. But after Mary, and especially after my second sister, Carol, came along…it was as if I was forgotten."

"That had to feel terrible."

"It did, Sheila, it really did. So many times I thought of running away, but I was scared. Where could I go? Who could I turn to? I had to do something."

"Had to, Catherine?"

Catherine voice choked up. "There was more."

I saw Sheila stiffen, as if she knew what was coming.

"Would you like some water, Catherine?"

Catherine shook her head. "It was him. My father! Right after my sisters were born. He saw me sulking, noticed my moodiness. That's when he began coming into my bedroom at night, 'to comfort me,' he said."

Sheila reached across to her. "You need say no more, my dear. Let us wait for a better time."

97

"No, Sheila, it's all right. I'll be all right. Just give me a minute," she said, turning her face aside.

"If this is too painful—"

"No, no, Sheila, I want to tell you. I need to tell you now that you've opened me up. I need to talk."

Sheila leaned back in her chair. "I'll listen as long as you like, dear."

Catherine's voice came forced. "He would put his arm around me and tell me how much he and my mother loved me, and how it was natural to give the girls all the attention because they were babies compared to me. That made sense to me." Her voice cracked. "He stroked my back and rubbed my shoulders. 'To make me relax,' he said. Then he started kissing my neck."

"You were frightened, naturally."

"No, Sheila, not really. Not that I remember, anyway. Of course, at the time I was only about...I don't know... six?... seven? He kept saying he loved me. I wanted to believe him. I needed to believe him."

"Of course you would."

"Gradually things became worse. He began touching me in places he said would soothe me and make me feel good." She lowered her head, tears starting in her eyes.

Sheila leaned toward her and touched her knee. "I understand, Catherine. I'm sure that was horrible for you."

"Oh, Sheila, you *don't* understand," she said, raising her head, her cheeks wet. "They *did* make me feel good. They *did*. I'm so ashamed." Sobbing, she buried her face in her hands. "Can you understand now? It was wrong, I know it now but I didn't know it then! I didn't know! Only later...."

"You were an innocent child, Catherine. It was no fault of

yours."

"One day he hurt me, Sheila, hurt me bad. I was crying and bleeding. I shouted at him. He squeezed my mouth shut with his hand. He said the police would put me in jail if I ever told them about what happened. He said who would believe me, a girl jealous of her father because she thought he loved her sisters more. I was afraid."

"Did the abuse stop then, Catherine?"

"Yes, for a while, but he got even with me in other ways. He knew how much I loved my dog, Skippy. He said Skippy ran away, but I knew he was lying. About a week earlier, the newspaper carried a story about a man who drowned his dog because it chewed the tire on his car. I know my father did the same thing with Skippy. Maybe he didn't drown him but he did something. That's where he got the idea. He also killed my parakeet. He said he found it dead in its cage." She took a deep breath. "I loved my pets, Sheila. I love animals. I wanted to be a veterinarian someday." Her watery eyes reflected pain.

"Did it finally end with that?"

"No. He became bolder, taking advantage of me while my mother was awake and busy doing chores elsewhere in the house. He'd trap me in the hallway or the cellar or a closet, touching me. When she went grocery shopping, he'd drag me into the bedroom with him. I wanted to scream so somebody could hear me, but somehow I couldn't. I just couldn't."

"And, of course, your sisters were too young to be of help?"

"They wouldn't help if they could. He scared them away by saying he was taking me into the bedroom to punish me for being bad and he'd do the same to them if they didn't behave and go someplace else to play."

Sheila listened, her face grim.

"I was almost sixteen before I was able to fight him off. He hurt me bad, twisting my arm and punching me in the stomach. I made up my mind then to tell my mother, tell her everything about what he had been doing to me and for how long." Her face twisted with the memory.

"Did she help you?"

"She slapped my face and called me a damned liar. She threatened to turn me over to the police for trying to ruin her husband's reputation and break up her marriage. She even picked up a kitchen knife and waved it around like a mad woman. So I ran, ran out of the house as fast as I could over to my girlfriend Louise's house down the block. She lives alone with her mother. I told them what happened. They were shocked and let me stay temporarily."

"You couldn't go back, of course, not after that."

"Never! Louise's mother, Ida, suggested I go to the church and talk to a priest and ask for advice."

"That seemed wise advice."

Catherine smiled, but it wasn't a smile at all. She laughed, but it was no laugh, either. Sardonic may be the word to describe it.

"Wise, yes, wouldn't you think so, Sheila? Oh, he was understanding, all right, that decrepit, sad-eyed priest. At first, that is. He even found me a part-time job on weekends and a few evenings helping clean those mansions for the rich people on Delaware Avenue."

"Are you disparaging the priest?"

"Disparaging him? Man of the church? Man of God? After he heard my confession he invited me into the rectory, saying he wanted to comfort me, to console me with the love of Jesus. Those were the words he used a week before he put his arm around my shoulder and led me to a big cushiony chair along the wall, where he sat me down and bent over me, petting my hair with his freckled hands, whispering words that burned my ears with his hot breath. But I wasn't the dumb, vulnerable child I had been. I ran, Sheila, I ran again, back to Louise and Ida. Ida had the extra room and offered to put me up for as long as necessary."

"That was kind of her."

"I was able to pay my way cleaning mansions every chance I got. I stayed till I finished school. That's how I saved my money and why I'm here."

"You've been through a great deal for one so young, Catherine."

"I'm still paying for it, Sheila. I'm tormented. Everything looks black." She scrunched down, hugging herself. "I don't want to think about it, but I can't escape what I feel."

"That's understandable, Catherine. Yet, despite those feelings, you're endowed with that mystical quality God reserves only for the young."

Catherine raised puzzled eyes. "Mystical quality?"

"Yes. It's called resilience. You have more strength than you know and you're obviously highly intelligent. Don't underestimate yourself, Catherine. You can overcome your past."

"I wish I could believe you, Sheila." She slumped. Her face darkened. "I've been depressed a long time. I really don't want to...to—"

Sheila reached across to her again. "Oh no, my dear, don't ever say that. Don't even think it. There's so much to live for, but you must give life a chance. Promise me you won't entertain any more such foolish thoughts. You've been living

101

with a painful past, but tonight you've exposed those bitter memories to the light. That in itself will start the healing. Nevertheless, exhaustion can bring on depression. It's not healthy. You need sleep. We can talk tomorrow." She reached over and patted her hand. "You must rest now."

She rose from her seat and smoothed her dress. Catherine rose with her.

"I'm sorry to have burdened you with my problems, Sheila. I truly am."

"Oh, tush," she said again, waving her hand as she walked out. "Do we have a date for tomorrow?"

Catherine smiled and closed the door.

It was close to midnight. All was still, except for those mysterious creaking and groaning sounds I make that seem to emanate from nowhere in the dark of night and feed rumors of ghosts haunting the passageways. Then I heard a soft clicking sound and noticed it was the door to Sheila Graham's apartment closing. In the dim light I saw her practically tiptoeing toward the stairs. Suddenly she paused and lifted her head, like an animal sniffing the air for danger. She moved close to Catherine's door, stopped and let out a scream.

"Call an ambulance!" she cried. "Somebody call the police!" She tried turning the doorknob, rattled and pulled on it, then began banging on the door with her fist, and calling, "Catherine! Catherine!"

Yapping dogs and slamming doors sent sleepy tenants staggering into the halls, rubbing their eyes and yelling, "What the hell's going on?"

When they heard Sheila shout the word 'Gas!' several tenants rushed to the second floor, the wooden floors and stairs echoing with their pounding feet. Startled awake, Huggs bolted

Frances R. Schmidt & James A. Costa

up in his cot, listened a moment before jumping to his feet and dashing out of the cellar in his underwear. He bounded up the stairs two at a time, knocking against a few tenants scrambling down to get outside.

"It's locked! It's locked!" Sheila cried.

Milling around, confused, the crowd parted and Sheila moved aside as Huggs leaped over the top step, broke into a loping run, lunged between them and hurled his body with a sickening thud against Catherine's door. He bounced off and did it again and again until the frame fractured and the door swung inward hanging by a single hinge. While others dashed in behind him to throw open the windows and turn off the gas, Huggs searched the dimness, calling her name over and over until he spotted her frail body sprawled across her bed. Panting with exhaustion, he bent over, snatched her up and staggered out of the apartment, where Jeb Morrison stood waiting to take her in his muscular arms and carry her limp body downstairs.

By the time they reached the front door, a police car and an ambulance with their sirens fading pulled up to the curb, where two men in white uniforms immediately jumped out and dragged a gurney from the back of the vehicle. Jeb handed her over carefully and stepped aside as they placed Catherine on it. By then, Sheila caught up with them.

"Where are you taking her," she cried, holding her throat, breathless, as they slid the gurney inside the ambulance. "What hospital?"

"Columbus Hospital," one of them shouted as he hopped inside the back and slammed the door shut.

Chapter 15

Of course I don't know what transpired at the hospital. I only know that Sheila visited her there early the next day, as did Sylvia, the waitress, who came with a geranium plant, which I later heard Catherine appreciated, saying it was a thoughtful and pleasant surprise.

Apparently, the ambulance arrived at the hospital in the nick of time to save Catherine's life. I heard the rest of the story several days later when she returned to her apartment after a two-day hospital stay. Sheila was sitting in the same chair she used the first night she visited, and Catherine was in her place across from her. A teapot rested on the small table between them.

"Do you take sugar, Sheila?" Catherine asked, filling their cups.

"No, thank you, dear."

Catherine settled back and pulled her housecoat over her knees. "I owe you my life, Sheila. Others told me if not for you—"

"Oh, tush tush," Sheila said, waving her free hand.

"When I was in the hospital, I don't remember if you told me how you knew I was in trouble. I was pretty groggy."

"You might call it the hand of fate, Catherine."

"Fate?"

"Yes, you see, ordinarily I'd be sound asleep by midnight, but I had much on my mind that kept me awake. Nathan, my fraternal twin, is quite ill and not likely to live very long. He's asked for my advice on certain family financial matters. It involves my moving back to Boston and taking over the family home. I had to decide rather quickly, for reasons I won't go into. Although I did have a bit more time, I thought it best to answer immediately." She sipped her tea. "So I wrote my letter and left my apartment about midnight to get it in the mailbox downstairs. I wanted to be sure I didn't miss the early morning mail pickup. But you see, my dear, as I was passing your apartment I smelled gas. When I realized it was coming from beneath your door, I became alarmed because I remembered your state of mind before I left you earlier that evening."

"My life was saved by a letter you really didn't have to mail right then?"

"You might say that, Catherine. It's as good an explanation as any. As I said, fate had a hand in it."

Catherine sighed. "Sheila, I do thank you, but—"

"Oh, tush. Let's drop the past and concentrate on the present. Catherine, I have a proposition to make, one I want you to seriously consider."

"A proposition?"

"Indeed. A very generous one, I think, but, of course, you'll have to decide for yourself." She sipped her tea. "Will you listen?"

Catherine nodded.

"Very well, then, here it is and to the point. I've made up my mind to return to Boston and accept my brother Nathan's plea for me to take the house we grew up in. Frankly, it's more than a house. Say, a mansion? It belonged to our parents, who have long passed. Being born with a crippling disability, Nathan never married, never had children. Having no other siblings, I was entitled to half possession with him, but being married to my dear husband Willard, who at the time was himself independently wealthy, I had no need for anything more. Unfortunately, my husband's life ended abruptly."

Catherine looked at her curiously.

"You see, Catherine, when the stock market collapsed in 1929, so did our fortune. Willard, like many others in his predicament, found his solution to the problem by exiting this world through a window on the 41st floor of a Wall Street building. I wasn't left penniless, but I wasn't rich anymore, either. For the past decade or more, I've managed to survive well enough." She paused. "I imagine you're wondering how I came to this place?"

Catherine nodded again.

"Actually, my parents were born in Buffalo, in fact, not very far from here. When my father invested in the burgeoning movie industry, he struck it rich and we moved first to New York City, and later to Boston. My mother's twin sister—as you can see, twins run in our family— her twin sister, Harriet, wasn't as fortunate and never prospered, as we did. Aunt Harriet was born the sickly twin, just as Nathan was mine, and Aunt Harriet's husband, Wallace, suffered from diabetes. Like my mother before me, I was able to provide them with private nursing and medical care while Willard was alive. They were looked after for many years. But once my husband Willard was gone, I could no longer afford the luxury of giving that service. Except for my brother Nathan, I had no other relatives in Boston, so I returned to Buffalo to care for them myself."

"And you stayed."

"I had no compelling reason to return to Boston. Willard and I lost our home there and I soon learned I was persona non grata in my former social circle. When Aunt Harriet and Uncle Wallace passed on here several years ago, I sold their house. At my age it would have been too much for me to keep up. Living here as I do now, in a neighborhood I know and have grown to love, I've reconciled myself to a reclusive life and the loss of those things that give life meaning. So much so, in fact, that I was quite prepared to turn down Nathan's offer." Her eyes twinkled. "That is, until I met you."

Catherine pointed to herself. "Me?"

"Yes, my dear, you. Now this is what I'm proposing and hope you will accept: I would like you to accompany me to Boston, as an aide, companion, whatever you wish to call yourself. You will, of course, live in. In return for your services, I will provide you with all you may need and a fair salary. I'll also provide tuition for you to attend a university nearby where you can eventually pursue a career in veterinary medicine, if that is still your wish."

Catherine' jaw dropped. "Sheila, why me? You hardly know me. I don't deserve—"

"Tush, my dear. You see, Willard and I were childless. Through no fault of our own, I might add. Again, it may be fate stepping in, but I've developed a special fondness for you, Catherine; I can't say why, but it's undeniable." She set her cup down. "Frankly, I had accepted my circumstances. My life was on hold, going nowhere, until the morning I saw you having breakfast. I knew there was something special about you, something you possess, a mysterious quality that is rare, almost, if I dare say it, ethereal. I knew immediately, if only intuitively perhaps, but convincingly enough, that our meeting was preordained. My words may appear to be the jabbering of a woman grown dotty with time and loneliness, but they're from my heart and I must speak them." She paused. "Would you like to mull over my proposition, Catherine, and give me an answer by this weekend?"

Catherine reached across and squeezed Sheila's arm. "Oh, Sheila, I don't need think it over. I can tell you now. Of course I'll go with you. No one in my life has ever—"

"Wonderful, Catherine," Sheila said, cutting her short and rising. "I prayed and believed you would accept. That's why I wrote the letter telling Nathan to set the wheels in motion, so to speak."

Catherine rose and wrapped her arms around Sheila and hugged her. "I don't know what to say. I—"

"No need to say anything, my dear. Just make any preparations necessary. We'll probably be leaving quite soon."

Both women had damp eyes when Sheila left Catherine's apartment.

A few days later I watched the taxi driver load several of Sheila's suitcases and Catherine's bag into the trunk of his yellow City Service cab. Sylvia, the friendly waitress, was standing in my doorway, smiling sadly and waving her handkerchief goodbye.

I've heard of people speak of fate before, of things that were 'meant to be,' but I never put much stock in it until Sheila and Catherine met. Apparently, fate brought together two women at a crucial juncture in their lives. One found a mother; the other found a daughter. Each gave the other meaning to her existence. I trust both women have found enduring happiness.

But the drama of the preceding week when Catherine tried to take her life didn't end for Huggs. He was teased mercilessly. Whenever he passed anyone in the halls, he'd hear comments like:

"Hey, Huggs, was that a diaper you were running around in,

or what?"

"Hey, Huggs, when you gonna get some hair on them skinny legs?"

"Hey, Huggs, what was that thing we saw jiggling down there when you come running up the stairs?"

Huggs didn't think their comments were very funny. He yelled back,

"You wise guys ain't never going to get no more hugs from me. And don't ask me for no favors, neither. Never!"

But neither was that the end of the story. The next weekend, my tenants threw a surprise party in Joe's restaurant for Huggs. They played loud, happy music on the juke box, festooned the ceilings and walls with colored ribbons and balloons and hung signs proclaiming him a hero for saving Catherine's life. They showered him with all manner of gifts, most notably, pants. A few gave speeches praising him for his heroism and the 'loving, affectionate' person he was, and Sylvia read a special letter to him from Catherine expressing her eternal gratitude for saving her life. The last speaker's final words were:

"Even without britches, Huggs is a damn sight better man than all the rest of us guys here put together!"

Everyone cheered.

I looked at Huggs, sitting proudly on a high, throne-like barstool in the middle of the room, with a golden paper crown cocked on his head. He was encircled by tables bunched together and filled with my smiling tenants clapping and swaying as they sang out,

"For he's a jolly good fellow,

For he's a jolly...."

It was the first and only time I ever saw anyone laugh and cry at the same time.

Chapter 16

For about a month after Catherine's attempted suicide, everything returned to normal. The special school bus that picked Rosie up in the morning also dropped her off home again about three o'clock. The only difference I noticed is when Gustav leaves for work in the afternoon, he stops at the top of the stairs, where little Rosie likes to sit, cuddling or disciplining Shirley, her dolly. Or she might be running her hands over Shirley's body, fitting her with a skirt or blouse. On a typical morning, I'd hear something like this:

"Hi, Mr. Gustav."

She always hears Gustav's door close, and recognizes his footsteps approaching. She knows he's on his way to work.

"Hi, Rosie. How's Shirley, today?"

"She was naughty, so I had to spank her, but not hard."

"That's good, Rosie, we wouldn't want her to be too spoiled, would we?" he said, taking a couple of pieces of taffy from his pocket and pressing it in her hand.

"Oh, thank you, Mr. Gustav. "

I could tell a great affection was developing between Gustav and Rosie. My guess is that she reminded him of his own little girl, Inga. Lizzie also noticed this pattern. Harmless as it appeared, and for whatever reason or reasons she had, Lizzie was apparently upset by the connection between Gustav and Rosie, upset enough, in fact, to send her knocking on Gustav's door. When Gustav answered, Lizzie said in a voice raspy but firm:

"Gustav, I hope you don't mind my busting into your private time for a few minutes, but I want to gab a little about my Rosie."

Gustav opened his door wide and glanced around. "Step inside, Lizzie, won't you?"

"Thank you, don't mind if I do."

"Can I offer you coffee or something else to drink?"

"I thank you kindly, but you won't want me to be staying after you hear me out."

Gustav looked at her curiously.

"What I have to say is short and sweet," she said, pulling a hanky from her sleeve and coughing softly into it. "Truth be told, I've noticed lately Rosie taking quite a shine to you, Gustav."

"The feeling's mutual, Lizzie."

"I'm sure. She's a loveable little thing. All the same, Gustav, I worry she may be getting too attached. She brings you up enough to make me uncomfortable when we're sitting eating, and she tells me how you brought her this or that, a little gift of candy or, like the last time, that glass bracelet with the pretty red hearts. All she did for hours afterward is run her hand back and forth over it, saying you gave it to her and how much she likes you. You gave her a real thrill with that one."

"I'm glad to hear it."

"Yes, but I'm not glad to say it. What I do want to get off my chest, Gustav, is what's going to happen to Rosie if you move out? I'm afraid that would break her heart."

"I don't intend to move, Lizzie."

"Maybe not, Gustav, but you never know about this crazy world. It's unpredictable. What if you come down with a sickness or, God forbid, get run over by a car?"

Gustav shrugged his shoulders. "What are you asking me, Lizzie?"

"It's a hard thing for me to bring up, Gustav, because you're obviously a kind man, but I'm asking you to back off and not be so friendly. Put some space between yourselves. Let her know you're just a neighbor with no special affection for her. In other words, break the connection however you do it, but do it. And the sooner the better, I might add."

Gustav looked downcast. "All right, Lizzie. I understand. You're her mother and of course, you have the last word, the only word."

"In fact, Gustav, I'm not her mother. I'm her grandmother. Her mother, my beautiful Jeanne, died giving birth to her."

Gustav looked taken aback. "I'm very sorry to hear that, Lizzie."

"And I'm sorry you brought it up, but it's true," she said irritably. "Rosie knows nothing of this. A time will come when she'll have to be told, but not yet."

"How about her father?"

Lizzie scowled. "What father? That scum never came forward. Jesus knows I haven't the slightest idea who he is or where he is, even if I wanted to see him. Jeanne never said."

"I understand, Lizzie."

"No, you don't, Gustav. You see, I'm not a well woman

myself. Rosie is the only thing that keeps me going with worrying about what will happen to her if anything happens to me."

Gustav tightened. "Forgive me if I'm overstepping myself, Lizzie, but I have to say it: those cigarettes I notice you smoking one after the other aren't helping. That cough doesn't sound very good to me."

"Don't I know it, Gustav? Don't I know it?" she said, glaring at him and backing out the door. "All I'm asking is that you separate yourself from Rosie so you don't break her heart someday. Soon, Gustav, soon."

Gustav nodded. "Goodnight, Lizzie," he said, hearing her hacking her way down the hall as he closed his door.

Chapter 17

About the same time, I looked into Jeb and Cotton's apartment. They were sitting at their table eating, with several books stacked between them.

"I think maybe you should come along, too, Cotton. Join the class."

Cotton set her coffee cup down. She shook her head. "I don' know, Jeb. Them books look mighty hard to me."

"It's 'those' books, Cotton, not 'them' books. And maybe it is a little hard, but you'll catch on, jes' like I'm doin'."

"I can hear the diff'rence in how you speak, Jeb. Why cain't I learn jes' by listenin' to you?"

"Well, I s'pose you can, somewhat, but together we can learn a lot faster, I think."

"Gib me a little time to think about it, Jeb. Some of my cleaning jobs is in the eve'nin', you know. Besides, we got a baby comin' along to think about."

"I know that, Cotton, but maybe we can work somethin' out. I know you'd like it. My teacher, too, Miss Coleman. She's real nice. I don't get no sense she resents colored folks."

"You mentioned some o' them other folks don' seem too friendly."

"You mean 'those' other folks,' Cotton, not 'them' other folks. Anyways, maybe not so much that they ain't friendly. I think it's because they never been used to sitting so close to a colored person."

"Didn't you tell me, Jeb, never to say ain't?"

"Why, I shorely did."

She laughed. "Well, you jes' did it yo'self, Jeb. I heard it plain as day. You said, 'They ain't friendly.'"

He broke into a hearty laugh. "Dogged if you ain't right, Cotton. Oops, I mean 'aren't right.'" He slapped the table. "Well now, don't you see, Cotton, you's learnin' already."

Cotton looked pleased. She picked up one Jeb's books. "This don' look nothin' like that skinny book they let us read out of back home."

"You are right, Cotton. That one was mostly religious readin'. The one in your hand is a whole lot better 'cause it actually teaches you somethin'. Personally, Cotton, I think those folks down home don't want us to get too smart. You keep people ignorant, then you never has to worry about guys gettin' out of the tabaccy and the cotton fields, and women washing white folks's clothes, and changin' things."

"So colored folks never can get nowhere in this world."

Jeb took a last bite and pushed his empty plate aside. "That's right, Cotton. We didn't have no chance down in Georgia, but here we do. It's gonna be diff'rent for us now. I'm bone-tired from work. It was a real hard day today. The boss did a lot of yellin' 'bout us being slow as molasses. We didn't get hardly no break at all."

"Can't you take this one night off from school, Jeb?" she asked, rising to clear away the dishes.

"No, Cotton. I gotta make every day count. Besides, Miss Coleman, she's been givin' me extra time."

"What's she like, Jeb? Is she pretty?"

"I reckon you'd think so. She got long hair the color of butter, and her skin is milk white and don' have no pimples like I see on some other women folk around here. I think she be older than me, too, but not too much so."

"Is she married, Jeb?"

"Now, Cotton, why you wanna go and ask me a question like that? I reckon maybe she's not hitched 'cause I don' 'member seeing no ring on her finger, but maybe she is. She's nice, though. Nice enough to me, and that's all that matters. She says I got a lot of natural brains but I gotta learn to use 'em proper."

'I coulda told you that, Jeb."

Jeb dabbed a cloth on his mouth, rose and came around the table, wrapped his arms around her and kissed her. "You sure know how to make a man feel good, Cotton. I'm sure one lucky fella, yes, sir, I shorely am lucky."

A few nights later they came to a decision:

"I been thinkin', Cotton, and I agree with you. I think it best you don't go to school wid me. Workin' days like you do, house cleanin', and wid the baby comin' along and all, well, you'd be just as tuckered out as me. But on days I don't go to school, I can teach you what I know." He smiled broadly. "I be the student and the teacher at the same time. Now ain't that somepin'! I mean, *isn't* that somepin'!"

Jeb suddenly grabbed her hands and pulled her into his arms. "C'mon, Cotton, honey, dance wid me," he said, laughing and whirling her and stomping around even after someone in the apartment below began banging a broom up against their ceiling. Jeb didn't stop until Cotton, out of breath, reminded him of the baby and her delicate condition.

As far as I could tell, Jeb continued to work days and go to school nights. He'd come home from work, wash the sweat and grime away, eat his supper, then head out with his books tucked under his arm. I often saw him come home, drop his books on the table, fall on his bed and pass out instantly. Cotton grew used to the routine. She'd pull the covers over him, kiss him on the cheek and turn out the light.

Several weeks later I looked in and saw them sitting on the couch together. Jeb was telling Cotton what happened to him on the way home from work:

"A whole mess o' people, Cotton, me included, we were all bunched up down by Shelton Square, standin' by the curb waitin' for the red light to change, when this ol' white man in a wheelchair, jes' sweet as you please, like he owns the street, ups and starts off across in front of us."

"Against the red light, Jeb?"

"Yeah, jes' like that, he's pushing his wheels with his hands, and not far down the block, here comes the big, ol' streetcar rollin' full speed ahead and swayin' back and forth wid its wheels squealin' and bell ringin' and clangin'."

"Oh, my, you're not goin' to tell me what I'm thinkin', are you, Jeb?"

"You jes' listen to me, Cotton, OK? There's a lot more to this story."

"I'm sorry. Go on, honey. I'm all ears."

"Well, everybody's standin', all froze like, watchin' the man tryin' to beat the streetcar, and seein' that streetcar barrelin' along like hell fire. He had time to make it, I thought, and he would've, but then I see his wheels are caught in the track

117

'cause the street is slushy wet."

"Oh, my."

"He's spinnin' those wheels a mile a minute wid his hands, but he's stuck good. And that streetcar is a rollin' right at him a mile a minute and bearin' down like it's aimin' to kill him."

"Don' tell me it hit him, Jeb, don' tell me that!"

"Widout a second thought, I jumped into action, Cotton, bolted right into the street. By then that streetcar's brakes was squealin' worse'n I ever heard any ten hogs gettin' butchered at once, but it's too late to stop. And too late for me to push that wheelchair out o' the way."

"So what'd you do, Jeb? What happened?"

"Now hang on, there, Cotton, hang on a minute. This is my story and I'm jes' gettin' to the good part."

"I'm sorry, Jeb. Go on."

Satisfied, Jeb leaned back smiling and crossed his legs. "So, like I been saying, Cotton, that streetcar's brakes is screeching like a hoot owl, but she's still comin' on full speed, and widout even thinkin', I jes' reaches over, jacks him up by the shoulders and jerks him out o' his seat right back into my arms. Jes' in time, too, 'cause that streetcar swooshed by so fast I could feel a blast of cold air 'crosst my face before it smashed that chair to smithereens. It even took the man's one shoe wid it."

"Jeb, you coulda been killed yourself!"

"That's what the man said. But I don' think so, Cotton. The Lord put me in that spot for a reason. I don't know why, but I don' believe he did it to save somebody's life, only to take mine instead."

"Oh, my, Jeb, you are a hero, for sure."

"Shucks, no, Cotton. Anybody woulda done it, but it happened so fast nobody had time to think."

"Nobody 'cept you, Jeb," she said, taking his arm and cuddling close to him.

"OK, Cotton, let me finish now, let me finish. You hear? There's still some more to this story."

"Go 'head, Jeb. You don' need to chop my head off. I'm not stoppin' you."

"I'm sorry, Cotton, I didn't mean to snap at you like that. Anyway, right about then, the people's collectin' around us and talkin' all at once, while the man's standing on one leg wid the shoe on it, and leanin' agin me. He's shakin' pretty bad, too. It wasn't but a minute later when a po-lice car swings over and takes him off'n me, talkin' and axin' him questions and fin'lly stuffin' him in the back seat of the car.

"Before he ducks his gray head back inside, he stares at me with eyes that look bulgy like a blue-eyed catfish's behind his eyeglasses and he says, 'You could've been killed but you risked your life for me, a perfect stranger. Why?'

"So I says, 'You can thank the Lord, mister. He was watching and he was the one what done it, not me.'"

"'What's your name, lad?' he axed me. 'Where do you live?'"

"I only told him my friends call me Jeb, and before he can axe me any more questions, the po-lice started buttin' in, and I jes' eased back and melted into the crowd and scooted on home." He put his arm around Cotton. "To be wid you, baby." He patted her belly. "And wid our little one."

"Jeb, maybe you should o' give him your address. Maybe he wanted to send you a re-ward for savin' his life. We could always use a little extra money, 'specially wid our baby on the way."

"Cotton, honey, I admit I did think that very same thing, too, but only for a minute. I did a good deed, thass all. You know a good deed don't need no re-ward for any reason whatsoever. Jes' doin' it is the re-ward itself. Didn't they larn us that in church down back home?"

After that, nothing more was ever said about it, at least not that I heard, and their lives went on the way they had before that dramatic event in their lives. Jeb was picking up correct English fast and passing what he could on to Cotton, who herself was a fast learner. The months were slipping by quickly.

They worked hard, Jeb at the warehouse, and Cotton cleaning houses. They saved their money and seemed to me to be as happy as any couple could be. Cotton was well along with her pregnancy and it wasn't more than a matter of weeks, even days, before their baby was due.

They constantly discussed all they were planning to do someday. Listening to their laughter and hearing the excitement in their voices reminded me of the book Alice had spoken to Agnes about, called, 'Of Mice and Men.' Something else, too, Alice said afterwards: 'If you want to make God laugh, tell him your plans. I wondered if Jeb and Cotton's dreams for the future were about to take a turn for the worse.

Chapter 18

Unfortunately, my intuitive fears weren't unfounded. The bliss the Morrisons were experiencing was soon about to evaporate, because on a bitterly cold night, Jeb burst into the apartment, dripping sweat and sucking in air.

Alarmed, Cotton reached out to him. "Jeb, honey, what's wrong!" she cried, taking his books from his hands. "What's wrong!"

Jeb ripped off his jacket and threw himself on the couch. He leaned back, sweeping his arm over his eyes. "Cotton, we got trouble. Big trouble."

"What kind of trouble you talkin' 'bout, Jeb? You didn't go sock somebody again, did you, same's you did back home?"

"Worse'n that, Cotton." He snapped up straight. "We got to pack. Now! Got to pack and run out of here fast as we can." He jumped up and ran to the closet, where he pulled out a battered leather suitcase and flipped it open on the kitchen table.

"Jeb! We can't go runnin' no place again. I'm almost ready for the doctor. Our baby's comin' any day now, maybe any minute. We got to be near a hospital. Jes' look at me."

"Hurry, Cotton, hurry! If'n they git their hands on me, they gonna lynch me, they gonna—"

The sudden thundering of feet on the stairs and shouting

voices echoing in the hall stopped him in his tracks. Moments later a night stick made a cracking sound on the door. "Police! Open up in the name of the law or we'll break it down!"

Jeb looked at Cotton. His arms dropped loose to his sides; his eyes filled with grief. "We're done in, Cotton. Done in good. Too late!" he wailed, crossing the kitchen. "Too late!" He looked back. "Jes' one thing, Cotton... promise me you won't believe anything the po-lice tell you. Whitey's gonna tell lies, every danged word they say. All black lies!"

Jeb opened the door and several policemen lunged at him, knocking over chairs as they grabbed and wrestled him face down to the floor, their knees pinning his neck and legs. They twisted his sweating arms behind his back and shackled his hands.

"Stop! Don't hurt him!" Cotton begged, rushing toward him. "Please! You're hurting him!"

Two policemen, straining and huffing, hoisted Jeb to his feet, pushed her aside and muscled him out into the hall.

"Cotton!" he cried, struggling against them. "Cotton!"

Cotton stood frozen, watching the police drag him away, hearing his cries. She staggered a step before her legs buckled beneath her.

"Jeb," she gasped as she collapsed and fell to the floor.

Barking dogs and angry voices sent Huggs flying up from the cellar in time to see the police pulling and half-hauling Jeb thumping down the stairs and out the front door. Followed by several others, Huggs dashed up the stairs and stopped. Through the partially opened door, he saw Cotton's legs with dark blood seeping out from under them into the hall.

"Call an am-blance, somebody! Quick! Call an am-blance! Cotton's dead! Cotton's dead!"

Actually, Cotton wasn't dead and she didn't die, but she did lose the baby. Rumors flew all over the place since the evening the police hauled Jeb off to jail. Conversations were carried on for days in Joe's restaurant:

'I don't know, he seemed like a nice enough guy to me, for a Negro.'

'You can't always judge a book by its cover, you know. I'll bet Jack the Ripper probably looked like a nice guy, too.'

'He was always polite and friendly to me. Remember how he helped carry that girl Catherine down to the ambulance that night after she tried to gas herself?'

"Always minded his own business, far as I could see. Never uppity like some of them these days. Still, something stinks bad about this whole thing.'

And so it went until Cotton returned home from the hospital a week later. Obviously still weak, she climbed the stairs, holding the banister and pulling herself up painfully slow. She kept her head low. I suspect it was because she knew what some people must be thinking, seeing her husband dragged off in handcuffs like that.

*Cotton picked up a newspaper someone had left in front of her door and carried it inside. Weary and breathing hard, she slipped out of the jacket a nurse at the hospital gave her to wear home and hung it on a hook behind the door. She laid the paper on the table and sat down. The first thing she saw scrawled in big, black letters across the front page was the incomplete message, **GET OUT NI**. On the lower half of the front page, prominently displayed, was a picture of Jeb, bent forward, handcuffed and staring wild-eyed into the camera. In bold letters the heading read **LOCAL MAN CHARGED WITH SEXUAL ASSAULT**.*

Cotton's breath caught in her throat. She struggled as best she could to understand the words on the page:

'Yesterday evening Buffalo police captured, without incident, rape suspect Jeb Morrison, a Negro, at his apartment on Niagara Street. The unnamed victim, a thirty-two-year-old white woman, has alleged that Morrison attempted to assault her after night-class at Grover Cleveland High School, where Morrison was enrolled in an adult education course. Morrison is presently being held for arraignment in downtown Buffalo. The police have offered no further details on the alleged crime, and....'

Cotton laid her head on her arms. "I don't believe it, Jeb. You tol' me they'd be telling lies. I believe you, Jeb. Oh, Lord, I believe my husband." She raised her head and looked up. "Please, Lord, help my Jeb. He's a good man. I know he didn't do nothin' like they say he did."

Neither Cotton nor I knew at the time that someone else was also reading the article with great interest.

Chapter 19

Sometime about then, one of my tenants, Jasper Didion, who'd been acting irrationally since he arrived about a month earlier, became even more erratic. I'd been watching since the first week when I saw him sitting on the edge of his seat, listening to the radio as if waiting to hear some dramatic news. Other times I heard him rummaging around his apartment. He'd open closet doors and run his hand over the shelves; look in his cupboards, moving cups and dishes aside; get on his hands and knees and peer under the living room chairs and couch. I thought perhaps he had lost something and was searching for it. Once, I even saw him coming home late at night, climbing the stairs and throwing punches at some invisible foe.

I had never seen such anxious behavior before and didn't quite know what to make of it until I overheard a conversation between Alice Wagman and her sister Agnes.

"Agnes, have you noticed that new tenant from the fourth floor, the one who wears those high-water pants that look like a barrel held up by suspenders?"

"Heavens to Betsy, Alice, yes, he is a sight to behold," she answered, pouring a cup of chopped onions into a soup pot. "I forgot to mention it to you, but just yesterday he almost bumped into me while I was downstairs getting our mail. He's really scary."

"I haven't personally witnessed anything, but I've been hearing rumors about him. What made him scary to you, Agnes?"

"Would you believe it? I simply turned to go back upstairs and he leaped out of my way with a cry that almost stopped my heart. I must have scared him as much as he did me. He was bent over, creeping along like an animal sneaking out of the building. I said 'excuse me,' but he just looked at me with wild eyes like I was something terrible he was afraid of, and ran off out the front door."

Sitting at their kitchen table, Alice squeezed her chin between her thumb and forefinger. "Hmmm."

"What is it, Alice? What are you thinking?"

"Yesterday I was reading the back cover of one of the books I was cataloguing in the library. There's a word for what you've described."

"You mean the way he was acting, creepy and sneaky?"

"More than that, Agnes. More like suspicious and wary."

"You're right, Alice, that is more like it. If you would've seen how his eyes darted around, so suspicious. He looked like a scared rabbit."

"Yes, that's exactly what I mean. The word is 'paranoia.'"

"I've never heard that word, Alice."

"It's a medical term. It describes a mental disease that afflicts some people. People who have it believe someone is after them. They're always looking over their shoulder, and hear threatening voices from people who aren't even there."

"Oh, my, Alice, that's a terrible disease to have. Do you think he really has it?"

"Not being a doctor, I can't really say, Agnes, but it sounds very much like it. You're not the first one to mention his bizarre behavior, either. Others have complained of him sneaking around the hallways and peeking out his door at all hours of the day and night."

Agnes shuddered. "Do you think he could be dangerous, Alice?"

"I don't know much more than what I read about it, but it's possible, especially if he thinks someone is out to hurt him. Then he could strike first."

"You mean to protect himself?"

"Exactly. That's exactly what I mean and it worries me."

It was early evening when I saw Jasper in the hallway outside his door, crouching and pivoting one way and another brandishing a kitchen knife. He was shouting threats and raving like a madman. Moments later his next door neighbor opened his door and stepped into the hallway to see what the commotion was all about. When he saw Jasper slashing the air with the knife, he quickly retreated into his apartment, slammed the door shut and locked it.

Hearing loud voices, Huggs dropped the comic book he was reading, hopped off his cot and rushed up the basement steps to the first floor. When he heard a woman scream, he bounded up the stairs two at a time. His shortened breath caught in his throat when he reached the fourth floor and saw Jasper facing him with his knife poised in the air ready to strike.

Huggs almost fell backwards, caught his balance, twisted around and leaped down several steps at a time until he reached the first floor, where he almost fell into Joe's arms. Joe had a small club in his hand.

"Easy, there, Huggs, easy," he said, pushing him upright.

Panting, Huggs gasped out the words, "That Jasper guy… upstairs… a knife… tried to kill me…."

"It's OK, Huggs, I know. I warned Mrs. Chapman last week this guy was cuckoo. Don't worry, I already called the cops. The hospital, too." He shoved him off. "Go sit inside with my customers and stay there. Tell everybody I said to stay put until this is over. Lock the door, too."

By then my tenants were poking their heads out of their apartments and yelling for someone to call the cops. Jasper was already down to the second floor when two policemen barged through the front door and almost collided with Joe.

"Upstairs!" Joe shouted, pointing with the club. "Watch out, he's nuts. He's got a knife!"

"What's his name?" the lanky officer asked.

"Jasper… Jasper something–or-other. I'm not sure."

The officer called up, "Jasper, come down with your hands up and you won't be hurt."

"You're lying,' Jasper shouted back. "You're with them. You can't trick me."

"With who, Jasper, with who?"

"Don't try to trick me. You know damn well who. Stay way!"

"We're not going to hurt you. We want to help you."

"You can't fool me. You're lying, I know it!

"We don't want us to come up after you, Jasper. We're here to help you, trust me. Throw down your knife and put your hands in the air."

"Liar! Liar!"

The lanky policeman held his billy club in one hand and laid his hand on his holstered gun with the other. He nodded to his partner, who drew out his own gun. Slowly, they ascended the stairs, the lanky one followed by his partner. When they reached the top step, Jasper lunged forth slashing at the first officer, catching only his coat sleeve before tripping and tumbling down the stairs. Before he could get up, both officers piled on top of him, slapping the knife away as they pinned him face down and clamped handcuffs on his wrists behind his back. Writhing beneath them, Jasper wailed his despair, crying for help.

Moments later a station wagon pulled up to the curb. Two men in white jackets jumped out and rushed inside.

"We'll take him from here, officer," the one with thick eyeglasses said. "He escaped from Forest Avenue. We've been looking for him for over a month." He reached down. "C'mon, Jasper, c'mon. We're going home. Your friends are waiting for you." They hauled Jasper to his feet. "Thatta boy, you're OK; you're safe now."

The other white jacket saw the blood on the lanky officer's arm where he had pushed up his sleeve. "Better get that taken care of. It doesn't look bad, just superficial, but it could get infected."

Joe piped up. "He seemed all right for a while before he started acting nutty, saying things like people were talking about him on the radio. At first I thought he was just trying to be funny."

"Jasper's a good actor, only he wasn't acting. He can fool anybody at first. Pretty resourceful, too. He robbed the bursar's office before he slipped away in the trunk of a visitor's car. This isn't the first time he made a break, but eventually he shows his true colors, alarms people around him and we end up catching him and bringing him back."

Jasper was mumbling incoherently when they helped him out the door into the station wagon.

Chapter 20

Two days after Cotton returned home from the hospital, a black Cadillac pulled up and parked in front of my entrance. I was rather surprised to see that. People of high caliber usually go downtown to the Hotel Statler for lodging. I watched the young driver pull a folded wheelchair out of the trunk, carry it up the few steps to the landing, set it down and unfold it inside the door. From there he returned to the car, where he helped an elderly man in a tan, camelhair coat out of the back seat. Looping the old man's arm over his shoulder, he guided him over the sidewalk and up the steps. Once inside, he lowered him into the wheelchair and pushed him into Joe's restaurant.

The driver, a slender young man with a rigidly arched back, and wearing gray gloves and chauffer's cap bent low, apparently to hear better what the man was saying, then left. I watched him check the names on the mailboxes, climb to the second floor and knock on Cotton's door.

Cotton opened her door part way and peered out cautiously.

"Mrs. Morrison?"

"Yes."

He handed her a business card. "Mrs. Morrison, Mr. Danbury begs your forgiveness for this intrusion; however, he didn't want to delay this meeting, so he's come personally. He is presently downstairs in the restaurant and hopes he is not inconveniencing you, but would like to see you now, if possible."

Cotton looked at the card in her hand. "Somebody wants to see me?"

"It's in regards to your husband's present incarceration."

"About Jeb?"

"Mr. Danbury is an attorney. You must have heard of him?"

Cotton shook her head. "No."

"Nevertheless, he's waiting. Shall I tell him you'll be coming down?"

"A lawyer man?"

"One of the best."

"For Jeb?"

"Yes, your husband."

Cotton hesitated. "I don't see what good it will—"

"I suggest you let Mr. Danbury decide that. You'll be down?"

She nodded, staring down at the card.

"Good. It would behoove you not to keep Mr. Danbury waiting. His time is valuable."

Five minutes later, wearing a white sweater over a dark dress, Cotton entered the restaurant, tentatively, and glanced around.

"Over here, Mrs. Morrison," Danbury called, waving his hand.

He offered her a seat across the table and introduced

himself as Rupert Danbury, of the Schlubb, Franks, Pendleton and Danbury Law Firm.

"We've never met, but I'm sure you know me from this," he said, patting the arm of his wheelchair.

Cotton's eyes widened. "You mus' be the man—"

"Exactly. The man in the wheelchair on the street. And I have a debt to repay. If not for your husband's actions, I wouldn't be here talking to you now."

Cotton lowered her head. "A debt? Jeb never expected nothin', Mr. Danbury. He says a good deed don't need repayin'."

"Good deed, indeed!" Danbury adjusted his thick eyeglasses and smoothed back a shock of gray hair. "First of all, Mrs. Morrison, I'd like to express my sympathy for your loss. I know it must have been devastating for you. I'm speaking of your baby."

She looked surprised. "You know about dat?"

"Knowledge is my stock in trade."

"Jeb doesn't know 'bout it yet. He mus' be worrin' his heart out not hearin' from me, but they wouldn't allow me no telephone call. He's gonna be hurt when I tell him I lost the baby. Awful hurt. He had plans for our baby. Big plans. They tol' me I can visit him tomorra."

"Let's forget your visit tomorrow, Mrs. Morrison. I'm posting bail for Jeb. You'll see him shortly, right here."

"Mr. Danbury, I don't know—"

"Please, enough said about that." He drew from an inside pocket a small pad and a fountain pen. "Now, to come to the point; I would like to represent your husband in this case. With your permission, of course."

She hesitated. "Mr. Danbury, I sure do appreciate your interest, but I don' think I can accept your kind offer. Jeb and I, we did save some money workin' hard, but we don' have a whole lot put away. Surely not near enough for a lawyer and goin' by what they say about everythin' else these days."

"Let's not think about money and what 'they say,' shall we, Mrs. Morrison? Let me worry about that." He unscrewed the cap of his fountain pen. "To begin, I'll need some information from you."

"Excuse me, Mr. Danbury, and with all due respect if I may ask, but Jeb tol' me he never gave you his name. So how did you come to know—"

"Not his full name, that's correct, Mrs. Morrison. But he did give me his first name, and I saw his picture in the newspaper. Of course, I recognized him immediately as the man who saved my life." He turned a page in his notepad.

Cotton sat silent for a moment, nervously twisting her thin wedding band, then looked up with sad eyes. "Mr. Danbury, sir," she said softly, "Jeb never did no crime, like they said he did. He never would."

"I know that, Mrs. Morrison. Over my many years in this business, I've developed a discerning eye for the rascals out there, and I've seen them crop up from every walk of life. But in that brief encounter with your husband, I saw a man with character, a good, decent human being, and I'm one hundred percent convinced he is innocent. I intend to prove to a jury that these are nothing more than baseless, trumped up charges. And once he is declared not guilty, we will proceed to file our own civil lawsuit against his accuser. They will pay for this travesty." He looked hard at her. "Believe me, they will pay dearly."

Cotton brightened. "Do you think you can do that, Mr. Danbury? Prove Jeb didn't do anythin' to that woman?"

"I know they'll never prove he did, or my name isn't Rupert Danbury! I've already begun my investigation ... Now, first question...."

After they parted, I watched Cotton climb the staircase with a far lighter heart than the one she came down with an hour earlier.

Chapter 21

It was about that time that I noticed a change in me, an odd sensation I didn't recognize until about a week later. Huggs had just set his bucket aside after mopping the staircase and lit a cigarette, when a young brunette emerged from the restaurant, holding the arm of elderly woman using a cane.

"The eggs were perfect, weren't they, Auntie? Golden yellow like the rising sun."

"My love, breakfast couldn't have been better. Thank you for bringing me here."

Huggs watched the couple go out the door. "Why can't I get a cute girl like that?" he asked, blowing off a stream of smoke. "I ain't so bad to look at like some people maybe think I am. "

Naturally, I assumed he said it aloud, but then I realized his lips hadn't moved. It suddenly hit me: Huggs didn't speak. He thought those words, and I had read his thoughts. I actually read his thoughts! I seemed to notice this phenomenon weeks earlier, but only briefly on a few occasions, which I attributed to my imagination. Now I was certain.

Reading the minds of my tenants was a new dimension to my life. I could not only think and feel emotions the way humans do, but now I could get inside their minds. Whether this would be a gift or a curse, I didn't know. I only know that at the moment, the revelation was both exhilarating and frightening. I didn't have to wait long before using my new found gift. About a month after Bob Sherman, the accordion player, and Willy Dee, the drummer, moved out of their apartments, two new tenants moved in several weeks apart.

A man named Mike McGurty took Bob's apartment. When he stepped inside, he looked around disapprovingly. He had a stringy mop of brown hair, a full, scruffy brown beard to match and a bloated stomach. He tossed his suitcase aside, dropped on the couch and pulled a paper bag out of his yellow, corduroy jacket pocket. He uncorked the bottle inside it, took a long swig and glanced around.

"The place looks better already," he thought, releasing a loud, reverberating belch.

Three weeks later a petite young woman named Grace Pulski set her bag down on the floor of Willy Dee's former apartment next door. She slipped out of her coat.

"Oh, gosh," she said aloud, glancing around and swiping some dust from an end table. Brushing off her hands, she wandered into the kitchen, the bedroom and finally into the bathroom. "This place could use a good cleaning. I will definitely have to call that fellow Huggs Mrs. Chapman mentioned. She said if I needed anything done I could find him down in the cellar where he lives."

It didn't matter to me whether these people verbalized their thoughts aloud or not, I heard them as clearly as if they were shouted. After a while, I realized the Miss Pulski talked aloud to herself all the time, which seemed odd to me for someone so young. I didn't learn why until much later during one of her conversations with McGurty, her new neighbor.

Huggs complained. "Darn it, Miss, I cleaned that apartment myself right after Mrs. Chapman threw that drummer guy out. I sure did, right after he made that big racket dragging those drums down the stairs."

"Well, I'm sorry to tell you, but I need it done better."

Huggs scowled. "If you say I gotta do it, I'll do it, but I don't have to like it."

"I'll pay you extra for it."

Huggs's face broke into a lop-sided smile. "You mean it? Heck, nobody ever paid me extra like that for nothing I ever did."

"Then this will be a first for you."

Huggs took a step toward her. "Can I give you a hug? To welcome you here like I do with everybody?"

Miss Pulski drew back. "A little forward, aren't you?"

"Just a quick hug?"

"Not on your life!"

Hugg's face drooped. "OK. I'll clean it up when you say. But you don't have to pay me extra. It's my job."

After a week or so passed, Miss Pulski was comfortably settled in. Huggs had cleaned the place to her satisfaction and she forced him to take a dollar for his trouble. She'd already begun a routine of making herself comfortable on the easy chair, with a book on her lap and a cup of tea or coffee on the table beside her. She would have been quite content, if not for the occasional loud music vibrating her wall. Exasperated, she finally decided to go next door and say something about it.

Nervous, she rapped on McGurty's door. The loud music inside forced her to rap again, harder.

"Who's there!"

His gruff voice scared her, but she stood her ground. "It's your neighbor, Grace Pulski."

The door swung wide. McGurty stood glaring down at her, a bottle of beer dangling by its neck between his thick fingers. "To what do I owe the honor of this call, Grace Pulski?" he asked, taking a swig of beer.

Grace girded herself. "If it isn't asking too much, Mr. McGurty, would you kindly turn your radio down? These walls are so thin the sound travels right through them."

"Maybe I'm a little deaf," he growled. "Did you ever think of that? Deef in one ear and can't hardly hear nothin' out of the other'n?"

"Oh. Oh, I'm so sorry? If that's the case—"

"Yeah, but it ain't the case. For your information, I can hear as good as anybody else. I got ears like a hawk."

"Well, praise the Lord for that. Then may I ask you to please be a little more considerate? I'm having a hard time concentrating on my reading. Will you please do it for my sake?"

He scratched the hair protruding from under his grungy jersey to his throat, and took another swig of beer. "Well, since you put it that way, OK, I'll think about it," he said, staring her straight in the eye in a way that made her shudder.

"Thank you," she said, turning away and leaving.

"Hey!"

She turned back. "Yes?"

"I forgot already. What did you say your name was?"

"Pulski. Grace Pulski." Under her breath she murmured, '*It was my name and it still is.*'

McGurty obviously thought about it and did turn down the volume on his radio. Not all the way, but enough to satisfy Grace. It was probably the following weekend, when Grace was startled to hear someone rattling her doorknob. Frightened, she rose from the couch and padded silently to the door. Now it sounded as if someone was jiggling a key in the keyhole. Then she heard a growling voice talking and a fist banging the door.

"Come on, damn you, open up!" The rattling and banging continued. "Open up or I'll break you down!"

Grace recognized the voice. She'd heard him yelling in the hall several times before. She called, "Mr. McGurty, is that you?"

"Of course, it's me. Who do you think it is, Santy Claus? The question is, who are you?"

"I'm Grace Pulski, your next door neighbor."

"Is that so? Well, tell me, then, Grace Pulski my next door neighbor, what the hell are you doing in my house?"

"For your information, Mr. McGurty, this is my apartment, not yours."

"The hell, you say!"

"It's true, Mr. McGurty. And please don't use that language. Look at my apartment number or go next door and you'll see."

She heard his heavy footsteps stomp away.

"Well, I'll be damned," he said, opening his squeaky door. "Damned if Grace Pulski- my- next- door- neighbor wasn't telling the truth!"

Grace heard his door slam. Relieved, she sat on her couch and picked up her book. "Such a strange man," she said aloud. "It looks as if old demon rum has him in its clutches."

The next afternoon Grace answered the knock on her door. "Yes, Mr. McGurty?"

McGurty averted his eyes and shifted his feet nervously. "I just stopped by to apologize for last night, Mrs. Pulski. Afraid I made a damn—excuse my French—afraid I made a fool of myself, disturbing you like I did."

"I understand, Mr. McGurty. And it's Miss, not Mrs. Call me Grace, if you like."

"That's mighty big of you, Mi— Grace. You can call me Mike."

"All right, Mike. And I thank you for not playing your radio so loud."

"It was only decent of me. I should've known better to begin with."

"Of course you couldn't know how sound travels here." She studied him a moment. "Are you feeling all right… Mike?"

"Not exactly chipper, I admit. It's called a hangover. It's a doozy, but I've had worse."

"Well, I'm glad you've recovering," she said, her hand poised to close the door.

"Uh, Grace, if I could make it up to you somehow… I mean, to kind of start off on a different foot for--"

"Think nothing more of it, Mike. It's all forgotten."

"Uh, if we could just talk a bit sometime. Over a cup of coffee, maybe?"

Grace hesitated.

"I promise I won't be like the same guy you heard last night, if that's what's worrying you."

It was obvious it was what was worrying her, but she didn't say so. "Maybe we can, Mike. We'll see."

"OK, then, Grace," he said, backing away. "Maybe pretty soon, huh?"

As Grace closed her apartment door she wondered if she was opening the door to future trouble. After all, it seemed fairly certain that Mike had a drinking problem. That could lead to trouble, big trouble, as she well knew from a few members of her own family. She decided she would think about it later. At the moment, she had other things on her mind.

Later that evening, Grace finished sorting the last of her things. She picked up the crucifix that had been lying on the nightstand and carried it over to her dresser, where she made the sign of the cross, kissed it and set it carefully up against the mirror. She remembered....

'Sister Grace, we wish you well.'

'Thank you, Mother Angela,' she answered, packing the last few items in her bag.

'We'll keep you in our prayers.'

Grace climbed into the back seat of the taxi and waved goodbye to the cluster of nuns standing at the entrance door, waving back, their sad faces framed in their white and black cowls.

Tears filled her eyes as she watched the convent fade from view. It seemed only yesterday she had entered that holy place and vowed to give her life to Jesus and the church. Now her heart was filled with guilt for betraying her vows. It hadn't been an easy life, but she loved it, much as she loved the children she was assigned to teach in the convent school. After her troubled early life at home, she had found peace at last. That, and all the happiness and contentment she'd ever craved until....

A ruckus suddenly broke out downstairs. A bellowing voice sang out amid other voices raised in anger.

"My wild, Irish rose…"

"Shut up, we're trying to sleep!"

"The sweetest flower that grows…"

"Hey, can it. Can it now or I'm calling the cops!"

"Search anywhere…"

Grace opened her door a crack and saw Mike McGurty stumbling up the stairs swinging a bottle of beer and singing at the top of his lungs.

"But none can compare… to my Wiiiiild IIIrish Roooose!"

"Will somebody shut that guy up before I kill him!"

McGurty had almost reached the top of the stairs, when he tripped and fell on his face. Sprawled out and moaning, he dragged his body onto the landing.

Grace rushed out and tried lifting him. "Mr. McGurty, Mike, you have to get up."

"Lemme go, damn it, lemme sleep. I wanna sleep right here."

Moments later Huggs came rushing up the stairs.

"Huggs, can you help me get Mr. McGurty to his apartment."

"I guess I can," he said, trying to catch his breath before reaching down to drag him. "We need his key to get in. Where's his key? You got his key?"

"Look in his pockets."

Huggs searched him. "It's not here, just some money. Maybe he must've lost it."

"Go try his door. See if it's open."

Still breathing hard, Huggs hurried over, pushed and pulled the door and rattled the knob. "Nope. It's locked, just like I thought."

Grace wiped her brow. "All right, then help me bring him in here, into my apartment."

Struggling together they dragged McGurty over the floor inside her apartment, where they strained to lift his unconscious body into the parlor chair.

"Dead weight," Huggs said, huffing. "Dead weight makes him even heavier'n he already is." Huggs straightened and pinched his nose. "Stinks like a brewery, too."

"Thank you, Huggs. And pick up that beer bottle he dropped in the hall, will you?"

"OK."

"I'll leave the door partially open in case anyone wants to look in on him."

"I don't know who that'd be," he said, leaving. "All I know is he's nothing but a bunch of trouble from the minute he moved in here last month. Big drunk. Mrs. Chapman's gonna hear about this. She'll throw him out just like she did that crazy drummer and accordion player. Yessir..." he mumbled, going out the door, "...throw him out on his ear just like she did them other troublemakers. Serve him right, too, always drunk and bothering people like that!"

Grace looked down at Mike, his head back, mouth open and his legs spread out. He was soon snoring.

"Mike," she whispered to herself, "didn't you promise just this morning you weren't going to be the same guy?"

Grace covered the lamp with a sheer scarf and sat on the

couch across from him. She pulled a light blanket over her legs. Having a man in her apartment overnight was grounds for eviction, but she felt sure the circumstances would excuse her. The partially opened door allowing anyone to look inside should avoid suspicion, too. She watched Mike a long time before dozing off. Occasionally, either his snoring woke her up or a short burst of unintelligible words that left him writhing for a few moments before he sank back into a deep sleep.

Morning couldn't come soon enough for Grace. At the first sign of light, she rose, tired and red-eyed. She went into the kitchen, set a pot of coffee on the stove and sat at the table. It was obvious to her that Mike was a troubled man, not the kind of person she wanted to get mixed up with. For three years her life as a sister had been serene and happy. She didn't want to return to the tumultuous existence that dominated her childhood. She made up her mind to have nothing more to do with him.

It was late morning before Mike opened his eyes and glanced around. He sat up. "What the—"

"Good morning, Mike."

"Hey, what's going on?" he said, looking around bleary-eyed and confused. "What's going on here? Where am I?"

"You lost your key, Mike. Huggs helped me get you in here, in my apartment."

Mike ran his hand through his hair. "I don't get it."

"I'm afraid you were badly inebriated when you came in last night."

He rubbed his eyes, trying to focus them. "Oh... yeah... I remember now.... You're Grace, right? Yeah, Grace. I did it again, didn't I? I said I wouldn't, but I did it again, didn't I?"

"I have coffee on the stove. It's quite strong. It should help clear your head."

Mike stood up on shaky legs. "Thanks, Grace, but no, I've imposed enough. I'm sorry for that, very sorry."

"No need to apologize, Mike. It was just one of those unfortunate situations."

"Yeah, well, I've been having too many of those, as you say, 'unfortunate situations' for way too long. Anyway, I thank you for your help and consideration. Maybe I can do you a favor sometime," he said, moving toward the door. "I hope my being here in your apartment all night isn't going to—"

"I'm sure it will be all right."

"Because if it isn't, I'll swear an oath to God that—"

"It won't be necessary, Mike. Huggs was here and the door was open all night."

"All the same—"

"I don't know how you're going to get into your apartment, Mike. Your door is locked and Huggs searched your pockets but didn't find your key. I'm sure our landlady has one you can copy if you lost yours."

Mike laughed. "It's not lost because I don't keep it in my pocket. Too easy to lose when I pull out my dough to pay for my beer. I learned that lesson a long time ago." He bent down and slid his fingers inside his shoe. "See?" he said, holding it up and twisting it in his fingers. He winked. "Pretty smart, huh?"

Chapter 22

After Mike left, Grace opened her purse and sat down at her kitchen table. It was time to land a job. The little money she had wouldn't last too much longer. She could have gone home to her parents' house, but she wasn't ready for an inquisition and having to explain why she left the Order again. She didn't want to hear any more of their questions or listen to their nagging.

Her first day out, she had to telephone and give them her new address, but she didn't want to argue with her mother about returning home 'where she belonged.' The phone call left Grace with the uncomfortable feeling of reliving a nightmare. She made up her mind to start a new life, free and independent. A subtle sense of excitement competed with the anxiety already giving her stomach problems.

She took a scrap of paper out of her purse and laid it aside. She would call first thing in the morning to see if the diocese would hire her as a teacher at one of the parochial schools. They didn't pay much, she knew, but it would get her by until she could make other plans.

Almost two weeks passed.

Grace was just finishing her second cup of morning coffee when she heard the soft rap of knuckles on her door. She thought it might be Mrs. Chapman finally coming to inquire about all the activity that had occurred earlier. The smile on her face faded when she saw a strange man standing there.

"Yes...oh...oh...." Grace stood with her mouth open. "Mike?"

"Yep, it's me, Mike McGurty. In person." He laughed.

"Mike McGurty."

"Didn't recognize me at first, did you? That's because I've changed, physically, mentally, and permanently, and that's a promise."

She shook her head.

"I knew I'd fool you. Took a while to sink in, didn't it? Look, Grace," he said, splaying his hands along his body. "New shirt, clean slacks. Trimmer, too." He slapped his stomach and patted his face. "No more beard and a fresh haircut. All showered up and ready to go." He laughed again. "How about that?"

Grace finally collected herself. "Very impressive, Mike. Really. After the way I last saw you—"

He threw his hands up and stuck his fingers in his ears. "Don't tell me about it, Grace, please. I can already guess. But believe me, I'm a new man now and I'll swear an oath to that."

They stood a moment, neither saying anything until Grace opened the door wide. "I just made a fresh pot of coffee. Would you like to come in?"

Mike shrugged his shoulders. "If it wouldn't inconvenience you none," he said, stepping inside. Grace left the door wide open to allow anyone passing in the hall a clear view of them in the kitchen.

They sat opposite each other at Grace's table, both feeling awkward; he, because of his recent actions and she, because a man was in her house, a relatively strange man, at that.

147

"If I may ask, Grace, are you from this neighborhood?"

"Actually I'm from the Broadway- Fillmore district. That's where my parents and most of my relatives live now." She sipped her coffee. "And you, Mike?"

"Me? I'm from everywhere. An over-the-road truck driver, laid off at present, but I'm originally from the South Park area. Lots of Irishmen and a bar for almost every one of them. Actually, there's a bar on every corner and some in between. That means lots of boozing and fistfights every Saturday night. I boxed for a while. Thought of turning professional, but seeing so many guys with mashed noses and cauliflower ears... not that I'm any beauty myself, but, well, they didn't look too pretty and I didn't care to join the 'pug-ugly' club, so I gave it up." He reached into his pocket. "Do you mind if I smoke, Grace?"

"Not at all," she said, not really truthfully. "I don't have an ashtray because I'm not a smoker, but this saucer should do," she said, sliding one over.

Mike thanked her and sat back in his chair. He took a swallow of his coffee. "Grace..." he balked. "Grace... I know I've been a nuisance since you've arrived here, but I'd like to make it up to you somehow." He blew a puff of smoke off to the side. "Do you by chance have a boyfriend, somebody you're seeing steady?"

Grace smiled. "No, Mike, but I think I should tell you something."

"Nothing to disappoint me, I hope."

"It depends what that would be."

"You got me there," he said, tossing his hands out.

"I was a sister."

His eyes opened wide. "You mean a 'sister' sister? Like one

148

of them in the church?"

"Until recently."

"I kind of thought all nuns or sisters were old and shriveled. At least that's the only kind I ever knew when I was a kid going to Catholic school."

Grace laughed. "The old stereotype. The truth is, though, we all start young and eventually get there."

"I guess you're right about that," Mike said, taking a deep drag on his cigarette. He hesitated a moment, blowing a stream of smoke upwards, then said, "Does that mean...? Uhh, what I'm trying to say is, being a sister and all...."

"You're asking if I can date men."

"Exactly, Grace, exactly. That's what I was getting at, that is, if I'm not being too personal."

Just then a rapping turned their attention to the apartment door. It was Huggs standing stiff and looking confused.

"It's all right, Huggs," Grace said. "Come in. We won't bite you."

"It's these, Miss Grace," he said, dragging his feet and holding up a couple of letters over his head. "I figured I'd save you a trip to the mailbox."

"Well, thank you, Huggs," she said, taking them from him. "Would you like a cup of coffee? Mike and I would be happy to have you join us." She nodded toward Mike. "Wouldn't we, Mike?"

Mike sat up straight. "Oh, yeah, yeah, happy to have you join us, Huggs," he said, snuffing out his cigarette.

Huggs backed away. "Oh, no, no. I got these other ones in my pocket to deliver. Nobody minds, except Mr. Gustav. He likes to get his own." He spun around on his heels and practically galloped off.

"He's a nice fellow," Grace said. "Always willing to help."

"Yeah, helpful, very helpful …uhh, Grace…" He took a deep breath and blurted out, "Do you think you'd like to have a date with me? Nothing fancy, you know, but maybe just a neighborhood show or something simple like that?"

Grace smiled. "Thank you, Mike, but I'm sorry. At the present time I can't."

The breaking smile on Mike's face faded. "I don't blame you if you're telling me you don't want to. It's OK, Grace." He started to get up. "I understand."

"No, you don't, Mike. I can't just now, but if you give me a little time to take care of some personal matters, I think we can work something out."

Mike broke out in a wide grin. "That's swell, Grace." He stood, pushed his chair under the table and started for the door. "OK if I check in on you? Say, in a week?"

"Fine, Mike," she said, walking him to the door.

"Thanks again for the coffee," he called back as he headed down the stairs.

Grace shut the door and went back to the table. Whether she'd see him again would depend on whether he stayed sober for the next week or so. She picked up the letters. One was from the diocese. She opened it.

'Dear Miss Pulski,

Since your request for employment at one of our parochial schools has been received by our office, we have requested and received transcripts of your past experience and qualifications as an elementary school teacher.

It is my pleasure to inform you that you have been approved by our review board for an opening at St. Columba's. A brief interview will be...'

Grace squeezed the letter in her hands. Now she would have a steady income, not much, but enough to be independent. Her new life was beginning. Laughing aloud, she sang and danced and pranced around the house all day.

The weeks passed quickly for Grace. She'd already started teaching third grade pupils and was quite content with her work. Creative, she was constantly making up puzzles, diagrams, riddles and games to make her classes interesting and entertaining as well as educational.

She had just put her school papers away, when Mike rapped:

"All set, Grace?" he asked, stepping inside.

"Give me a minute," she said, gathering up her jacket and purse.

"No walk in the park tonight, Grace. No coffee and doughnuts or neighborhood show, either. We're going big time for a change."

"Is the opera in town?" she teased. "Or the Russian ballet?"

"No. I wouldn't go if they were. Too high-class for me." He held her hand going down the stairs. "It's downtown for us. Shea's Buffalo. I heard it's a great movie playing. Humphrey Bogart's in it. I like him a lot."

"What's the name of the movie?"

"I heard it's got romance in it, so I took a chance you'll like it."

"I'm sure, but what's the name of it?"

"Casablanca."

"You mean white house."

"Huh?"

"White house. 'Casa,' house; 'blanca,' white. That's what Casablanca means. The Spanish put the adjective after the noun. Translated literally, it's 'house white.' We do it ourselves, but only occasionally, as in, Hotel Statler, instead of Statler Hotel." She laughed. "That's the teacher in me coming out."

Mike looked a little mystified. "Oh, yeah? Interesting. Anyway, I hope it's not one of those foreign movies. I don't like having to read all those...those..."

"Subtitles?"

"Yeah, that's it, subtitles."

"I doubt it's a foreign movie, Mike. Not if Humphrey Bogart's in it."

I didn't know what happened after they left the building. It wasn't until later that night when they returned to their respective apartments that I got the full story. Grace poured herself a cup of tea and sat in the big parlor chair, the same one Mike had slept in a month or so earlier. She was disturbed and I wondered why until she put her head back and relived the evening, moment by moment.

After the movie they took a leisurely stroll down crowded Main Street, past the little shops and big department stores, like Kobackers and J.N. Adams, with their window displays of male and female mannequins all decked out in the season's latest fashions. When they passed AM&A's department store window,

Mike said,

"Too bad it isn't Christmas time, Grace. I really like the big holiday displays."

"You and everybody else in Buffalo, especially the kids," she said. "Seeing Santa Claus, the elves, the reindeer and all the other things moving and performing as if they're actually living creatures is beautiful."

"I heard they call it animation, Grace. It's really amazing how they do that. Keeps the sidewalk crowds hypnotized watching all those things waving and bowing and spinning around. Who knows what they'll come up with next."

They sauntered along and went back to talking about the movie.

"That Casablanca was really a good movie, wasn't it, Grace? It even had a good love story with what's her name?"

"Ingrid Bergman. I didn't care for the sad ending, though," she said.

"It didn't faze me. But girls like happy endings, I know."

She looked at him slyly. "Oh, do they?"

"Hey, and what about those lodges? Neat weren't they, the way the seats recline?"

"I didn't mind the cigarette smoke, but the cigar smoke bothered me."

"Darn it, Grace, why didn't you say something? I paid extra for that smoking section. We could've moved to another spot."

They carried on their conversation about one thing or another and finally caught a City Service cab back to the neighborhood.

"It's still pretty early, Grace. The stars aren't even out yet.

How about we take a slow walk around the block before going in?"

"All right, Mike. If you'd like."

"Can I ask you a question, Grace?"

"It depends on the question."

"A couple of times I passed your door and I heard you talking. At first I thought it was the radio, but I know your voice and I didn't hear any other one. I know it's none of my business, and you don't have to answer if you don't want to, but who the heck were you talking to? I know you don't have a dog or a cat. Or even a bird. Don't tell me you're practicing a Charlie McCarthy act?"

Grace smiled. "No, Mike, I'm not learning to be a ventriloquist. I was talking to myself."

"To yourself?"

"I've been doing it for quite a while."

He looked closely at her. "You're not going cuckoo on me, are you, Grace?"

She laughed. "No, Mike. You see, for several years, along with other sisters, I was forced to maintain silence for hours and hours on end. It was hard." She looked up to him and smiled. "Now that I've found my voice again I'm making up for lost time."

"Oh, I gotcha," he said, nodding. "I gotcha now. I'm relieved to know that you're not off your rocker, like I thought at first."

They were halfway down Potomac Avenue when a man wearing a black suit and a hat low on his forehead suddenly jumped out from behind a tree and startled them.

"I want to talk to you, Grace. "

Grace gasped. "Howard!"

When he stepped forward and took her wrist, Mike reached out and grabbed his arm. "Hey, get your hands off her or I'll break your back!"

"This is none of your business." He turned cold eyes on Grace. "Tell him, Grace, tell him."

"Mike...."

"I don't care who you are or what your game is, Buster, but you make one move toward her and I'm gonna turn you into a funeral."

"Grace, tell him!"

"Mike, let him go! I know him."

"Yeah, well, I don't like the way he introduced himself." He pushed the man away. "Just keep your hands to yourself."

"Go away, Howard, go away."

The man named Howard backed off. "All right, but I'll be in touch, Grace. All right for now." He turned and started across the street. "I know where you live. You'll be hearing from me," he said, calling back and wagging a finger.

Grace and Mike began walking again.

"You want to tell me what that was all about, Grace?"

"Not now, Mike."

"What did he mean by saying, 'Tell him, Grace'?"

She ignored his question. "Let's go back, Mike. I'm tired."

Baffled, Mike shook his head. "OK, Grace, whatever you say. I guess you got your reasons."

Chapter 23

Later that evening Grace sipped her tea, remembering and still shamed, remembering Howard— Father Howard Bevins— sitting beside her on the rectory couch without his black suit jacket and white collar. He was so handsome with his piercing blue eyes and his thick, black hair.

"This is wrong, Father. So wrong. Please stop," she pleaded, trying to wriggle from under his arm looped around her shoulder. "I only came here to talk. This has to end."

"It's Howard, Grace, call me Howard. Don't fight me," he said, pushing her down on her back.

"Howard...don't—" He smothered her words with his mouth.

Grace first noticed Father Bevins during vespers, those evening prayers when she'd catch him staring at her, or, to be more precise, when she 'felt' his eyes burning holes in her back. Soon afterward he found excuses to be near her, to talk to her. Gradually his attentions became more intense, so much so that she feared the other sisters would notice, particularly the way he inserted himself into situations where priests didn't usually belong.

She should have stopped him, threatened to report him to the bishop, but she didn't. Secretly, she enjoyed his attention, savored the feeling he gave her of being special, desirable. She had never known so wonderful a sensation before. Together they worked on the Christmas play and other school activities, and with each meeting, he moved closer to her, often saying things she should have objected to as being too personal.

Cloistered at night, she prayed on her knees to God to give her the strength to resist him, but even as she said those words, she knew she wasn't sincere. She wanted him. She wanted Howard more than she'd ever wanted anything in her life. For weeks, guilt struggled with desire. Ultimately, desire won.

Their affair had begun, surreptitiously, at first, then more openly, carelessly, until it came to the attention of the bishop....

Trembling, Grace entered the rectory, where she saw the bishop sitting behind his ornate, mahogany desk with a book opened before him. Slowly, he raised his shaggy head. Gesturing to her to sit across from him, he studied her with eyes that seemed heavy with sorrow, eyes conflicted in their understanding of human frailties and the values of the church both had vowed to uphold in the name of Jesus Christ. The sharp lines carved into his face suggested a mortified existence and world-weariness.

His gray head nodded with his last words. "… and as bishop I'm obliged to deliver a decision my heart is reluctant to deliver, but my duty requires it," he said, his voice quiet but firm. "You've broken your vows and in the process, unfortunately, stained the reputation of this holy institution, as well as yourself. I see your tears and understand your remorse and sorrow, sister, but there is nothing more to be said or done. I must ask you to leave immediately. I pray God forgives you…."

Grace left the meeting, her head bowed in tearful shame. A week later, those sitting in judgment dismissed her and transferred Father Howard Bevins to another parish. She'd

157

always heard it was a man's world but didn't realize how much until that moment, when she was forced to leave, while he was merely assigned to another parish. She didn't know whether the bishop's commitment to the church would allow him to forgive her in his heart, but her sisters, except for a few, definitely did, waving goodbye with tears in their eyes as she drove away. Expelled from the church, she had no choice but to go home to her parents. Even for the short time she was there it wasn't pleasant.

Her mother called from downstairs. "Grace, will you come out of your room and speak to us? Your father is very upset."

"I will. Give me time."

"For heaven's sake, how much time do you need? You've been hibernating since you came home. Grace, are you listening to me? We have questions we'd like answered. What happened? Why are you here? Maybe we can help."

Grace knew they couldn't help, especially since she missed her period, something she dared not reveal. She had to leave the house now. She would return to the church, plead for help. Under the circumstances they couldn't refuse her. When she left, she told her parents she was returning to the convent. They seemed relieved and asked no more questions.

As she expected, the authorities didn't refuse to take her back after she gave the facts to Mother Superior, who then passed the information up through the proper channels. Grace was allowed to remain in the convent until the time of her delivery. She stayed aloof as much as possible, ashamed to be in the presence of the other sisters. Initially, she thought she'd be treated as a pariah among them, but most showed no sign of disapproval. Nevertheless, she believed she was an abomination in the eyes of God and the sisters who tended to her.

On a dark, dreary day, her labor pains came, the ambulance came and the baby came, all in proper order. But she never saw the baby. She never even knew its gender. They said it was to prevent her from becoming attached. She knew it would be placed in an orphanage and eventually put up for adoption. It was there that one of the nurses who sympathized with her said her situation was not unusual, and told her she had seen many such similar cases. Not only did the knowledge not make Grace feel any better, but it left her disillusioned with the church she loved so much. Yet, she couldn't deny or hide from the fact that she herself had contributed to the dark sinfulness kept secret by the hierarchy.

Grace's parents never knew of her pregnancy. She only contacted them after she found the apartment she now occupied. She thought she was content, as much as she could be, but her contentment was shattered by the appearance of Howard earlier that evening while she was walking with Mike. Did she still love Howard? It was a question she couldn't really answer, not after all she'd been through. But she had gained strength over the months. Confidence, too. She could stand on her own two feet and didn't need anyone. There was something exhilarating about that.

Weeks passed and she occupied herself with school work. She made time to see Mike, but not too often. She knew he was disappointed with her apparent lack of interest or even what he considered her aloofness, but he didn't complain. It only showed in his sad face whenever she turned him down. She was grateful he never brought up the incident with Howard, even though she believed it had to prey on his mind and bother him.

It was early on a Saturday afternoon, when Grace made a last minute decision to go to the A&P store to pick up coffee and a few staples she needed for the weekend. Ragged black clouds hanging over the city dropped cold rain that stung her face when she stepped outside, where she struggled to open her umbrella against an icy wind howling off Lake Erie, intent on blowing it inside out, and her along Niagara Street.

Once inside the store and anxious to get home to work on a new school project, she rushed around picking her items quickly, handed her money to the clerk, took up her shopping bag and was preparing to open her umbrella, when she felt a strong hand grip her shoulder.

She swung around. "Howard!"

"I told you I'd be in touch, Grace."

She shrugged his hand off. "Howard, I want you to leave me alone."

"I can't, Grace. I love you. I have to see you. I want us to be together again."

Snapping her umbrella fully open, she hurried down the few steps and started walking briskly.

"Grace, you have to give us another chance. I've left the priesthood," he said, stumbling along to keep up with her under the driving rain. "Yes, I did, I gave it up for you. For us. We can make it right. We're both free now. I've been miserable without you all these past months. I love you, Grace. I need you. I want to marry you."

"It's too late, Howard. I have a new life. I have plans and I don't want them spoiled."

Rain spilled off the brim of his hat as he hung close beside her. "Is it because of the guy I saw you with last time? Is that it, Grace? Do you love another man?"

"I'm not answering any more questions, Howard. My life has been ruined once already. I'm content now. I'm asking you to go and leave me alone."

"I can't, Grace. We belong together. Don't you understand?

I've given up the priesthood I swore an oath to for you. The things we said, the things—"

She turned on him. "I'm going to call a policeman if you don't stop bothering me. I mean it, Howard. Please!" She stepped off the curb into the water streaming along the curb and scurried across the street.

"Grace!" he called, darting after her. "Wait!"

A horn blared and tires squished over the pavement with the squeal of brakes as a truck barreled down on him.

Grace looked back and saw him pinned under the wheels of a dump truck skidding sideways and smashing into a parked car, blowing out windows and scattering glistening glass shards over the wet pavement. She screamed, dropped her umbrella and rushed back across the street, spilling a trail of scattered groceries. "Howard! Oh, Howard!"

Grace remembered little except having heard the sickening thud of metal hitting flesh and the hysterical truck driver climbing out and crying over and over again to the gathering crowd, 'He ran out in front of me, I couldn't stop. He ran out in front of me.' Wide-eyed, panic-stricken, he rushed from one bystander to another, grabbing them by their collars. 'You're my witness. You saw it, didn't you, the way he ran out? Didn't you see it? You did, didn't you, the way he....?'

Stunned, Grace stood drenched in the soaking rain, her limp hair flat and stringy hanging down dripping over her shoulders, watching men work to free Howard's body from under the chassis and cover it with a tarp. She saw his blood mingling with rainwater trickling pink to the sewer along the curb. Voices called over one another. As she wandered away, she heard someone shout, 'He's alive!'

Grace spent three sleepless nights reliving the gory images and haunted by the belief that it was her fault Howard was hit.

She prayed for him to live and for her own salvation. After making several phone calls she learned he'd been taken to General Hospital, the same place her baby was born; however, no visitors would be allowed until the next day. On the morning of the fourth day she dressed quickly and called down the stairs to Huggs.

Huggs emerged from the cellar and came around to the staircase and called up.

"You want me for something, Miss Grace?"

"Yes, Huggs. Will you please do me a favor and call a taxi? Here's the nickel," she said, tossing it down. "I'll be ready in a few minutes."

Twenty minutes later she arrived at the hospital and hurried to the admission desk. She gave her name and said she was Howard's fiancée. When she asked for Howard's room number, the receptionist checked her sheet and told Grace she'd first have to talk to the doctor. Minutes later as she anxiously paced the floor in the waiting room, the doctor came in and introduced himself.

"How is he, Doctor Zeffner?" she asked, alarmed by the grim look on his face. "Is he going to be all right?"

A lanky man with a soft voice, the doctor shook his head. "He's been gravely injured, Miss Pulski. Frankly, his condition is dire."

"Can I see him, doctor?"

He hesitated. "All right, but only briefly. Rest is crucial at this point. He's suffered multiple internal injuries and lost a great deal of blood."

Tears welled in her eyes. "Doctor Zeffner, is he critical?"

He nodded. "We've done everything possible. It's up to God

now." He indicated the way to the room, escorting her down the corridor. "Remember, only a few moments. He's not a pretty sight," he said solemnly. Try your best not to get emotional when you see him. It won't be easy for you, but we can't afford to upset him."

When she opened the door, the smell of antiseptics assaulted her senses. She peeked into the room and tiptoed over to his bed. Shocked, her breath caught in her throat when she saw him completely swathed in white bandages, except for his eyes, nose and mouth. Tubing ran everywhere like rubber snakes. She moved to the side of his bed.

"Howard?" she whispered, "Howard, it's Grace."

His eyelids fluttered. "Grace," he mouthed without sound.

"I'm sorry, Howard, so sorry."

A hint of a smile touched his lips.

She spoke softly. "You're going to be all right, Howard. The doctor said so."

She had to lean over the bed close to his lips to hear.

"No."

"Yes, Howard, oh, yes. The doctor said it's going to take a little time, but you'll get stronger. Just a little more time. Howard, I'll help you. I'll look after you, I promise." She looked up. *Oh, God, if I could only save him. Please God, spare his life.*

Howard's lips moved.

"What, Howard?" she asked, trying to read his lips. She bent low, trying to hear his whisper. "What?"

"I waited… for you…."

"They wouldn't allow me in until now, Howard. They said

163

you... you weren't ready for visitors."

"How...long?"

"Four days. They made me wait four, excruciating long days. But I'm here with you now, Howard. I'm here."

A tear surfaced in the corner of his eye and traced a path down to his pillow. He breathed out the words, "Pray with me."

Grace straightened up. "I will, Howard, I will." Gently, she clasped his hand between her hands.

His hand was cold and limp.

"Howard..." She looked into his blue eyes, already clouding over. "All right, Howard, all right."

Together they began to say the Act of Contrition:

"Oh, my God, I am heartily sorry, For having offended thee, And I detest of all my sins, Because I dread the loss of heaven and the pains of...."

Howard's mouth fell open. His eyes closed. A long breath rattled from his lungs, faded and stopped.

"Howard. Howard, no!" She turned and cried out, "Doctor! Doctor Zeffner!"

Chapter 24

"Come in," Grace called. She knew it was Mike.

He opened the door. "Here I am, just like I said."

"Mr. Dependable." She smiled. "Come in, Mike, and sit down. Leave the door open."

He came in and sat opposite her at the kitchen table. She poured their coffee and sat down. "It's been a while. Two months, in fact."

"Actually, seven weeks and four days, Grace," he said, stirring in a spoonful of sugar. "I really missed you, but I think I know what you were going through with the death, and all. It had to be hard."

"I apologize, Mike. I've also really been busy with school work. They like to pile it on."

"I can imagine."

She paused and gazed across to him for a long time before speaking. Finally, she said, "Mike, I think I owe you an explanation."

He looked surprised. "An explanation? For what?"

"For what happened that time we were taking our walk. And everything after that. It's long overdue."

"You mean with your friend...what's his name....? I forgot all about it."

"I don't think you have, Mike, so—"

"Grace, you don't have to explain anything to me. It's not my business."

"I owe it to you, anyway. What happened was rude and might have been dangerous to you."

"Grace—"

"Mike, listen to me. I was a sister in the Catholic church."

"Yes, sure, I remember you telling me that. So what does—"

"Hear me out, Mike...."

Grace proceeded to tell him about her involvement with Howard and how she was ignominiously discharged from the Holy Order. She told him everything except the most intimate details and having a baby.

Mike listened without showing any emotion. When she finished, he shrugged. "Well, Grace, it's all in the past, right? Like they say, 'Water over the dam.' Or, 'Don't cry over spilled milk.' It hasn't anything to do with now. It's done and over with. I forgot it already."

"You're very sweet, Mike."

"Aw, shucks, Grace." He laughed. "Hey, did I sound like Will Rogers in that movie we saw a while back?"

"All you need is a lariat, a cowboy hat and a horse."

They laughed together.

Mike drained his cup and sat back. "I have some news, Grace. Might as well break it out now."

She looked at him, curiously. "Good news, I hope."

"Not exactly." He drew an envelope from his pocket. "Greetings from the president. President Franklin Roosevelt himself."

"Mike, you've been drafted?"

"Yep. I go for my physical next week. Gotta get even for that dirty sneak attack they pulled on us in Hawaii."

"It's everybody's duty, I suppose."

"Grace, it's a little awkward for me to say this, and I know we haven't known each other all that long, but would you mind if I ask for your picture?" He pointed. "The one on the table there?"

Grace reached over and picked it up. "It's not much of picture, being so small. I was close to nineteen when it was taken."

"Still, it's you, Grace. I'd really like to have it to remind me of… of home while I'm gone."

"Certainly, Mike." She removed it from its cardboard frame and handed it over. "Maybe it'll bring you good luck, at least I hope so."

"Thanks, Grace, I really appreciate this." He opened his wallet and slid it carefully inside. "Maybe I'm asking too much now, Grace, but would it be OK if I wrote to you once in a while… just to see how you're doing, you know, with your teaching job and all, and let you know how things are going with me?"

"Of course, Mike. I'd like that very much."

"I mean, it's not like we're engaged or nothing like that, but I feel we got kind of close over the past couple of months or so."

"We did, Mike, didn't we? It was a little touchy in the

beginning, though, wasn't it?"

They both laughed

"I was a real jerk then, wasn't I?" he said, slapping his forehead. "But now, Grace, I mean, I'm not holding you to anything or—"

"I know what you're saying, Mike. We have grown close. You're thinking of me dating other men."

"I know I don't have the right, Grace, but—"

She reached across the table and patted his hand. "We'll write, and I'm sure I'll still be here and unattached when you come back. In fact, Mike, I'm going to be very busy. I'll be starting classes at UB when the next semester begins."

"The University of Buffalo? What for, Grace. You already got a teaching job."

"Let me confess to you, Mike." She leaned close to him. "I already told you about Howard, right?"

"Yes, I appreciate your taking me into your confidence, Grace. That wasn't an easy story to tell."

"It was a harder one to live. Anyway, Mike, I didn't give you all the details or background, but I feel responsible for Howard's death."

"Grace, it wasn't your fault. You had nothing to do with that. For gosh sakes, he got hit by a truck!"

"Oh, Mike, I know, but there's more to it than that, so much more. When I saw him in the hospital, I felt horrible because I was responsible, and I couldn't help him. Not directly responsible, perhaps," she said, shaking her head, "and I suppose that's true, but however you look at it, if not for me, Howard would be alive today. I watched him die, Mike. I watched him take his last breath."

"That can't be a pretty picture, I'm sure. So then what are you getting at, Grace?"

"I'm saying that I'm going back to school, eventually to medical school."

His eyebrows went up. "You want to be a doctor?"

"Not *want* to be doctor, Mike, I *will* be a doctor. Being a woman is a disadvantage, and I know it won't be easy, but I'll do it. I'll do it if it kills me."

"An actual medical doctor! Wow, Grace, that's some ambition."

"I couldn't save Howard, but maybe I can save other lives someday. In a way to make up for...to atone for—"

"Stow it, Grace, stow it," Mike said, shaking his head slowly. His face softened and his whole demeanor showed his admiration. "Grace, it's no wonder I lo... I mean, I think the world of you."

I could see that it was a sad and awkward moment for both Grace and Mike. Whether anything would come of their relationship, I couldn't know at the time. The odds seemed against it, but if I've learned anything at all over the years, it's that the lives of humans and the plans fate has in store for them are definitely unpredictable.

Chapter 25

One morning I was listening to some gossip in Joe's restaurant, when through the door came Barney Fulton, a middle-aged, knobby-boned tenant who exuded the dead-meat smell of the slaughterhouse where he worked.

"Mornin', y'all," he muttered matter-of-factly, and making no eye contact as he passed between the tables on his way over to the counter.

"Help you?" Joe asked, wiping a damp rag in circles on the countertop.

"Two roast beef sandwiches on kummelweck rolls to go. One rare. Horseradish on the side."

Barney's fingers tapped his impatience as he waited for the sandwiches to be made. Head lowered, he glanced around, his mouth twisted in its usual sour shape. He was a naturally grumpy fellow who lived upstairs with his wife, Belinda. They kept to themselves and never had visitors, not that I'd ever seen. Occasionally, I'd hear them arguing, but it would soon go quiet.

"Here you go," Joe said, handing him the bag, taking Barney's money and giving him change from the tarnished-gold cash register that opened with the pretty 'cha-ching' Joe called his 'money song.'

Barney headed up the stairs with the greasy bag dangling

from his hand. Sitting on the top step was Rosie, who recognized my tenants by the sound of their footsteps.

"Good morning, Mr. Fulton," she said.

Barney grumbled past her.

Rosie whispered in her doll's ear. "I don't think he's a happy person, Shirley, because he never has a smile in his voice." She tittered. "I hope that roast beef sandwich I smelled has a fly in it."

Later that evening, when most of the daily activity had died down, I heard someone knocking on Gustav's door.

"Who's there?"

"It is me—Wilhelm" he said in a hushed voice. "Open up."

The door swung open and he stepped inside.

"Wilhelm. It's dangerous for you to come here, you know that." Gustav peeked out quickly before closing and locking the door. "We agreed to meet at city hall. You might have been followed."

"I was very careful to come a roundabout way." Wilhelm pulled off his hat and strode to the table. "You have coffee?"

"Of course," Gustav said, rushing to the stove to turn the gas on under the pot. "But you didn't come here for coffee, Wilhelm. Tell me, what is it?"

"No, it is not for the coffee."

"Is it good news for me?"

Wilhelm brushed the melting snow off his shoulders before peeling off his overcoat and sitting down. He removed his eyeglasses from his suit pocket and began slowly polishing them with his handkerchief, as if to give himself time to think. "No, Gustav, I'm afraid it is not good news for you."

171

"Greta? The children?"

Wilhelm nodded sadly. "We have received word they have been taken by the Gestapo."

"Taken! Taken where?"

"To my understanding, it is Buchenwald."

"Wilhelm, they say Buchenwald's a death camp for Jews. But we can't be certain of that, can we?" he asked hopefully, his hand trembling as he lifted the hot coffee pot from the stove. "So many rumors have proven to be false."

"I don't know, Gustav. As I told you, they were sweeping the towns for all Jews, your town included. I do not wish to be pessimistic, Gustav, but we have an informant, a very reliable one who's proven his worth several times over."

Gustav poured the coffee. "What can we do, Wilhelm? What can I do?"

Wilhelm shrugged. "We can only wait, Gustav. We have no choice."

"Wait? Wait for what! Wilhelm, can I go back? Is that possible?"

"Not anymore, I'm afraid. Not since a few days after Pearl Harbor when our gloriously insane Fuehrer declared war on America."

"Wilhelm, I must get back. Can I be smuggled into Germany? I must save my family!"

"I don't think it's possible anymore, Gustav. Anyway, it would be extremely dangerous."

"There must be a way, Wilhelm, there must be a way! I should never have left them behind, even for a short time. What was I thinking! Those butchers will murder my family!"

Wilhelm nodded his head in sympathy. "I understand your feelings, Gustav."

"No, you don't!" Gustav shouted, slamming his fist on the table, rattling the cups. "You can't know. It's *my* family!"

Wilhelm pushed his chair back. He stood and put on his coat. "I'm sorry, Gustav. I am the bearer of bad news. I know that makes me an unwelcome guest in your house, but you had to know how matters stand. I was the only one who could tell you." He moved to the door.

Gustav rose quickly. "I'm sorry, Wilhelm," he said, clutching his arm. "Forgive me, it's my nerves. Please stay a while."

"I do understand, Gustav." He pulled his arm away and patted Gustav's shoulder. "It is better if I leave. If and when I get further news, I will let you know. But not until I get something definite.... One more thing, Gustav— just to be safe— is there a back door to this building?"

"Yes, on the first floor. Go to the end of the corridor past the restaurant doors and the cellar door, then turn right. It opens to a weed lot."

After Wilhelm left, Gustav shuffled back to the kitchen table, sat down and glared through the window to the lights blinking on over the neighborhood, and the industrial smokestacks smudging the sky along the Niagara River beyond. His chest heaved and his clenched fist beat the slow rhythm of his tortured thoughts on the table.

Chapter 26

Gustav slept fitfully in his rocking chair, dreaming of Greta and the children. They had taken the Crystal Beach boat across to the amusement park in Canada, where Inga and Hans skipped along with other children, licking their ice cream cones or nibbling from bags of popcorn. They rode the bumper cars and screeched their delight on the wilder rides. They begged Gustav to let them go into the house of horrors. They weren't afraid, they said. He and Greta smiled their approval, paid their tickets to someone in an ugly clown costume, and waited outside.

After a short while, the crowd emerged, but Hans and Inga were not with them. He called their names: 'Inga! Hans!' He could hear them calling back, crying, 'Daddy!' He tried rushing inside, but something kept him out, some invisible wall he couldn't penetrate. 'Daddy's coming,' he called over and over, 'don't be afraid, Daddy's coming!' He heard Greta crying, but now she too was inside. 'Help, Gustav, help us! Gustav! Gustav!'

"Gustav!" The call was accompanied by a series of hard knocks on his door.

Jarred awake, groggy, he answered. "What? Who is it?"

"It's Lizzie. Sorry if I woke you up. Your newspaper was on the stairs. My Rosie could've tripped on it. Lazy good-for-nothing paper boy. I could slap the bejesus out of him!"

"Thank you, Lizzie. Leave it by the door."

"Whatever you say," she said, dropping the paper and scuffling away.

Gustav looked at the wall clock. It was already eight o'clock. He had slept hard but it was a troubled sleep and he was glad to be awake. He rubbed the lingering pictures from his eyes. After returning from work the night before, he made a sandwich and started to read a book, but being so tired, he fell asleep in his chair without ever waking to put on his pajamas.

He rose, set the coffee pot on the stove and padded across the room, where he cracked the door enough to reach down and pick up his newspaper. Wearily he sat at the table, spread the sheets and ran his finger down the page. Apparently satisfied, he muttered a few words, folded the paper, set it aside and got up for his coffee.

Gustav nursed his coffee and his bruised psyche, wishing Wilhelm would contact him with some good news. The endless waiting was hard to bear. Perhaps he could corner him at the next Bund meeting, but with so many prying eyes and keen ears around, it could be dangerous. Frustrated, he pushed his cup aside and got up to look out the window. A steady flow of traffic moved along Niagara Street. A rapping on his door turned him around.

Still out of sorts, he answered. "What is it now, Lizzie?"

The rapping continued.

"Lizzie?"

Again no answer. Suspicious, he went to his closet and drew out the gun he had found on the stairs. He walked quietly and put his ear against the door.

"Who is it?"

A soft voice replied, "A friend."

"You have the wrong apartment."

"Gustav Schwartz?"

"Who are you?"

"I said, a friend."

"I have no friends. Leave now!"

"Does the name Greta mean anything to you? Or Inga? Or Hans?"

Gustav mind raced. Was this some kind of trick?

"What if it does?"

"I have important information for you."

Gustav held the gun in his right hand behind the door. With the other hand he turned the catch and the knob, opened the door a crack and peeked out.

"Who are you?"

"I must talk to you. It's important and it's in your interest."

Torn, Gustav hesitated. This could be a ruse, a trick to catch him off guard and take him in. Or kill him.

"How do I know I can trust you?"

"I said I come as a friend." He flashed his open wallet. "You'll have to trust me."

Holding the gun behind his back, Gustav stepped aside, opened the door and, with his head, motioned the man in. He glanced out quickly to be sure no others were hiding before closing the door and locking it again.

"Now, Mr. FBI…" he said, brandishing the gun, "…*if* that

isn't a fake badge, what do you want from me?"

The man smiled. "I'm Noah, and I'm legitimate. You can put the .38 down now, Mr. Schwartz. It has no bullets in it anyway."

Gustav waved the gun. "Don't kid yourself. It's loaded all right."

Noah nodded toward the gun. "Take another look."

Gustav brought the gun up close. "What the— I know there were bullets in the chambers when I hid it away!"

"Correct."

Gustav looked dumbfounded. "Then…then…."

"All in good time, sir. Can we sit?"

"Sure," Gustav said, bewildered, "sure," still staring at the gun in his hand.

Of course, I immediately recognized Noah as the clean-shaven man with the swarthy complexion sitting so many times in Joe's restaurant. Apparently, Gustav had been in the FBI's sites for some time.

Opening his coat, Noah pulled out a chair, sat and set his hat aside. "I'll come to the point, Mr. Schwartz."

Gustav pulled up his chair across the table from him, laid the gun in front of him and covered it with his hands. "Since you seem to know me, you may call me Gustav."

"Thank you. Incidentally, for now, Noah's the only name you'll know me by."

"OK, I get it, FBI secrecy. So, Noah, what's the point you're coming to? Is it on the legit or is it a ploy to arrest me?"

"Relax, Gustav. I have a proposition to make, one that will

benefit both of us."

"A proposition? That's interesting. OK, go ahead, I'm listening."

"First, let me make a few things clear to you. We know you belong to the Bund, and we've known it almost since the time you joined up. That in itself interested us and raised grave concerns with the Bureau. We also know you've lived in Germany and that your wife Greta and your children are still there. You are presently employed as an engineer by the Curtiss Aircraft Company, obviously placed to obtain information or to plot some sort of sabotage in the future. This fact alone, of course, invited much closer scrutiny of your activities.

Gustav listened, his eyebrows raised. "You know a great deal. Are you here then to arrest me for espionage? If you are, I can assure you, Noah, I never turned over any information of value to them."

"I said I was here to make you a proposition."

"All right, you have my complete attention."

"We know you are desperate to have your family rejoin you here in the United States, where they belong and where it's safe."

"Yes, yes, that's true," Gustav said, squeezing his hands around the gun in front of him, "but you're too late to help. I've learned that they've been taken away to a concentration camp."

"What if I told you you're wrong? That we can help."

Gustav looked at him with tortured eyes. "Oh, God, if only you could. I would do anything, anything."

"That's what we're counting on. So this is what we want from you, Gustav. Any information you can get from the Bund, their plans, who and where their agents are, their contacts in

Germany, other organizations cooperating with them— in other words, anything that can be helpful to break up this suspect espionage ring and prevent sabotage in the United States."

"And in return?"

"We will get your wife and children back to you."

"I think it's impossible. I told you, I've been informed they've already been interned in a concentration camp called Buchenwald."

"You are mistaken."

Misery twisted Gustav's face. "I wish I were. I have it on the highest authority they have been taken."

"Many Schwartzes have been taken. It's a common name. Your family is not one of them."

"You know that?" Gustav cried. "You know that for sure! You are certain? Do I dare hope it?"

"They are being sheltered and hidden at this very moment by a sympathetic German family."

Gustav reached his shaking hand across the table. "Can you get them here, Noah? Get them here safely?"

"Of course, anything can happen and there aren't any guarantees, but we are quite confident we can. We work with various government agencies that coordinate their activities and share information. We have partisan contacts inside Germany working for us at this very moment."

"But how will I pass any information I gather from the Bund to you? They're watching me, I know. They don't trust me because I was born in America. Lately I've been chastised for not bringing useful information to them from my job."

"Don't let it concern you, Gustav. We've anticipated that.

We'll provide you with documents that will appear to be important, but they won't be. In fact, they may contain material contrary to their interests and advantageous to us. As for them watching you, you needn't worry. We're watching them."

"That makes me not just an ordinary spy, but a double agent."

"It makes you a loyal American."

"I always was."

"We know that, Gustav." He rose. "You needn't worry about contacting us. We'll be in touch with you soon and provide you with instructions. Check your mail every day as soon as it's delivered. In the meantime go about your normal business. In a few days you will receive classified documents in the mail you can pass along to the Bund."

Gustav stood up. "Thank you, Noah. I have hope again." He walked Noah to the door. "Are you sure you can protect my family from danger? Get them here safely?"

"Luck's always a factor in such matters, but with a little bit of it and God willing, I'm sure we can."

Gustav took Noah's hand and squeezed it. "Thank you, thank you so very much."

Noah smiled. "By the way, did you forget about something?"

"What?" Gustav glanced around. "I don't think so."

"The gun?"

"Oh, the gun! Yes, the gun. I know you said it wasn't loaded but I know it was, and you're right, the chambers are empty. It isn't loaded. How can that be?"

Noah stepped across the kitchen to the radio setting on the

cupboard. He picked it up, slid the cover off the back and turned the radio to Gustav. "What do you see?"

Gustav peered inside. "Some wiring, tubes…"

He tipped it. "Look closely."

Gustav squinted. "What is that?" he asked, pointing.

"We call it a bug."

"A bug?"

"A transmitter, Gustav. We've monitored all your conversations, particularly those with your friend, Wilhelm. We had it planted while you were at work."

Gustav's eyes opened wide. "So that's how you know so much?"

"Yes, that's how we knew you had a gun, too. While you were at work, your radio was *fixed* by our undercover repairman. Knowing you had a loaded gun, we disposed of the bullets to ensure you didn't get into trouble with it. What's more important, listening to you, and to Wilhelm, as well, the transmitter proved you're both loyal American citizens who can be trusted." He turned to go.

"Incidentally, Gustav, send no more money. It never would have done you any good, even if you'd have sent a million dollars. What you've already sent has been stolen. And you should be careful, even about whispering to yourself. You see, we know you've accumulated a great deal of money playing the stock market. After hearing you talk to yourself and rattling your newspaper, we checked your financial records, both with the Erie County Savings Bank, and with Bache, your brokerage firm. You are a very shrewd speculator, Gustav, or a very lucky one."

"My, God, you know everything about me!"

"J. Edgar Hoover leaves no stone unturned." Noah gave a wink as he headed out the door. "We'll be in touch."

After hearing the conversation between Gustav and Noah, I remembered the workman who was so neatly dressed climbing the stairs. It must have been he, a government agent, who planted the microphone and unloaded the gun in Gustav's apartment. Had I not been distracted at that moment by the surly new tenant who didn't appreciate Huggs's welcoming gesture, I might have known the story beforehand. And at last I finally understood what Gustav was doing with his little book and why he would either smile or growl when he read the newspaper. He was looking at the stock prices, which explained the source of the large amount of money he was giving to Wilhelm to buy his family safe passage to America.

Chapter 27

Boris Spasinsky was an interesting tenant who occupied the small apartment behind Joe's restaurant since at least the early 1930s. A quiet, almost secretive man somewhat past middle age, Boris emigrated from Russia in 1918, soon after the end of WWI. Despite his age when he arrived here, he obviously had a good education and, for a foreigner, spoke fairly good English. As far as I knew, he never had a wife or children, and no friends that I'd ever seen, but on the city streets, he was a popular figure known and loved by many, especially the children, who called him the hurdy-gurdy man, and often gathered around him to see him crank out his music.

For those who don't know, a hurdy-gurdy is a guitar-like instrument that grinds out music by turning a handle, rather like an organ grinder. Boris traveled around on foot playing his instrument for coins people would drop into the hat he would either pass around or set on the ground. He'd been doing this ever since I can remember. You might have seen him at any time of the day or evening, his white mustache and eyebrows twitching with his smiles as he pumped out pleasing strains of music on Buffalo's streets entertaining the public.

A private, reclusive man, apparently content with his solitary existence, Boris was always a mystery to others who lived in my apartments. He avoided all adult relationships, never complained, never bothered anyone, and always paid his

183

rent on time. *If not for one heartbreaking event, most would never guess he even existed, much less lived here.*

It all came to light one evening when the most cavernous howl I ever heard issue from the depths of a human being's soul broke the relative silence of my corridors. Then I saw him burst through his apartment door into the hall, wild-eyed, half mad, tearing at his clothes and wailing his despair. His cries reverberated off my walls and filled the building up to the fourth floor:

"My money! My money!"

Hearing the hysterical ravings, Joe barged out of his restaurant, almost running into him, and caught him by his shirt. "What is it Mr. Spasinsky, what is it?"

"Who did it!" he cried out, ripping the sleeve off his shirt as he spun himself out of Joe's grip and clawed at the wall. "Who did this to me? Who!"

Joe grabbed him again and held him tight. "Who did what, Mr. Spasinsky, who did what?"

"They robbed me," he sobbed. "My money! It's gone! They robbed me!"

By then, dogs were barking while my tenants, aroused by the shouting downstairs, poked their heads out of their apartment doors, crying,

"'What's all the yelling about?"

"What's happening down there? Who's getting killed?"

"Can't I ever get any peace and quiet around here, dammit!"

"Somebody shut that guy up!"

Joe, still gripping him, shouted over his shoulder, "He says he was robbed. Somebody get on the phone and call the cops."

Again Boris broke from Joe's hold and again threw himself against the wall, moaning and wailing as he pounded it with his fists and his head and kicked holes in the plaster.

Joe pulled Boris along, dragging him into the restaurant and forcing him into a chair. He told others who followed him in to keep him down until he could get him some coffee.

Boris's head dropped to the table. Groaning, choking back swallowed words, his torso heaved with spasms as his fists beat the table. Joe hurried back with a cup of hot coffee and set it beside him.

"Drink some of this, Mr. Spasinsky. It's black and strong with a shot of whiskey in it. It'll help calm you down."

Boris swung his arm across the table, sending the cup and saucer flying.

"Hey, Mr. Spasinsky, for crying out loud!" Joe exclaimed, moving away quickly to get a mop.

The police arrived within minutes and took charge. Annoyed, Joe continued cleaning the mess, while the other tenants backed away. The cop, a burly man with hunched shoulders and puffy eyes took Boris by the collar and straightened him up. The other cop, young enough to be a rookie, shooed everyone out of the restaurant.

"First tell me your name and then your problem," the burly cop said, pulling a chair up next to Boris.

Joe piped up. "His name's Boris Spasinsky."

The cop glared at him. "Did I ask you?"

Embarrassed, Joe backed off and busied himself sweeping up the glass.

The cop turned his attention back to Boris. "Is that your name, Boris Spasa…Spasasinsky?" he asked.

Boris had his face in his hands. "Yes, yes!"

"You want to tell me what happened?"

Boris lifted his head and stared at him with haunted eyes. "Somebody robbed my house."

"Do you know who did it? Or have any idea who might have robbed you?"

Boris shook his head miserably. His voice quavered. "I don't know, I don't know. I was robbed. I know nothing else."

The cop took out his note pad and scribbled in it. "Lots of people get robbed," he said, obviously bored with a familiar complaint.

"My life savings!"

"What? You keep your life savings in your house?"

Boris nodded. "Yes, yes, everything, all of it."

"What's the matter, don't you believe in banks?"

Boris raised his head defiantly. "Don't you remember 1929? Wall Street? The banks!"

"OK, OK, yeah, the stock market crash. Just take it easy."

"Don't you understand? My life savings. All gone. Somebody stole it all!"

"All right, I gottcha, I gottcha. You say somebody stole your life savings. How much money we talking about?"

Boris looked around. "I don't want to talk here. I want you to take me to your headquarters."

"Look, Mr. Spasininisky… however you say your name… you don't give me orders about what you want."

Boris bolted up to his feet. "I demand to see your superior officer!" he shouted. "I demand it as a United States citizen!"

The cop looked up to his younger partner and sighed. "OK, settle down, for crissake, not that they can do any more for you there. But first I want you to show me the scene of the crime and where you keep your money. Or kept it."

Boris staggered on weak legs. "Come, follow me," he said, teary-eyed. "I'll show you."

Boris led the two officers into his apartment over to a closet. He pointed to the floor.

"There. You see? They tore up the boards. Somehow they knew. They knew and they took it. All of it!"

"Who else knows you hide money in this spot?"

"Nobody!" he moaned. "Nobody! Only me!"

The cop made a note in his pad, then turned. "Anything else missing?"

"I don't know," he moaned, shaking his head, his voice cracking, "I don't care."

"All right, let's go," he said, lifting him by the arm. "Hold his other arm, Neil. He don't look too steady on his feet to me."

That's all I knew at the time, and all anyone knew. Everything we learned after that we took from the newspaper. The investigation that followed revealed nothing useful. The police weren't able to determine who stole the money, how the thief or thieves entered the premises nor how they knew where Boris's money was hidden. The only possible and probable explanation came from Boris himself. He told the police he went out on a vodka binge as he always did every year at this time to celebrate his birthday. His last memory was of being at DiTondo's tavern. He said he blacked out and remembered nothing more of that night. It's most likely he revealed his secret to a stranger during one of his bar-hopping stops and brought him home with him.

Because this became a human interest story, the newspapers ran a series of articles based on interviews Boris had given a number of years earlier, including a smiling picture of Boris posing with his hurdy-gurdy and surrounded by grinning children. The public was shocked to read that Boris had converted almost all of his savings into gold and silver coins estimated to be worth over 125,000 dollars, an incredibly huge sum for the times, when a workingman's weekly wage was about twenty dollars.

The articles went on to tell how Boris had arrived from Russia as a relatively young man almost twenty years earlier. The last of four children— and the only one not stricken with hemophilia, the family curse— he was the pampered child of a wealthy family with ties to royalty. However, shortly after the Bolshevik Revolution in 1917, the government seized the family's extensive land holdings and their estate. They confiscated the silverware, the artwork decorating the walls and anything else of value they could find. Stripped of their dignity as well as their wealth, Boris's parents were left destitute, barely able to survive, especially after the secret police arrested his father and hauled him off to a gulag, never to be seen or heard from again. His mother, already a frail woman suffering from tuberculosis, now with a broken heart, soon after succumbed to her afflictions. With nothing to hold him back, Boris gathered his meager belongings and escaped the country. With the help of kind strangers, he trekked through the by-ways, towns and backwoods of Poland, Germany, Belgium, England, Scotland, and finally to America.

While in Scotland, he met a friendly old Scotsman who offered him shelter and interested him in his hurdy-gurdy. Boris fell instantly in love with the instrument and acquired one. When he arrived in Buffalo, he wasted no time earning money by strolling up and down the streets, playing his music from morning to night seven days a week throughout the neighborhoods. Apparently, the several years of deprivation in Russia turned him into what most people today would call a miser. I'm sure Boris wouldn't have labeled himself that way. To him, hoarding and hiding his money was being frugal and wise, a way to protect himself from the government and strangers and the vicissitudes of life. After the robbery, I heard Boris complain that he'd escaped the clutches of one kind of thief, only to fall into the arms of another kind.

Boris no longer traveled the neighborhoods playing his hurdy-gurdy. The joy of playing he always felt in his heart was gone. His once exuberant soul shriveled, dried up and died. To survive, he sold the music box along with what few other possessions he had.

Lizzie Shanahan, little Rosie's mother, though lately ailing, would, like several others, occasionally bring food to him. Joe would often bring him a sandwich or sometimes a hot meal from his restaurant. Mrs. Chapman lowered his rent to almost nothing.

Father Dominick from Holy Angels heard of Boris's personal tragedy from one of his parishioners and tried on several occasions to visit him. The last time he knocked on his door, he called:

"Mr. Spasinsky, this is Father Dominick. I would like to speak with you. Please let me in."

"Go away!" Boris cried from inside his apartment. "I told you before, go away!"

"Only for a few moments, if I may, Mr. Spasinsky."

"I don't want no priest. If ever a God was, he's dead. No loving God would do this to a good person. I was a good person!"

"You are wrong, Mr. Spasinsky," he pleaded. "So wrong.

You must trust in Jesus Christ, in God Almighty. He has reasons for what happens to us here on earth. Despite all our misfortunes and suffering, like Job, we must have faith."

"Go away! Do you hear me? I don't want to hear no more lies about God. About a loving God. Go away!"

Father Dominick implored him with all his heartfelt passion until Boris, unable to contain himself any longer, jerked open the door, shouted a profanity in his face, and slammed the door shut. Ultimately, deeply saddened, Father Dominick departed, calling out that he would continue to pray for him and would always be there should Boris change his mind.

Boris soon became a wreck of a human being. The happiness he once knew had long deserted him. Nightmares dominated his sleep, often waking him up in the middle of the night, crying, 'Who? Who?' Each week, without fail, he visited police headquarters:

'Have you found him yet?'

The officer behind the desk would shake his head. 'No. I'm sorry, Mr. Spasinsky, we have not.'

And the next week: 'Have you found him yet?'

A sad shake of the head. 'No. I'm sorry, Mr. Spasinsky, we have not.'

Weeks passed. Then months. Boris haunted police headquarters until it became a ritual familiar to everyone: 'Have you found him yet?' And always the same words with a negative shake of the head. 'No, I'm sorry, Mr. Spasinsky, we have not.'

After a year words were no longer needed. Boris would step inside the precinct doorway, battered hat in hand, his tragic eyes fixed with rheumy hope on the sergeant behind the desk. And as always, the sergeant would tilt his head up and shake it sadly from side to side.

Boris scavenged for empty bottles he could return for pennies. He rummaged through garbage barrels for items he could sell to the ragman who regularly drove his horse-drawn wagon through city streets, calling, 'Rags a rags. Rags a rags....'

Two years came and went. Boris wasted more with each passing day. His body smelled rank, and his bones showed through his blue-veined and withered flesh. He grew stooped and took to using a cane. His scruffy beard grew out a dirty gray and his clothes hung loose and shabbier on his skeletal frame. Any time of the day or night, you could see him scuffling along in his broken shoes roaming the streets of Buffalo, alarming strangers he'd grasp by the arm, peer up to them with desperate eyes, and ask, 'Do you know who stole my money?'

One day, Huggs discovered that Boris's apartment was empty. I didn't see him leave. No one saw him leave, nor did anyone ever learn where he went after he left. I later heard that up until the day he stopped haunting police headquarters, he never gave up hope the thief would be caught and his money returned. Boris apparently died alone somewhere, a tragic figure who never found the justice he sought so desperately while he lived. I hope to never witness such human misery again.

Chapter 28

The trial of The State of New York vs. Jeb Morrison was over. Jeb was a free man. In his cross examination, Jeb's attorney, Rupert Danbury, shredded the plaintiff's testimony:

"Isn't it true, Miss Coleman, that you once accused your college professor of a similar offense?" Danbury asked, his thumbs hooked into his suspenders, his eyes under bushy eyebrows peering over his horn-rimmed glasses and pinned on the plaintiff. "Be careful how you answer, Miss Coleman, we have the transcripts."

"Yes, but—"

"The question, Miss Coleman, just answer the question. And isn't it a fact that you also accused your eighth grade elementary school teacher of the same offense?"

"I can explain—"

"Again, Miss Coleman, we have the records...."

The way I heard it later, the examination went on for a blistering hour or more, until an hysterical Miss Coleman stumbled from the witness box blotting the tears smearing black mascara over her face as she rushed to her seat in the courtroom and buried her head in her lawyer's shoulder. The trial ended the way Danbury predicted, with the plaintiff, Miss Coleman, completely vanquished and the defendant, Jeb

Morrison, completely vindicated.

Chauffeured home, with Danbury in the passenger seat, and Jeb sitting with Cotton in the back seat, they rehashed the high points of the trial.

"I sure do appreciate more than words can say how grateful we are for what you done for Cotton and me, Mr. Danbury," Jeb said.

Danbury half turned in his seat. "Not nearly as much as you did for me."

"Seems to me, you getting stuck on the streetcar tracks was the best piece of good luck I ever did have in my whole life."

Danbury smiled. "And you getting me out of the streetcar tracks was the best piece of good luck I ever did have in my whole life, too," he mimicked.

They all laughed, including the chauffeur.

Danbury turned serious. "We're not finished yet, Jeb."

"I don't gather your meaning, Mr. Danbury."

"We're suing. There are penalties for what that woman did. You've been damaged, seriously damaged. Your character's been impugned, and our charming Miss Coleman is going to pay dearly for it."

"You mean you want me to sue Miss Coleman?"

"That's exactly what I mean and that's exactly what we're going to do. That callous woman would have put you behind bars and left you there to rot, forever if necessary."

"Maybe so, Mr. Danbury, but after she accused me, she probably couldn't go back on her word. Maybe even the po-lice wouldn't let her. I don't think she's a really mean person, leastwise, I never saw any such side of her."

"You could be right, Jeb; nevertheless, she put you and your wife through hell and there's going to be compensation for that."

They drove a while without anyone saying anything until Jeb spoke:

"Mr. Danbury, with all due respect, sir, I don't want to go through with no more court case like we just did."

"Oh, it won't be so bad, Jeb. This is a civil suit involving money and it will be easy to prove. It won't be nearly as much pressure, either, because your life won't be on the line this time."

"I don't mean that."

Danbury turned around in his seat. "Well, what *do* you mean, Jeb?"

"Well, sir, it seems to me Miss Coleman is just a plain, pathetic soul. I think she just never had nobody love her the way she needed to be, so she went after me, like she did with those others you mentioned in court. Didn't have to be me this time, could've been anybody that was nice to her."

"That's a beautiful sentiment, Jeb, but you were the injured party and she was responsible for that. It's a simple matter of justice."

"I understand what you're saying, sir, but sometimes justice has got a different kind of look to it. There's a human angle to it, if you gather my meanin'. It's somethin' more than gettin' even, or hurtin' somebody back who hurt you. That's why I'm askin' you to forget it. It's all done now. That woman's reputation is ruined and, sure as shootin', she's gonna lose her job if she already didn't. Besides, she did teach me much and made me know I'm smart as I needs to be to do whatever I needs to do. I owe her somethin' for that."

Danbury nodded to Jeb's words.

"I can't say anythin' more, Mr. Danbury, except I believe Miss Coleman's got enough misery in her life which is goin' to dog her for years to come. I'd say that's payback enough and I'd just as soon let it go."

The limousine pulled up to the curb in front of my entrance, and the driver got out and opened the back door.

Danbury turned around to shake hands. "Jeb, you are one in a million." He looked at Cotton. "That's quite a man you have there, Mrs. Morrison."

Cotton smiled. "I know that, Mr. Danbury," she said, sliding out behind Jeb, "and I appreciate you seeing it, too."

Danbury spoke out his side window to Jeb, standing on the curb. "Jeb, I know you were fired after all this made the news. I'll be contacting your company tomorrow to make sure you're reinstated with back pay."

Jeb bent down to talk. "Thought about it Mr. Danbury, me and Cotton, but we don't intend on goin' back there. We already made up our minds, that is, supposin' you set me free, which you did. Not headin' back to our hometown in Georgia, neither. That wouldn't be good thinkin'. We be moving on to Alabama for a fresh start. Cotton's got kin there, too. Aside from workin' a job, I 'pect I be goin' to school down there and finish my education. One thing, though, Mr. Danbury, before we leave, it'd help very much if you can see to it they mail me the pay I got comin' from afore I was let go."

"Consider it done," he said, reaching out to shake Jeb's hand. "If I can do anything else for you, Jeb, anytime, just let me know." He motioned the driver to move. "You have my number."

Both Jeb and Cotton waved goodbye as the car pulled away down the street.

Chapter 29

I have a story I'm reluctant to tell because it is such a tragic one. In its own way it's worse than the story of Boris Spasinski, the hurdy-gurdy man whose fortune was stolen. This is a tale the hypersensitive reader may choose to skip because it is very dark and depressing. It has to do with Barney Fulton, whom we saw earlier ordering roast beef sandwiches in Joe's restaurant. He and his wife, Belinda, carrying little baggage, moved from Tennessee in the later years of the Great Depression into one of my apartments. It was soon obvious to others who crossed paths with him that Barney was not only an anti-social man, but a surly one, as well.

Occasionally, I heard the couple argue, but as far as I could tell, their shouting matches were harmless and short-lived. A private, almost secretive couple, they had little, if anything, to do with any of their neighbors. They kept to themselves and rarely went out. I never meant to eavesdrop, but from time to time I couldn't help pick up bits of information.

I learned that after a tornado tore through their rural town and destroyed their trailer park home and the meat-packing plant where Barney worked, he and his wife, Belinda, decided to move north. One of Barney's down-home friends who preceded him here, told him the stockyards in Buffalo were hiring experienced men and paid 'good money.' Being an experienced butcher, Barney landed a job with one of the big companies on William Street the day after he and Belinda arrived.

Having little money to start with, they filled the apartment with used furniture, an old gas stove, an ice box, table and four chairs, a bed, dresser, couch and the other odds and ends needed for living. Even though they did well enough financially over the next three years, they never changed the décor of the apartment. Tacked to the walls were magazine pictures of movie stars like Vivian Leigh and Clark Gable, and country singers like Roy Rogers and Gene Autry. One wall had a picture all to itself of President Franklin Delano Roosevelt.

Belinda kept the place clean and always had bright-colored artificial tulips in a vase standing on a table in the corner of the kitchen. On a shelf above it, a radio forever tuned to a country music station was playing. The twangy nasal strains of country music that tug at the heartstrings and bring tears to the eyes was an ironic counterpoint to what was happening in the Fulton kitchen:

'...another bee-yootiful day in bee-yootiful Lincoln County, down here in Kentucky, yes-sir-ee, another fine Juu-ly morning coming on the next hour till high noon, with Tex and the gang here at WKLD bringing you the music that says it all....'

It was another record hot day for Buffalo, with the temperature soaring into the low 90s. In one corner of the kitchen, a fan swiveled lazily, circulating the sticky air. I saw Barney sitting at the kitchen table, wearing a sweat-stained undershirt and boxer shorts that exposed his hairy legs. He wore neither shoes nor socks. Belinda wore pink underpants and a matching pajama top tight over her plump body. A small crucifix hung from a slender faux gold chain around her neck.

Waiting impatiently, Barney blotted his neck and partially bald head with a big, square, blue and white polka dot handkerchief in his hand. The other hand wiggled a fly swatter ready to squash any fly that dared land near him. To me, he and his wife, Belinda, reminded me of what I heard others refer to as 'hillbillies.'

At that particular moment, Belinda was standing by the stove scooping eggs out of a frying pan onto a plate, while Barney glared across the room at her.

Barney's lips twisted sour with his words. "You ain't much for talkin' this mornin'."

Belinda smoothed back her dyed-blond hair. "Ain't much mornin' left for talkin'," she answered, setting his plate down before him and pouring their coffee.

He tossed the swatter aside and stared down at the eggs on his plate. "Damn! Busted 'em again."

She sat across from him and stirred sugar into her cup. "You'd be bustin' them anyway with your bread, so what's the diff'rence?"

"The diff'rence is I don't like seein' 'em busted 'less'n I do it myself."

"Try 'em. You'll see they don't taste no diff'rent, busted or not."

He grunted. "Well, they do me."

This couple had changed a lot since they first moved in. They used to be civil to each other most of the time, even when they argued. But lately, it seemed they were forever at each other's throats over one thing or another. I felt, even from that early moment, that I was watching a drama play itself out.

Belinda's leg, crossed over the other, nervously bobbled the white slipper on her foot with her red toenails showing through the open toe. She kept stealing glances at her husband as she sipped her coffee. I almost turned my attention to Joe's restaurant downstairs, but decided to listen for a while longer.

"I didn't hear you come in last night, Barney. What time was it?"

"Twelve or thereabouts, I reckon."

"Or maybe three-thirty, thereabouts?"

Barney slammed his fork down. "Damn it, woman, why'd you ask if you know?"

"Wanted to see if you'd be tellin' me the truth."

"Coulda been I made a mistake out of habit. I was tired. I ain't perfect you know, never said I was."

Belinda scoffed. "That's for sure. And I suppose you're gonna tell me you was workin' till then."

"That's right, that's 'xactly what I'm a-tellin' you. Charlie Eagle took sick, they needed a fill-in and I was elected."

"Then why'd you lie for and say twelve o'clock when you knowed it weren't. You punch a time card don't you?"

Barney bristled. "Goddamnit, woman, I ain't gonna stand for you makin' me out a liar, when I'm out there bustin' a gut to bring home the bacon whiles yer livin' sweet- as- you- please, sittin' on yer lazy ass and listenin' to yer soap operas and suckin' down booze all day?"

"That's a lousy thing to say, Barney."

"Well, jus' ain't it, though!"

It was obvious Barney was very angry and agitated, not only by the way he was talking, but by his actions— slapping butter on his bread and knocking the utensils around. Neither said anything for a while. Only the radio was talking:

199

'...and ain't that sweet to the ear, folks? Don't it just make your heart smile and fill you with gladness to be alive?...Now here's a special ditty for all you true country music lovers out there in cow pasture land and beyond that's sure to bring a warm memory to your heart and sunshine to your soul. Here's Cliff Bruner and his boys singin', 'The Girl You Loved Long Ago....'

"And last Saturday. Did Charlie take sick then, too?"

"Damn it all to hell, woman, how long you gonna be nettlin' me with this garbage talk? Now, I don't want to hear no more about it, you hear me? I'm wore out already with this hellfire heat and don't need to worsen it with firin' up my temper. Enough's enough!"

"Well, don't be getting' mad at me, Barney. I'm just askin'. A woman's got a right to know where her husband's been till all hours of the morning, don't she?"

Barney wiped his face with his big handkerchief. "I told you all there is to know. Now pour me some more coffee and let that be an end to it once and for all!"

Belinda got up to get the coffee pot off the stove. "I'm sorry, Barney, but I still think I got a right to know. A woman ain't a thing like she used to be, no more'n a piece of furniture that her man could sit on anytime he pleased and not get no complaint from. These days a woman deserves some respect?"

"Trouble with you, girl, is you been listenin' to too many of them radio shows that keeps agitatin' folks about where they be goin' wrong in life. Ain't solvin' nothin', jus' workin' up all kinds o' discontent, causin' trouble and makin' women more miserable than ever they knew to think they was before."

"All the same, Barney, I can't be honest and say I b'lieve you no more. I tried, Lord knows, but too many times you been comin' home late and tellin' me stories that frazzle my mind tryin' to sort out the facts and lies and figure which is which." Her trembling hand spilled some coffee as she poured it into Barney's cup.

Barney scraped his chair back. "Hey, watch it, goddamn it! You tryin' to scald me or somethin'?"

"It'd be in the right place if I did."

He exhaled a long breath. "I'm telling you, Belinda, I'm getting mighty tired listenin' to your babblin'. I work hard, damn hard, and you know it. And you can't deny I done it for you. Kep' food on the table and a roof over your head without fail all these years."

"Don't be changin' the subject and beatin' around the bush, Barney. I want to know who you been seein'."

Barney clenched his fork. "You jus' don't never let go, do you? Jus' keep bitin' and bitin', bulldog-like. Well, let me tell you something you ain't gonna like hearin', and wouldn't hear if you didn't force me to it now. If I was carryin' on with another woman— which I ain't admittin' to— but if I was, who could blame me? Take a gander at yerself in the mirror sometime and tell me if that fat floozy with the corn-yella straw you call hair lookin' back at you wouldn't drive away any man with eyes to see."

Belinda gasped. "That's a hard thing to say, Barney. I always tried lookin' nice for you, you know that."

Barney blotted up his eggs with a piece of bread. "Hard thing to say, maybe so, but true."

"I wasn't always fat like this. I was trim once. Had a nice figure any girl'd be proud to own, 'specially my legs." She turned sideways, stretched her leg out and ran her fingers along it. "Lots of boys told me so. Told me so yourself, Barney, more times than once."

201

"What was once don't cut no ice now," he said, stuffing a piece of bread in his mouth and brushing a fly away from his face with his other hand.

"Still coulda been if I didn't bear you six little ones, which you wanted. How's a woman to keep her girlish body doin' that?"

"Lotsa women bring in whole litters o' kids and don't blow up hog-fat doin' it."

"You're mean, Barney, snake mean, and jus' lookin' to get yourself off the hook makin' 'scuses and turnin' things around so's to blame me. But you ain't fooled this ol' gal, not by a long shot. I got eyes to see and they seen them long, stray hairs stuck to your clothes, times when you come staggerin' home drunk. They was red ones last month. And I got a nose that can whiff cheap perfume a mile off. You're just a cheatin' man, Barney. And a lying one to boot."

Barney tore another hunk of bread off the loaf. "Spoil my appetite with your poison tongue, go 'head. I'm 'aginnin' to think yer getting' addle-brained in yer old age."

"I been addled for some time now, Barney, but no more. I still want to know what slut you been courtin'. Or I reckon maybe there's more than one."

"You got a nerve saying that to me, 'accusin' and insinuatin' the worst when you got no proof. Remember where *you* was when I found you."

Belinda stiffened and pinned him with cold eyes. "You drop that trash talk, mister, drop it now! You knew everything. I didn't keep no secrets from you, though I dare say I wisht I had brains enough to. You ast, remember? You jus' had to know ever' damn thing, all the dirty details. I didn't lie to you then, Barney, and never have since, not in all the years I been caterin' to your every want and need. And I been true, Barney, true blue, through and through." She pushed a damp lock of hair off her forehead.

Barney smirked. "You can give it all right, but you can't take it, can ya? If'n you don't like it, get off my back and let me finish eatin' in peace!"

"You're the cause o' this fightin', Barney. Wouldn't be happ'nin' if not for you."

He slapped his fork down on the table. "Goddamned food's all gone colder'n crap now!"

Belinda reached across the table and laid her hand on his arm. "Oh, Barney, I'm sorry. I wish I could b'lieve you. I honest-to-God do. I wish it could be like when the kids was small fry and you and me'd talk, 'member, Barney? And me massagin' your neck and back all achin' from work? And late at night after they was sleepin', us makin' love, Barney, remember? The cool summer breeze blowin' the bedroom curtain, and us jus' layin' there smokin' cigarettes afterwards, feelin' so good? An' how you made me promise I wouldn't never be frigid? An' I wasn't, Barney. You know it, never once the whole time."

Momentarily caught up in her rapture, Barney softened. "I do remember. Them were good days, I admit."

Belinda gazed across to him, squeezing his arm. "You was diff'rent then, Barney. You paid attention to me. Used to ask all the time how I felt, if I was tired with the cookin' and washin' and stuff. And sometimes sittin' together out on the porch swing in the evenin', the way it used to squeak, makin' us hope nobody thought somethin' funny was goin' on. Made us laugh to think it.

"Remember all that, Barney? Us rockin' easy, drinkin' beer and not sayin' much, just hearing the crickets chirpin' and seeing the fireflies sparking in the dark and smelling new corn waftin' in off the fields." She sighed. "And lookin' up at the moon if there was one shinin' through that big ol' maple tree, but us feelin' jus' on top o' the world because we was together, and how you'd take my hand in yours jus' to hold it. You tol' me I had nice hands." She raised them, turning them over and studying them. "You ain't done that in a long time, Barney. A long, long time."

"Things don't stay the same. They change."

"But why, Barney? Why do they have to change? We're the same people. I'm the same girl you married and said you loved and who gave you babies like you wanted, good healthy babies, each and every one o' them. Why do they have to change?"

"No reason. 'Tweren't nobody's fault. Stuff happens. Couldn't nobody stop it if they tried. Jus' the way life is. It don't stand still no more'n the sun or the moon can stand still."

"It ain't like that with your friend Luther and his—"

"Luther ain't nothin'! I don't want to hear about that Bible thumper and his doin's."

"I was only gonna say—"

"Well, don't. I ain't Luther and you ain't Millie, and that's an end to it."

'...and now from that singing romantic himself, Jimmy Davis, praising his love with, 'You Are My Sunshine.'

Belinda filled their cups again. "Barney, I don't want fightin' between us, just an honest clear-the-air talk. I'm the forgivin' kind, you know that. Comes natural to me, always has. Besides, my Christian duty obliges me," she said, unconsciously fondling her crucifix. "I love you, Barney, always did, always will. You're my man, and I'm willin' to forget it all if you promise me an end to the lying' and chasin' around."

204

Barney pushed his plate aside and leaned across the table toward her. "Well, since you opened this can o' worms, I guess now's as good a time as any to tell you somethin' you ain't gonna be happy hearin'."

"What're you fixing to tell me you ain't already said to hurt me, Barney?"

"I'm fixin' for a dee-vorce."

Stunned, Belinda sagged back in her chair. "You don't mean it, Barney. You can't mean it. You're jus' sayin' it to scare me quiet."

"I mean it jus' as sure as chickens lay eggs. Already talked on the phone to a counselor out west in Reno. Done it yesterday. Wired him some money up front, too, like he wanted for gettin' the pro-ceedin's started."

"You wouldn't, Barney. I been good to you, an honest, loyal wife. You can't jus' up and toss me aside like an old shoe. We got children to think about, too."

"They's all growed up and gone." He thrust his face out. "Face it, Belinda, we're done, finished. It's all over. I got plans for a new life. Gonna do things I always hankered after, see places I never been. I ain't wastin' the rest o' whatever time is left to me bein' badgered and accused ever' time you get a bug crawling up yer fat ass."

"Well, I won't allow it, Barney! I put in too many years, too much time and sacrifice. Many's the day I never so much as stepped foot outside our door, sweatin' from sunup to sundown, for cleanin' and cookin' and diaper washin'."

Barney blotted the sweat beading his own forehead. "'Tweren't 'xactly no picnic for me, neither."

Tears flooded Belinda's eyes. "I'll fight it, Barney. I ain't lettin' go. I'll get my own lawyer."

"Won't do you no good." He sat back sneering under a smug look. "Face it, woman, I'm gonna be a free man soon and where I'm goin' you ain't never goin' to find me. No more answerin' to you as to who I see or where I been. No more henpeckin' 'bout every nigglin' little thing comes to your 'tention about my habits you don't like." He slapped the table and jerked to his feet. "And you can tell the young'n's any lyin' thing you want, too. It ain't gonna change nothin' 'cause I ain't gonna be around to hear nothin'. It's over between us and that's final!"

Belinda sat cold and rigid. "Maybe I cain't stop you divorcin' me, Barney, but I surely can stop you being free." She crossed her arms and glared at him triumphantly.

Barney scoffed and sat down again. "What, you gonna kill me?"

"I should. You almos' nearly killed me."

"What the hell you gettin' at, woman?"

"Our Jacob's little angel, that's what I'm gettin' at, Betty Lou, who ain't stepped foot or showed her face where we lived for five years before we moved here. Our granddaughter."

Barney stiffened. "What about her?"

"How could you, Barney?" she sneered. "How could you?"

"How could I what! You're plumb crazy, woman, and I ain't stayin' to listen to no more crazy talk." He started to rise.

"Only ten years old. No more'n a baby. You took her, Barney. You know it. I didn't want to b'lieve it when she told me, not even the time she come to me cryin' and showin' me her bloody underpants. Told myself it was jus' her period startin'." Belinda went on, her eyes tearing and her voice breaking. She dabbed at her eyes and blew her nose into the hanky she drew from her sleeve.

"I never said nothin' to you nor nobody, Barney. I was too ashamed to make myself think such a black thing could be true, 'specially about my very own husband, Betty Lou's very own grandfather, but it jus' kep' afesterin' underneath and I couldn't make myself not b'lieve. Near killed me holdin' it in all this time. Would've kep' it buried still and said nothin', the past being the past and whatnot, and wouldn't do no good to bring it up, 'cept you forced me to it now."

Barney swiped his handkerchief over his sweating face. "Lies! All goddamned lies. Nobody'd ever believe a cockamamie story like that. Nobody!"

"Won't they, Barney? Well, even if the po-lice don't, our Jacob will. He's got that crazy hot temper, you know. He'll come up here, Barney, take his shotgun and find you no matter where you go or try and hide, and when he does he's gonna blow you open with both barrels and splatter your guts all over the floor. You're gonna be dead as a doornail and won't be takin' no trips like you been talkin' so proud about, sure as certain. Betty Lou is his special angel, and when he finds out you defiled her—"

'...and I hope you good people out there enjoyed that number as much as I did. Sure tells it like it is and warms the cockles of your heart, don't it, folks, the happiness we bring to one another to make life richer than the good Lord already made it? Now for all you Ernest Tubb fans out there—and who ain't?—here is....'

Barney smashed his fist down on the table and lurched to his feet. "Woman, you are a sour, lyin', goddamn bitch tryin' to wreck my life 'cause I don't want no part o' you no more."

Belinda pushed her face toward him defiantly. "If you can wreck my life after all the years I put into givin' you babies, makin' your meals, sweatin' and slavin' and waitin' up nights worryin' about you, and then toss me aside like a mangy cur, I reckon I can ruin yours, too!"

Barney lunged across the table and took Belinda by the throat. "I'll kill you first, you bitch! You rotten lyin' bitch!"

Belinda struggled against the hands gripping her throat. "…can't…breathe…ca…."

Enraged, Barney pulled her around by him and pressed her head against the table, his fingers clamped tight. "I won't let you ruin my life. Never!" He squeezed harder. "Never!"

Distressed, I rattled my pipes and windows and shook my walls as Belinda thrashed, kicking over her chair and struggling to breathe until she went limp and slid to the floor, dragging part of the tablecloth with her. As if in disbelief, Barney stared down at her crumpled body at his feet for a long moment, then at his hands. He walked slowly around to the end of the table and, in a spasm of unspent rage, swiped it clean of the few dishes still there, sending them clattering over the kitchen floor. He seemed to crumble sitting down at the table, wet with spilled coffee, clawed his face and laid his head over his folded arms. I saw his shoulders heave and heard his breaking sobs before they were drowned out by the radio:

'…so ends another hour with all you bee-yootiful folks out there in country music land. We thank you for sharing your time with Ol' Tex and the gang, and listening to the music that puts joy in our heart and makes our eyes wet with knowing how much we love and are loved in return. So, till tomorrow….'

Feeling my walls shake and hearing the shouting and arguing between Barney and Belinda brought my other tenants out of their apartments demanding to know 'What the hell is going on!'

It didn't take long for the police to arrive and storm the place. Sobbing, cursing and raving like a lunatic, Barney fought and resisted until they overpowered him, jerked him to his feet and hauled him away in handcuffs, much the way I saw them take Jeb Morrison away not long before that.

The ending this time, however, was much different. In all my years of existence, that was the first and only murder ever to occur on my premises. In the space of an hour, I learned what could happen when human emotions are rubbed so raw they can erupt into extreme violence. I hope to never see the likes of such a tragedy again.

Chapter 30

At first all I could see were a couple of suitcases, a purse, a gift box and what looked like a hatbox being juggled through my front entrance. Not until she bumped into Richard and dropped the box hiding her face did I recognize Sarah, Lilly's niece.

"Oh, I'm so sorry." She stooped over to pick up the box.

"It's OK," Richard said, scooping it up before she could grab it. "Let me help you."

"Thank you," she said, trying to pull everything together.

"Where to?"

"It's all right, I can handle it from here."

"If you had an extra arm and could see where you're going, you probably could."

She laughed. "Well, if you insist."

"I do," he said, handing over the box and taking the suitcases from her.

He started up the stairs ahead of her. "Second floor? Third? Fourth?"

"Second, number two."

He paused. "Hey, that's Lilly's apartment... hold on a

minute...you must be her niece. Sarah, right? She's been waiting on pins and needles for you to get here."

"I'm her niece, yes. Then you know my aunt Lilly?"

"I sure do," Richard said. "We broke bread together not so long ago."

"Broke bread?"

"Well, actually, we had tea and cookies."

"And you're...?"

"I'm Richard. Didn't your aunt ever mention me?"

Just then the door sprang open. "I heard the commotion. Sarah! Come in, Sarah, come in. You, too, Richard."

The suitcases collided with the doorway as they entered. Sarah dropped her boxes and threw her arms around her aunt. "It's wonderful to see you again, Aunt Lilly."

Richard set the suitcases aside as the two women hugged and kissed each other's cheeks.

"I'm so glad you were able to make it, Sarah. I've been looking forward to seeing you again since the day you answered my letter and said you'd try."

Richard cleared his throat. "Well, I guess—"

"Oh, Sarah," she said, grabbing her hand and Richard's. "This is Richard.... Richard...?"

"Belmont."

Lilly smiled up to him. "Belmont, of course. Richard Belmont. Richard, meet my niece, Sarah."

"I think I've already had that privilege downstairs, Lilly."

"Yes, I crashed into him and he helped me with my boxes." She stuck out her hand and laughed. "Nice to meet you,

Richard. Formally, that is."

Sarah's brown eyes flashed as she took in the boyish man standing there with a grin on his smooth, youthful face. His baby-blue eyes sparkled when he spoke:

"The pleasure's all mine, madam," he said, clicking his heels and bowing.

Lilly piped up. "Richard's a graduate student at the University. If you haven't already guessed, he's studying acting."

Sarah's eyes widened. "An actor?"

Richard put on a big smile. "Indeed, aren't we all actors on the stage of life?"

"You see, Sarah, he's also a philosopher."

Again Richard bowed. "Ladies, I'm afraid I must depart. You two have much to discuss, I'm sure."

"Thanks again for your help, Richard."

"Anytime, my fair lady, anytime."

Lilly took Sarah by the arm. "Richard, we'll have you down for supper with us after Sarah's settled."

"That's very kind of you, Lilly," he said, backing out the door. "I'll look forward to it."

Lilly shut the door behind him. "Sarah, dear, you can put your things away and freshen up after your long trip. I got your phone call from Cleveland. You're here a little earlier than I thought. Do what you need to do. In the meantime I'll put a nice lunch out for us. I know you like tuna salad."

"Love it," Sarah, said, picking up her suitcases and heading into the bedroom. "How do you know Richard, Aunt Lilly?" she called over her shoulder.

"Very much the way you just did, Sarah. I was coming home from the store one day loaded with a bag full of groceries. The wind and the rain started blowing so badly I had a hard time juggling it and my umbrella, so by the time I reached here my paper bag was pretty soggy. I almost made it up the stairs to my apartment and, wouldn't you know it, that's exactly when it decided to fall apart, sending my oranges, vegetables, bread and a few cans bouncing merrily all the way down. It sounded like an army marching. Usually Huggs is Johnny-on- the spot, but he wasn't this time and, as luck would have it, Richard came into the building at the perfect time to help me gather them up."

"And that was the beginning of your beautiful relationship?"

Lilly laughed. "He hasn't been here all that long, but we've become good friends. I have him down for lunch every so often. He's a bachelor living alone, so I know he appreciates it."

Sarah came into the kitchen drying her hands.

Lilly smiled slyly. "He's rather good-looking, don't you think?"

"Oh, I don't know," Sarah said. "I've seen better."

Lilly winked. "Not much, I'll bet," she said, putting plates on the table.

"Looks aren't everything; you know that Aunt Lilly."

"Of course, but it doesn't hurt. He's also a really a nice boy." Lilly took the pickle jar out of the icebox and put it on the table. "As you probably already noticed, he's very personable. Ambitious, too."

Sarah looked askance. "An actor, Aunt Lilly? Really?"

"If he can't make it in the theater, he can always do something else. He'll have his education— architecture, I believe he said— and he's young, only twenty-one. Your age."

"Old enough to vote. In another six months, I'll be old enough, too."

They made their sandwiches and Lilly poured their tea. "Have you decided how long you intend to stay?" Lilly asked, stirring milk into her cup.

"It was almost a week's drive here, Aunt Lilly, and it will be the same going back to Oregon. I'm between jobs right now, so I guess two or three will do." She looked over at her aunt. "That is, if you want me here that long."

"If I...! Oh, my dear, you can stay a month, a year, two years, forever if you like. I'd be overjoyed." She reached across and squeezed Sarah's hand.

As they ate, Sarah talked about her long trip across country. Soon after that, Lilly said, "I think you're going to find Richard interesting, Sarah. He's very likable, but underneath that façade of carefree cheerfulness, I sense something I can't quite put my finger on, something hidden that doesn't want to see the light of day." She paused to take a sip of her tea. "I'm pretty good at that sort of thing you know."

Sarah looked at her aunt, thoughtfully. "I remember you had a sixth sense. Didn't it have something to do with my cousin Ben?"

"You've a good memory, Sarah. You were only a little girl then. But, yes, you're right. It was the day Ben said he was going swimming out to Angola with a couple of friends. I remember feeling a strange chill when he told me, but I blamed my instincts on the weather. I said to him, 'Ben, I don't like the way the sky looks with those dark clouds. Why don't you wait till tomorrow? I think it's supposed to be a better day.' He scoffed and said, 'Don't be a worrywart, Aunt Lilly. I'm almost as good a swimmer as Johnny Weissmuller.' He laughed, saying, 'Maybe even better.' He went out the door yodeling like

Tarzan.

"You know the rest of the story. The way his friends told it, Ben went out in the lake, got caught in an undertow, and disappeared before anyone could even try and save him. It was tragic. He was only fifteen then. Absolutely tragic."

Sarah finished her sandwich and dabbed her napkin to her mouth. "I remember liking him, even though he used to tease me."

"He was devilish, but he was so likable. But as I was saying, Sarah, Richard is likable, too, in a different way. He has a warmth about him, but a…oh, I don't know. I'm not quite sure I know what I'm trying to say."

Sarah gave her aunt a smirk. "Are you trying to say I should get closer to Richard?"

Lilly smiled innocently. "Well, I don't think it would do any harm."

Sarah sat back in her chair. "Aunt Lilly, do you remember the last time I was here, how I started to tell you about my fiancé leaving me flat?"

"I remember saying you don't have to rehash the past, yes."

"It was a painful experience, Aunt Lilly. I'm not sure I'm over the hurt yet."

"Well, then, Sarah," she said, rising to clear the table, "maybe Richard is the answer to that."

"You don't understand, Aunt Lilly. I'm not sure I want to have anything to do with men, any man, now or ever. I've been burnt once, burnt badly, and once is more than enough."

Lilly sat next to Sarah and patted her hand. "My dear niece," she said, "do you remember when I told you to capture that moment in life that's waiting to be appreciated?"

"I do, Aunt Lilly, but it's hard. So hard."

"Of course it is. Life at its best is sometimes hard. But because of one man from the past who betrayed and hurt you, you're still grieving, wallowing in despair."

"I know, but—"

"I also told you to never let anyone like that live in your brain. If you knew someone at your door was going to torment you, would you invite him into your house?"

"That's what it's been, Aunt Lilly, torment."

Lilly reached over, turned Sarah to face her directly and dabbed her eyes with her napkin. "Now listen to me, Sarah, I may be old and not long for this world, but I learned a few things along the way. Remember the dish?"

"The dusty dish, yes. I keep it on a shelf in my kitchen."

"Have you forgotten, Sarah? Remember how I told you it reminded me I had to endure? I wanted you to take that message to heart. And more than that, I want you to thrive. Now is the time to do it." She patted her hand again. "There now, let's get off that dreary subject and on to something more pleasant."

Sarah rose with her and helped her with the dishes. They made some small talk. Sarah asked how her aunt's kidney condition was and was relieved to hear it didn't get worse. After that, Sarah settled herself in. As she sorted her clothes in the dresser drawers, she thought about Richard. He was good-looking and she liked his friendly manner and the soft tenor of his voice. He seemed genuine...but didn't all two-faced Romeos appear that way?

Chapter 31

They had just finished having dinner, the three of them: Aunt Lilly, Sarah and Richard.

Richard set his napkin aside. "Sarah, that was an especially delicious meal."

"Thank you, Richard, but it's hard to go wrong with a good pork roast."

"Your gravy makes it even better, Aunt Sarah."

"Thank you, dear. Shall we go into my humble parlor and have coffee there?"

"Sounds good to me," Richard said, sliding back his chair and moving over to help with Sarah's.

When they were seated, Richard said, "So tell me, Sarah, what have you been doing since you arrived last week?"

Sarah tucked her beige skirt over her knees. "Aunt Lilly and I have had a wonderful time together. Besides talking each other's ears off and poring over old photos, we've taken walks in the park, went to the zoo and...where else did we go to, Aunt Lilly?"

"We went window shopping on Main Street, and don't forget the nice movie, we saw. 'Gunga Din' was the name of it, wasn't it Sarah?"

"Yes, with Cary Grant and Douglas Fairbanks, Jr."

"And Sarah's been a great help to me right along, doing chores my body won't allow me to do myself anymore."

"Even that was fun."

Richard stood up and dug his hand into the pocket of his sharply creased pants. "Lilly? Sarah? I have two tickets I'd like to give you. It's for a play we're putting on over at the school."

"Really, Richard?" Lilly said, reaching over for them. "For us?"

"Absolutely. I'd like very much for you both to come."

"What kind of a play is it, Richard?"

"It's a musical, Sarah. Very popular. It's been around a few years. By Cole Porter. 'Anything Goes.' You've heard of it, haven't you?"

"Of course, Richard," Lilly said, standing up, "of course." Her eyes twinkled as she swiveled her hips, made a motion with her hands like moving windshield wipers and began singing: 'In olden days a glimpse of stocking was looked on as something shocking, now heaven knows, anything goes… The world has gone bad today and looks sad today and…and….' She laughed and said, "That's all I know."

"Oh, that's so pretty, Aunt Lilly," Sarah said, laughing. She turned to Richard. "Are you in it, Richard?"

Richard sat again and bent forward in his chair, his forearms on his knees. "Yes, Sarah, I am." A lock of his blond hair fell over his eyes.

"A big part?" Lilly asked.

"Big enough."

"And do you sing in it?" Sarah asked.

Frances R. Schmidt & James A. Costa

"Yes, I do, but don't compare me to Bing Crosby."

Their conversation went on over coffee and pastry for a couple of hours or more. Finally, Richard looked at his wristwatch.

"Holy smoke," he said, getting up and tucking in his white sport shirt. "Ten o'clock already. You ladies must be very tired from all the work you put in. I just want to tell you how much I appreciate your inviting me over." He looked at his watch again. "Getting late. I'd better get a move-on."

The women stood up with him. "I'm so glad you could come, Richard," Lilly said. "We'll do this again before Sarah leaves."

Richard looked disappointed. "Are you leaving soon, Sarah?"

"I don't know exactly when, Richard, but while I'm here I'm going to make the most of it, starting with seeing your play."

"That's nine days away," he said, moving to the door, "but it'll be here before we know it."

The nine days did pass quickly for Lilly, but not for Richard, and not for Sarah, who lay in bed trying to understand her feelings. She hardly knew this man, yet, handsome though he might be, she found nothing particularly attractive about him. Still, she couldn't stop thinking about him, the way he would look sideways and smile at her, as if they were sharing a secret. She felt herself being drawn to him against her will. It was an unfamiliar sensation that made her uncomfortable. She preferred to stay hidden behind the wall she had built after Jeff, her fiancé, walked out on her, a private place where she felt safe.

Her mind danced between her undeniable attraction to

219

Richard, and to Jeff, the man who rejected her, and to her Aunt Lilly, and the words she uttered their last time together, 'Sarah, capture that moment in life that's waiting to be appreciated.'

I heard Lilly and Sarah discuss what happened the night of the play and read their minds as if seeing a movie of the nuances involved: After the play ended they found themselves standing on the sidewalk outside on the UB campus hall, where the crowd spilled out chattering around them.

"Well, how'd you like the play?" Richard said, coming up behind and surprising them.

They whirled around together. "Richard!" Lilly cried. "It was wonderful, absolutely wonderful."

"I agree, Richard. I loved it. Such beautiful songs, particularly when you sang 'Easy to Love.'

"You have a beautiful tenor voice, Richard," Lilly said. "I expected you to be good, but you were simply out of this world. Yes, and better than Bing Crosby, too. I loved when you sang, 'All through the Night.'

Richard blushed. "That's called hyperbole, Lilly, but I thank you anyway."

"She isn't exaggerating, Richard, not one bit."

He turned to Sarah. "Well, I thank you both for coming and for your kind words." He looked over their heads. "Someone's calling me. I have to get back inside." He looked at Sarah again. "Sarah, do you think you'd have a little time to spend with me tomorrow. We can discuss the play, if you like."

Sarah didn't hesitate. "I'd love to, Richard."

"Great," he said, starting away. "I'll call on you tomorrow afternoon, if that's all right. About two o'clock?"

Lilly hooked her arm in Sarah's and smiled. "She'll be waiting."

Chapter 32

*It was one of those days when everything seems to happen at once. The morning newspaper ran a banner headline reading, **German Bund Cell Exposed**. At the same time, Gustav was downstairs tearing open a letter from FBI agent Noah. As I started reading along with Gustav, a huge disturbance changed my focus immediately.*

Standing in the hallway, hugging her doll and crying for her mother, was little Rosie. Within minutes the place was crowded with tenants rushing around, asking questions and finally barging into Rosie's apartment, where they found Lizzie Shanahan on the kitchen floor, convulsing and gasping for air.

It wasn't long before a squad car pulled up and two policemen raced up the stairs. Seconds later an ambulance skidded to the curb. Two medics rushed out, grabbed a stretcher out of the back and stumbled awkwardly up the stairs with it. Shouting for everyone to get out of the way, they squeezed through Lizzie's apartment door and disappeared inside. Minutes later they emerged carrying an unconscious Lizzie strapped to the stretcher.

One of the policemen herded the growing crowd toward the stairs.

"Clear the way and go back to your apartments, people. Nothing to see here. Move along, folks, break it up and move along."

Chattering between themselves, reluctantly they obeyed the order.

The other policeman knelt on one knee and placed his notepad on the other. "And the lady is your mommy?"

Rosie rubbed her knuckles into her wet eyes. "Yes."

"And what did you hear your mommy say?"

"She only called my name, that's all. Then she fell down."

"Does anyone else live with you?"

She wept. "No, only Mommy and me."

"Do you have any relatives that come to visit? An aunt or an uncle?"

"No."

"Any good friends?"

"Nobody. Only Mr. Gustav."

"Mr. Gustav?"

"That would be me," Gustav said, having just arrived home and coming quickly up the stairs, "Gustav Schwartz. I live in the next apartment."

The policeman turned and stood up. "Well, Mr. Schwartz. Since there doesn't seem to be anyone else.... Do you think you can watch this young lady until we can get social services involved? It shouldn't take long. If not, we'll take her with—"

"I want to stay with Mr. Gustav, please."

"Of course, Rosie, you can stay with me until your mommy comes home."

The policeman looked from one to the other. He lifted his

hat and smoothed back his hair. "OK, that settles it for now, I guess, until we can work things out. You'll be hearing from social services before long, I'm sure."

"Well be here waiting, won't we, Rosie?"

Rosie wrapped her arm around Gustav's arm. "Yes," she said, pressing her face and smearing her tears against Gustav's sleeve.

When the policemen left, Gustav guided Rosie into his apartment and led her to the kitchen table. "Wait till I get a pillow for you to sit on, Rosie."

"Will my mommy be all right, Mr. Gustav?"

"I'm sure she will, Rosie," he said, taking a quart of milk out of the icebox and filling her glass. He brought a plate of cookies out of the cupboard and placed it next to her glass. He took her hand and moved it toward the milk.

"That's OK, Mr. Gustav, I know how to get it without knocking the glass over."

While Rosie nibbled at her cookies, Gustav sat opposite her and pulled from his pocket the letter he received from Noah. It was short and to the point: he was to report downtown to Noah's office at eleven o'clock on Monday morning. Gustav frowned, wondering what news Noah had for him.

He watched Rosie for a few moments, then said, "Rosie, I'll call the hospital later and find out when we can visit your mommy. I know she'll be anxious to see you."

"Mommy's very sick, I think, Mr. Gustav."

"The doctors will make her well, Rosie. She'll be up and around before you can say, jibble jee jibble, bibble bee bibble, one, two, three, skidoo."

Rosie giggled trying to repeat it.

Gustav studied her a few moments. She was a beautiful child with golden braids and blue eyes that couldn't see, but seemed to have light trapped inside them. She was a few years younger than his Inga, but looked enough like her to be her sister.

When Rosie had finished, Gustav told her to take a nap on the couch while he went downstairs to make a phone call. A quick search located Lizzie at the General Hospital on High Street.

The first thing Gustav did the next morning is take Rosie down to Joe's for breakfast. The restaurant was crowded, but Sylvia rushed their order, per Gustav's request. Half an hour later they were in the back seat of a taxi on their way to General Hospital, all three of them, Gustav, Rosie and her doll, Shirley.

A nurse led them to Lizzie's room and peeked in. She whispered, "She's sleeping lightly now. Don't keep her too long, she needs her rest." She leaned close to Gustav's ear. "Doctor Nesbitt will here shortly to talk to you."

Gustav held Rosie's hand as they came in quietly together. They stood next to the bed, listening to Lizzie's shallow breathing.

"Are we going to wake Mommy up, Mr. Gustav?"

Lizzie's eyes fluttered open. "Rosie? Is that you, my baby?"

Rosie burst into tears. "Yes, Mommy, it's me."

Lizzie turned her head slightly. "Gustav?"

"It's me, Lizzie, yes."

"You have my Rosie?"

"Yes. I'm keeping her till you get home. She's been anxious to see you."

Lizzie voice was scratchy and alarmingly weak. "Gustav."

Gustav leaned over the bed, very close to her lips. "Yes?"

"Gustav," she whispered, "I'm worried."

He patted her frail arm. "Don't be."

Just then a slight man with a thin mustache and a wispy comb-over of gray hair stepped into the room. A stethoscope hung down over his immaculate white jacket.

"I'm Doctor Nesbitt," he said, extending his hand to Gustav. "And you're Mr. Schwartz?"

"Nice to meet you, doctor."

"And I suppose this is Rosie? How are you, Rosie?"

"Is my mommy going to be all right?" she asked, hugging her doll to her breast."

"Yes, of course she is." He cranked the bed to prop Lizzie up higher, then turned to Gustav. "Mr. Schwartz, may I see you in my office?" To Rosie, he said, "Rosie, stay and talk with your mommy until we get back. Can you do that? I'll send a nurse in, too."

Gustav followed the doctor past the nurses' station and out through the corridor to his office. "I had visitors this morning, Mr. Schwartz, a Miss Fenlow from social services, and Police Officer Dowd. He was first on the scene yesterday and gave us his account of what happened. He contacted Miss Fenlow immediately because a child is involved."

Gustav listened.

"Miss Fenlow will be visiting you very soon to consider some kind of temporary placement for Rosie. It will be difficult because she's, what, eight or nine years old? And particularly because of her affliction. "

"I see," Gustav said, "but only until Lizzie recovers and is released."

The doctor directed Gustav's attention to the wall behind him. "This is the reason I asked you to come with me." He walked over and flipped on a switch. "The film you are looking at, Mr. Schwartz, is an X-Ray of Mrs. Shanahan's lungs. Notice the shaded areas."

"Not good?"

"Worse than that. You're looking at an aggressive form of cancer. You see how the mass has metastasized into these areas?" he said, pointing. He clicked off the screen.

"And that means...."

"Exactly, Mr. Schwartz."

"How long, doctor? How much time does she have?"

"I can't give you the exact time, but she won't be leaving this hospital. It's a miracle she's lasted this long with her condition."

Gustav shook his head. "Poor Rosie. Lizzie's all she has in this world."

"What makes it worse, Mr. Schwartz, is that she's blind. It will be virtually impossible to find adoptive parents for her."

"Do you think I can speak with Lizzie alone?"

The doctor tapped Gustav's arm. "Of course," he said, indicating the door to the corridor.

When they entered Lizzie's room, a nurse was standing beside Rosie, removing her nurse's cap from Rosie's head.

"Nurse, why don't you take Rosie out by your station and show her how it is to work in a hospital and help sick people get better."

"Of course, doctor. Do you want to come with me, Rosie?"

"Is it OK, Mr. Gustav?"

"Yes, Rosie."

"But I can come back by Mommy again, can't I?"

"Of course, Rosie."

After Rosie, the nurse and the doctor left the room, Lizzie beckoned Gustav before he could speak. "Gustav, I don't have much time, do I?"

"Lizzie, of course you have time, as much as I do."

"That's a lot of blarney, Gustav, and you know it," she said, her voice fading. "I know my time's up. I've been ready. But, Gustav, a favor, if you will, please."

"Of course, Lizzie, anything you say."

Lizzie's pale eyes, red-rimmed and watery, pleaded with her words. "This is the moment I've dreaded for a long time. When I'm gone, Rosie will be placed in an orphanage or an institution for the blind. I'm afraid for her, Gustav. I can't bear to think it." She raised her hand to touch his hand. "And Gustav, I'm sorry for the harsh way I spoke to you about being so close to Rosie. Maybe I was only jealous. For sure I didn't expect this, at least not so soon.

"Please forgive me and promise me, please, Gustav, say you'll visit her once in a while, keep track of her, watch over her? To make sure she's faring well. Or well enough. I'm asking a lot, Gustav, I know, but you know Rosie thinks the world of you. In fact, I think she loves you for your kindness and being the father she never knew." She squeezed his hand. "For a dying woman's sake, please, please promise me."

He patted her hand as he slid his away. "I promise, Lizzie."

Lizzie exhaled a breath of relief. "Thank you, Gustav. God bless you." She closed her eyes and her arm slid to her side.

"I'll bring Rosie in to say goodnight, Lizzie."

She nodded.

On the way back home, Gustav tried to put on a cheerful face, but knowing Lizzie had very little time left made it difficult. He didn't want to think about the effect it would have on Rosie when Lizzie passes.

Gustav's mind was also occupied with thoughts of his family. Monday couldn't come quickly enough for him to hear what news Noah had of them.

Chapter 33

At ten o'clock Monday morning, Huggs came dashing up the stairs, shouting, "Mr. Schwartz, a phone call for you downstairs! A phone call for you downstairs! They said it's important!"

Gustav told Rosie to wait while he answered the call. He was certain it was Noah calling to cancel the appointment or to give him bad news.

"Hello."

"Mr. Schwartz?"

"Speaking."

"Mr. Schwartz, this is Miss Fenlow. Has General Hospital called you this morning?"

"No one's called me."

"I'm sorry to bring you bad news, but the hospital notified me that Mrs. Shanahan passed away at five a.m."

Gustav felt the blood drain from his face.

"Mr. Schwartz, are you there? Are you all right?"

"Yes… yes, I am."

"As you know, I'll be the social worker in charge of her daughter."

"I'm aware of that, Miss Fenlow. So what's the next step?"

"Since you're not biologically related, we'll have to take Rosie into custody until we know how and where we can place her, if possible."

Gustav was numb. "When is this supposed to take place?"

"As soon as possible, Mr. Schwartz. Since there are no known living relatives, she is now a ward of the state and it's our responsibility to ensure her safety and well-being."

"She's safe with me."

"Of course, we realize that, Mr. Schwartz, but we have protocol to follow. You understand."

"Protocol, yes," he said sarcastically, "I understand."

"We can pick her up and bring her down to our social services department on Franklin Street in Buffalo. Or you can bring her to us. Either way, we need to have her clothing and other possessions ready."

"I'll bring her myself."

"That will be fine, Mr. Schwartz. And, uh, Mr. Schwartz, do you want someone here, one of our counselors to break the news to her of her mother's passing?"

"When do you want her, Miss Fenlow?"

"I believe I said, as soon as possible."

"I'll need a little time to go through Mrs. Shanahan's apartment with Rosie to see what needs to be taken."

Miss Fenlow hesitated. "I know you mean well, Mr. Schwartz, and if it were up to me, I would say do so, but since you're not related except through friendship, that may pose a legal problem, if you understand what I mean. You can understand the reason for that, can't you?"

"I'm more than a friend."

"I understand how difficult this must be for you, but I have my duty and responsibilities in such cases. However, let me discuss this with my superior and get back to you sometime later today. As to my other question, do you want one of our counselors to break the news to her?"

"No, I'll handle it."

The phone call depressed Gustav. He knew Lizzie didn't have much time, but this was more sudden than he imagined. And how was he going to tell Rosie that Lizzie was dead?

With little time left to make his appointment with Noah, Gustav rushed Rosie along and headed out of the apartment. On the way down the stairs they ran into Alice Wagman, the librarian.

"Good morning, Mr. Schwartz. Good morning, Rosie." She made a motion with her head toward Lizzie's apartment, which Gustav understood.

"Lizzie's doing well," he said, shaking his head side to side. "Right now I have to run an errand downtown."

"I see," she said. "Well, listen. I brought some wonderful children's books home from the library that I have to make catalogue cards for. If Rosie doesn't need to be with you, do you think she might want to spend a little time with me and read a story or two while you're gone?"

"What do you think, Rosie? Sounds like a nice offer Miss Wagman's making, doesn't it?"

"I even have some peanut butter cookies we can share, and chocolate milk, too."

Rosie hugged her doll. "I think Shirley and I would like that very much."

"Wonderful, dear," she said, taking her by the hand. "My, what a pretty bracelet you're wearing. Such lovely red hearts."

Rosie jiggled her wrist in the air. "Mr. Gustav gave it to me a long time ago."

"Enjoy your stories, Rosie," Gustav said, moving away. "I'll be back soon."

All of what came later I either witnessed or heard from all the people involved.

Chapter 34

A matronly secretary greeted Gustav when he arrived, told him to have a seat and said Mr. Blanchard would be with him shortly, pushed up her horn-rimmed glasses and went back to typing. Gustav looked around the office. It was comfortably furnished, but it had a feeling of oppression about it. Was he feeling the weight of a government agency that wielded great power over people? It felt intimidating, but at the same time, it offered a sense of security. These employees, these secret agents, were watching out for him, for everyone, protecting the country against possible enemies. But what would it take, he wondered, for an evil person like a Stalin or a Hitler to take it over and use its power against the people? Could it happen here?

*In the corner of the room stood the American flag. On the far wall hung the circular FBI seal. Gustav studied it, taking in its various parts. Around the top were the words **Department Of Justice**; around the bottom, **Federal Bureau Of Investigation**. A shield occupied the center with red and white stripes bracketed by a couple of branches. Beneath that was an unfurled banner with the words Fidelity, Bravery and Integrity written on it. 'Ah, so maybe that's where the acronym FBI actually comes from,' he thought, 'not Federal Bureau of Investigation.'*

Gustav was certain the seal was filled with all kinds of

symbols. He was trying to figure out what they were when he heard his name called.

"Come in, Mr. Schwartz," Noah Blanchard said, holding open the door to his office.

Gustav snapped out of his reverie. "Good morning, sir," he said, rising quickly and stepping in before him.

Noah sat behind a dark, highly polished desk, barren except for Noah's nameplate, a stapler and a tray with paper clips and a miniature American flag poking up from the center. On the wall behind him hung a small replica of the agency's symbol. In the corner stood another American flag, a mate to the one in the outer office.

Gustav sat and leaned forward in his captain's chair. "I hope you have good news for me, Noah. It's been a couple of months."

"I'm sorry I haven't kept you up to date, Gustav, but things have been rather hectic with one thing or another going on. You know, of course, that the Bund has been neutralized."

"Yes, Noah, I know. I read it in the papers. I hope you'll see to it that nothing happens to my friend Wilhelm. He wasn't involved in their doings any more than I was."

"We're well aware of that, Gustav. He's been questioned and released, although I should tell you there's talk that many Germans are going to be rounded up and interned, simply because they're Germans."

"Wouldn't that be un-American, Noah? After all, this isn't a dictatorship."

Noah shook his head. "Not yet, it isn't, although Japanese citizens in California are facing the same threat," he said, taking a folder from his desk drawer. "But as I mentioned, I've been buried in work here, so I apologize for being out of touch so long."

"With the war and all and everything else you have to do, I suppose you couldn't help it."

"I'm glad you understand."

In fact, Gustav didn't understand. Inside, he was angry and impatient. Too many nights had passed, too many weeks, waiting for a phone call or a visit from Noah or news from Wilhelm, only to be disappointed on both accounts again and again.

Noah laid aside the folder and stood up abruptly. "Come with me, please."

Startled, Gustav rose slowly. It sounded like an order. 'Are they arresting me?' he thought as he followed him to the door of an adjoining room."

Noah held the door open and said, "Enter, please."

Warily, Gustav stepped in ahead of Noah and suddenly froze. Stunned, disbelieving his eyes, he saw across the room, sitting in three chairs facing him, his long-lost family— Greta, Inga and Hans.

"Gustav," Greta cried, rising and rushing across the room to him.

"Daddy," the children shrieked, leaping out of their chairs, and flying to him.

They embraced each other, locked arms and rocked together, laughing, crying and talking all at the same time.

Noah looked moist-eyed watching them. It was obviously a moment he would never forget.

Shortly after leaving the FBI building, the cab pulled up in front of my entrance. When they got out to gather their meager possessions, I heard the taxi driver tell Gustav that, judging by the sound of all the excited chatter in the back seat of his cab, he thought ten people were packed in instead of four. Standing inside with a mop stick in his hand was Huggs, smiling at the family procession jabbering away and carrying their little bags past him.

"Good afternoon, Mr. Gustav," he said, watching them pass and march up the stairs in pairs.

"Good afternoon, Huggs," he answered back. Then to his family climbing with him, he said, "That's Mr. Huggs, the building hero. He saved a woman's life right here on the second floor."

"Hello, Mr. Huggs," they sang out together.

Huggs's chest visibly swelled. Beaming, he cupped his hands around his mouth and said, "Call me if you need me, Mr. Gustav."

Inside the apartment they set their belongings aside and gathered around the kitchen table. Gustav spoke.

"This is a dream come true. I still can't believe it," he said, looking from one to the other with loving eyes.

"We almost didn't make it," Greta said. "The German border guard took our fake papers and was comparing them. I could see he was very suspicious by the way his cold eyes kept studying our faces, one to the other. Then he said he'd have to check with authorities and ordered us to wait while he went inside his kiosk."

Hans spoke up. "We were all shaking, Dad, because we thought we were caught, but then maybe a fight broke out or somebody was trying to escape or something— we never knew what— and the other guards suddenly started rushing away from us shouting back and forth to each other."

Greta finished for him. "Our guard ran out, shouted an order for us not to move, and dashed off to see what the disturbance was. That's when our driver stepped on the gas pedal and broke through the wooden gate and raced over the narrow bridge to the Swiss side."

Hans piped up excitedly. "Then they started shooting at us, Dad," he said. "We had to duck down in our seats. I could hear the bullets whizzing by and some were hitting the car. One bullet smashed through the back window and through the front window and just missed the driver's head." He beamed. "I wasn't scared, though, Dad, not one bit." He laughed. "But Inga was," he said, poking his sister. "She was scared to death and shaking like a leaf."

"I was not!" Inga shouted, slapping back at him. "Don't believe him, Dad."

"All right, all right," Gustav said. "Calm down, both of you. You're here now, safe and sound, thank God for that, so just be quiet. We have to consider some things. If I'd known you were coming, I'd have made arrangements, but this was totally unexpected. The FBI never told me you were on your way."

"We didn't know it, either, Greta said, "We were as surprised as you were when you came through that door."

"OK," Gustav said, glancing around. "We have to stay here tonight. It will be cramped, but we'll do it. First thing tomorrow I'll find another place for us to live."

"In the meantime I'll set up and try to make us as comfortable as possible," Greta said, starting to rise.

"Sit, Greta, sit, there's one more thing." His voice was serious.

Greta eased herself down again. They all looked at him expectantly.

"It's a long story, but basically this is it: A lady passed away here this morning and I've more or less become responsible for her daughter. Actually, she's her granddaughter."

"You?" Greta said, surprised. "You are responsible?"

"Not legally, of course, but yes. I'll give you the whole story later, but right now, another lady here named Alice Wagman volunteered to watch her while I went downtown this morning."

"So she's an orphan, is that it, Gustav? Has she no relatives to take her in?"

"Correct, Greta, she has none. I befriended her a long time ago after she did me a great favor. She might have saved my life."

"So, what are you saying, Gustav?"

"I would like us to adopt her."

Greta looked bewildered. "But Gustav, we already have two children to raise. Isn't there an agency that can place her in a good home, to parents who want a child? How old is she, anyway?"

"Well, Greta, that's the problem. She's seven, almost eight. She would be hard to place."

"Gustav, that's not too old. She's still a young child."

"She's also blind."

Greta slumped back in her chair. "Blind?"

"A wonderful child, Greta. Truly wonderful. And I still have to tell her that the grandmother she thinks is her mother passed away this morning."

"Oh, Gustav."

Gustav got up. "I'll see Alice now and ask her if she can

keep Rosie— that's her name, Rosie— if she'll keep her overnight. I'll also break the sad news to her. Alice can comfort her. Rosie knows her." He looked at Greta. "Tomorrow we can decide what to do with her." He started for the door.

"Gustav?"

He turned. "Yes?"

"If no one objects, we can take her. We've seen families rounded up and hysterical children torn from their parents' arms. We understand what it's like to be alone and afraid."

Gustav broke into a huge smile.

Excited by the idea, Inga said, "You mean I'm going to have a baby sister?"

"What!" Hans whined, "another girl?"

Rosie wept in Gustav's arms as he held her close, stroking her hair and speaking softly. 'Your mommy's with God, Rosie. He took her so she wouldn't suffer anymore. Right now she's looking down at us from heaven and she's smiling. She's saying she wants you to be brave. Can you hear her, Rosie?'

Rosie lifted her head. Her cheeks wet with tears. 'Mm hmm. I hear her, Mr. Gustav.'

'And she wants you to grow up good and strong and happy. Will you do that for her?'

'I'll try, Mr. Gustav,' she said between sobs, snuggling closer. 'I'll try.'

Alice comforted her as best she could and said she and her sister Agnes would be happy to keep her overnight, or longer if Gustav wished. Before leaving, Gustav told Rosie she would be living with him and his wife, Greta, and that his two children, Inga and Hans, were anxious to welcome her into their family. A big smile broke over Rosie's face. You mean I'm going to have a

239

for-real brother and sister?'

Stimulated by all that had transpired during the day, Gustav and Greta didn't sleep much that night and lay awake a long time talking. Greta told him how a kind German family, at risk of their lives, took them in and hid them in the attic behind a false wall, how they had made two failed attempts with the underground and were almost captured, and how, finally, they were smuggled out under very adverse conditions by masked men through forests, across streams and over mountains close to the Swiss border, where a car was waiting for them.

Eventually their conversation came back to Rosie.

"From what Lizzie told me, I gathered that Rosie's blindness could possibly be corrected. Obviously, Lizzie couldn't afford the expense of the kind of specialists she needs. I wonder, Greta, if we could look into that later."

"I think so, Gustav." She gazed up to the ceiling, her eyelids fluttering. "Isn't it strange, Gustav, how things happen? If Rosie's grandmother hadn't died, and if we hadn't escaped to be able to take her in, Rosie would probably never have a home to live in or a family of her own to live with."

"Or have a chance to see again. It's as if it were ordained, Greta."

"Yes, like she was meant to be raised by us. She'll take the place of the child we lost when I miscarried shortly after you left Germany, and the Nazis were hunting us down."

In the early morning hours, exhausted, they fell asleep in each other's arms.

Chapter 35

"Lilly, that chuck roast was absolutely scrumptious," Richard said, dabbing his mouth with a cloth and pushing a lock of silvery blond hair off his forehead.

"It really was, Aunt Lilly. I can't take another bite."

"Thank you. Now are you both ready for dessert and coffee?"

"Richard and I have decided to take a ride to the falls. Can we take a rain check, Aunt Lilly?"

"Why, of course," she said, rising to take her plate away.

"Would you like to join us?"

"No thank you, my dear, but I think it's a marvelous idea. Do you remember being there, Sarah?"

"I remember how high and noisy the falls were, like thunder."

"You were just a child then. You'll appreciate it so much more now."

Richard stood up. "I wanted to borrow my uncle's car, but Sarah insists we take hers."

"Leave everything as it is, Sarah," Lilly said, taking the plate out of her hands. "I'll clean up. Why don't you two go now? It's early enough and a beautiful day for a nice drive like that."

"I think we should go over the Peace Bridge and follow the river along the Canadian side," Richard said. "I think it's a prettier route."

"Oh, yes, be sure to do that," Lilly agreed. "Too many factories on the American side."

After they left, Lilly went about her chores absent-mindedly. Her thoughts were of Sarah, and how wonderful it would be if she and Richard could click as a couple. Most likely Sarah would then remain in Buffalo and get married. 'I'm not so old I couldn't be a grandaunt yet,' she thought, smiling to herself.

When Sarah and Richard returned later that evening, they sat at the kitchen table having their chocolate cake and ice cream dessert.

"The falls were really beautiful, Aunt Lilly. I wish you would have gone with us."

"Oh, my dear, I've been there so many times. Besides, you know the old expression, 'Two's company, three's a crowd.'"

Sarah blushed. "Oh, Aunt Lilly…. Anyway, it was an almost perfect trip until we were half way home. We had a flat tire."

"Oh, my."

"But Richard changed the tire in no time. Can you imagine, Aunt Lilly, I drove all the way from Oregon without anything going wrong with my car, and now, on just a short ride, my tire decides to go flat."

Richard pointed to a little bag beside Sarah. "Aren't you going to show her?"

"Oh, I almost forgot," Sarah said, taking an iridescent metal plaque from the bag.

It depicted a golden sunrise with the Peace Bridge spanning the sparkling Niagara River. On the blue water a Native American Indian leans forward in his canoe, his paddle poised to dive. Behind him in the distance is a frothy representation of Niagara Falls in bas-relief.

Lilly took it in her hands, studying it. "It's a beautiful souvenir. Thank you both so much. I'm going to place it right here on the shelf where I used to keep my dusty dish."

Richard was on his feet, ready to leave. "Dusty dish?"

Sarah took him by the arm and walked him to the door. "It's a long story, Richard. Remind me to tell you about it sometime."

Later that night, Sarah lay awake, thinking. She'd been at her Aunt Lilly's for almost three weeks, not long, but during that time she'd grown quite close to Richard. They'd been out together a number of times, going for walks, seeing him after one of his plays and talking about it for hours, visiting the Museum of Science and the Albright Art Gallery. In fact, they saw each other every chance they had. She had to admit to herself she loved being with him, and that's what worried her.

She had felt the same way toward Jeff, and he ended up betraying her and breaking her heart. If Jeff taught her anything at all, it was to never trust a man, especially a sweet-talking man. Richard seemed honest, but was he? How could she be sure? He was an actor, and constantly surrounded by beautiful, talented girls. Could she trust him? He seemed sincere enough, but so did Jeff when he whispered beautiful words of love in her ear. Like Jeff, Richard was good-looking, but not in the same dark way.

The only real difference she noted between the two is that, while Jeff was always trying to draw her closer, Richard would often reach a point when he'd back off, as if he'd run into some kind of mental wall. Was he unconsciously revealing he didn't care for her? Was he playing some kind of mind game? Was he harboring some dark secret?

Sarah tossed and turned, unable to sleep. She felt herself falling in love with Richard. An actor! Was he acting when he kissed her on their third date? When he seemed content to hold her in his arms and tell her she was special? His words thrilled her, and that scared her. It was all so sudden. She didn't want to be taken in, not again. A week earlier she watched him play Hamlet, and she remembered the words from his soliloquy: 'To be or not to be, that is the question.' Now she heard it as, 'To trust or not to trust, that is the question.' If she could trust him, if she knew he could be trusted, she could open her heart completely because she already loved him in a way she never loved Jeff.

They'd only known each other a ridiculously short time, yet she believed he was her soul mate. He endeared himself to her with his gentleness, his understanding, too, when they discussed world events and, more particularly, when they discussed the misfortunes of people like Lizzie Shanahan and poor Mr. Spasinsky, the hurdy-gurdy man who died heartbroken after his fortune was stolen.

The following Friday evening they headed out the front door together and made their way to Sarah's car, parked a half-block down Potomac Avenue. All that happened later I learned from listening and reading Sarah's thoughts.

Richard turned in his seat to Sarah as she shifted into gear. "Now are you going to tell me where we're going, Sarah?"

Sarah smiled at him. "This should be right up your alley, Richard. It's a play I hope you haven't seen."

"Well, that's a pleasant surprise. What is it and where is it playing?"

"Lafayette High School."

"A high school play?"

"Have you seen 'Peter Pan'?"

Richard frowned. "No, but I know the story, of course."

"You don't look very happy," Sarah said, glancing over at him as they cruised down the street.

"It's only because I wasn't expecting that when you said you had a surprise for me."

"Being an actor, I thought you'd be pleased."

Richard forced a smile. "Oh, I am, Sarah, I am. You caught me off guard, that's all."

Minutes later they parked on the street and moved with a group of people along the sidewalk, in through the front door of the school toward the auditorium. A young student took the tickets from Sarah and they passed through the inner doors down the aisle toward their assigned seats.

"You have to let me reimburse you for the tickets, Sarah."

"My idea, Richard, so it's my treat," she said as they found their seats in the center about ten rows from the stage.

The auditorium filled up quickly, mostly with parents of the students. The curtains parted, the lights went down and the play began. Sarah sat through the first act with a beatific smile on her face, while Richard looked restless and uncomfortable. .

"Are you enjoying it so far, Richard?" Sarah whispered.

Richard straightened up in his seat. "Yes," he said. "It's well done. It's obvious a lot of work went into whipping these kids into their roles."

"I love them. Back in Oregon we often have the children

from my Bible class act out the religious scenes. They're so adorable; I just love watching them. These children are older, of course, but they're still beautiful to see."

They made small talk between the acts, rose and clapped with the audience at the end of the play as the students took their bows, shuffled out with the crowd and walked to Sarah's car.

"It's almost nine-thirty, Richard," Sarah said, pulling away from the curb. Do you have to get up early tomorrow morning?"

"I do, but if you'd like we can drop into Santasiero's for a drink."

"Is something wrong, Richard?"

"Wrong? No, Sarah, nothing's wrong."

"Is something on your mind? Something bothering you? You seem far away, Richard, ever since I suggested seeing the play. Did I say anything to upset you?"

Richard turned a troubled face toward her. "Nothing like that, Sarah. I guess I...I guess I'm feeling a little... I don't know. Anyway, do you want to stop for a drink?"

"I don't think so, Richard," now herself looking rather sad. "Let's call it a night, shall we?"

Richard had a pained look on his face. "Sarah, I don't want to spoil your evening. It was nice and really thoughtful of you to do what you did, planning this and getting the tickets and all. Please, don't blame yourself for anything. You know how temperamental we actors can be. It's part of our emotional makeup I guess, but it doesn't mean anything."

"All right, Richard. I understand." She turned and smiled at him. "I think."

Almost a week passed after that evening and Richard hadn't called on Sarah. That was strange and unusual. Sarah was certain now something had happened to Richard the night of the play, but she couldn't imagine what it could possibly be. Was he getting cold feet, or beginning to show signs that he didn't love her anymore, if he ever did? Five days passed and not a word from him. It could only mean he wasn't interested in her, that she was just a passing fancy or momentary infatuation.

Hurt and confused, she made up her mind. She could no longer bear not knowing where she stood with Richard. She decided to hide her feelings from him the next time they meet, but she had to know where their relationship was going, if anywhere. She prayed he'd been sincere and his recent behavior was, as he said, no more than an actor's emotional temperament. If he didn't love her, however, she made up her mind to embrace her pain and return to Oregon immediately, even though it would mean disappointing her aunt Lilly.

The following Saturday, Sarah and Lilly decided to treat themselves to breakfast downstairs in Joe's restaurant.

"You're rather quiet these past few days, Sarah. Is something wrong between you and Richard?"

Sarah set her coffee cup down. "I didn't think so until the evening we went to see the Peter Pan play. I haven't heard from him since."

"That's odd, isn't it?" Lilly said, studying her niece's face. "I've noticed lately you haven't been quite yourself. You seem rather upset, even now."

"I am, Aunt Lilly. I'm worried… I'm thinking…"

"That there's another woman?"

"Yes. I didn't want to say it, I don't want to think it, but yes, that's my greatest fear."

"My dear, then there's only one thing to do," she said,

setting her fork aside, "and that's to be direct. Ask him outright and clear the air."

After finishing their breakfast they spoke briefly to Joe when they paid their bill and passed out into the foyer, where Richard happened to be coming down the stairs. He looked as embarrassed meeting them as they were meeting him.

"Good morning, Richard," Lilly said, with a slight bow.

"Oh, good morning, Lilly. Good morning, Sarah."

Sarah nodded.

They stood for a moment, as if at a loss for words, when Lilly spoke up. "You two may want to talk. I'll go on ahead upstairs, Sarah," she said, starting away.

Richard started to talk. "Sarah—"

Sarah interrupted him. "Richard, have you been as busy as I have?" she asked, forcing a broad smile. "I believe it's been a week since we've seen each other. Where did the time go?"

Richard looked a little perplexed. "I, uh … I've been pretty busy myself, rehearsing for our next play."

"Another musical?"

"Not this time. It's Eugene O'Neill's comedy, 'Ah, Wilderness!'"

"Oh, that sounds wonderful, Richard," she said. Then, as if suddenly thinking of it, she asked, "Richard, how would you like to go for a picnic lunch tomorrow, the two of us?"

Again, the same facial expression. "Well, uh… I'm not sure…"

"All right, then, skip it. Another time, maybe."

"Oh, no no no, Sarah, it's OK. What time do you want to

meet?"

Sarah hesitated a moment, then said, "Let's make it noon. I'll pack the lunch and meet you down here at twelve sharp. Is that all right with you?"

"If you really want to, Sarah."

"Well, of course, I do, Richard," she said, a little testy. "Would I ask if I didn't?"

"Okay. See you then," he said, moving toward the door. "I have to run over to the school right now."

Sarah gave him a little wave and headed up the stairs.

The next morning they met downstairs as planned.

"Good morning, Sarah," Richard said, taking the picnic basket from her. He was wearing a gray pullover sweater and blue pants.

"Good morning, Richard," she said, following him out the door. She was wearing a brown skirt and a tan woolen sweater. A thin, yellow scarf circled her throat.

"A little chilly this morning," he said as they walked down Potomac Avenue to where his Oldsmobile was parked at the curb.

Neither said much as they drove up River Road toward Niagara Falls Park, where they would spend the next few hours. Except for a young couple looking through their binoculars across the river to Canada, and an elderly man sitting on a bench feeding peanuts to the squirrels scampering around his feet, the park was nearly deserted when they arrived.

Holding hands, they strolled alongside the Niagara River, its cold waters churning past in a frenzied torrent of iron-gray fury. Sarah saw the river as a parallel to her own emotional turmoil.

They found a bench, set their basket on it and sat down to rest. A brisk breeze sent a trail of dead leaves swirling around their ankles.

"You've been pretty quiet, Sarah. It's pretty obvious something's on your mind."

"You've been pretty quiet yourself," she said, her voice as chilly as the air. "Are you troubled by anything?"

He paused. "Sarah, I think we mentioned something about honesty in one of our conversations, didn't we?"

Misty eyed, she turned to face him. Her lip trembled. "Did we?"

"We did, yes. Or did I just imagine it?"

"Richard, you been avoiding me for a week. It probably would've been longer if we hadn't bumped into each other yesterday morning."

He nodded. "Okay, Sarah, I think it's time to set the record straight."

"Richard, I know we've barely just met, but our time together has been intense. I need to know, do you love me?"

He balked.

"I see," she said, starting to get up. "This is just a waste of time. Will you take me home? Now, please?"

Richard laid his hand on her arm to hold her back and she sat again. He spoke softly. "No, you don't see, Sarah. Believe me, I do love you. I've been trying to avoid this moment, but I suppose I do owe you an explanation, if you want to hear it."

"Richard, if you love me and I love you, what is there to explain?"

His jaw tightened, as if he was reluctant to open his mouth.

"OK, Sarah, but it's not easy. I'm not sure where to start."

"Try at the beginning, Richard."

"I suppose that's the most logical place." He took a deep breath. "A little over twelve years ago my father, mother— my beautiful mother— and my younger brother, Chip, and I were taking a drive in the country. We did that every Sunday as long as the weather was good. Sometimes we'd stop at a farmhouse and buy a gallon of milk from a farmer. The milk was always still warm and fresh from the cows in the barn. Then we'd cruise along, taking turns drinking it right from the jug and singing songs like, 'I've been working on the railroad.' My father would always try to harmonize with us, even though his voice sounded like someone gargling gravel. We'd kid him about it and beg him not to sneeze and spray us with stones.

"It was a Sunday like so many before it, when we piled in our car—it really was a pretty, black 1931 Packard. The sun was shining and, as usual, we were all in a cheerful mood, sailing along at maybe thirty miles an hour with the windows open and the wind blowing our hair all over the place, enjoying the smell of the country air and heading toward Batavia, when suddenly we heard this train sounding its horn and coming up parallel to us on our left.

"It was gaining on us and making such a heck of a roar when it was running beside us that we had to yell to hear each other. I remember sitting in the back seat, waving out the window and the engineer waving back. Then our boyish competitive spirit kicked in, and Chip and I kept shouting, "Beat him, Dad, beat him!"

My father got caught up in the spirit of the thing, stepped on the accelerator and our car lurched ahead.

Every time we yelled, 'Hurry, Dad, hurry!' The motor roared as Dad went even faster. Looking over his shoulder I could see the speedometer needle bouncing around 65 miles an hour. My mom was such a wreck she kept crying, 'Arthur! Slow down! Arthur!'

"My dad, Chip and I were laughing and that shrill train whistle was blowing so insistently I thought I'd go deaf listening to it. My mother kept shouting to my father, 'Arthur, slow down! Slow down!' But my father wasn't haven't any part of it. He was hunched over the steering wheel, and the last words I heard him say—or should I say, heard him growl— were, 'Oh, so you want to race, huh, buddy?'

"When I looked up I could see the crossbucks of a railroad crossing on the road ahead getting bigger, closer. With the speedometer needle already wavering around 70 miles an hour, my dad pushed the pedal to the floor and we were pulling slowly ahead of the locomotive. As we got closer to the crossing, Dad didn't slow down and neither did the train. I could see the engineer's arm yanking a cord, which sent out intermittent blasts of the horn, ending with one, long, shrill wail blending with the roar of the engine bearing down on us.

"All I remember after that is feeling the rumble and bouncing of our car on the tracks beneath us, and seeing for an instant the headlight of the engine looking at me like a giant eye through my side window, and then hearing a terrible grating, screeching sound of metal being shredded."

Richard's lips moved but no sound came from them. He bent down to pick up a handful of small stones. It took a few moments for his voice to return.

"The next thing I remember is opening my eyes and seeing my bandaged arms and a priest standing beside my hospital bed. Months later, midway through my recovery, I learned that I was the only survivor. My family was killed instantly, all three of them."

Sarah laid a gentle hand on his arm. "Oh, Richard, I'm so very sorry. Such a horrible experience."

Richard waited a moment, then said, "Aren't you going to ask what that story has to do with your question?"

Sarah looked at him curiously.

"About my loving you?"

"Yes, Richard, of course, but reliving such trauma, I didn't think now would be the right time for you to answer."

"It's as good a time as any." His voice took on a harder tone. "Yes, I do love you, Sarah, more than anything in the world."

"Well, then—"

"But I can never marry you."

Sarah looked dazed, confused. "Richard, why not? If you're feeling so guilty that—"

"That might have been reason enough, but it isn't."

Her eyes searched his face. "Why, then, Richard, why?"

"Because I was severely hurt in the accident."

"Richard, you're fine now, anybody can see that."

"Sarah, didn't you tell me you teach Sunday school back in Oregon?"

"Yes, I do, but—"

"And I know your desire is to become a teacher."

"Is something wrong with that, Richard? Do you resent me for that?"

Richard took her hand. "Of course not, Sarah. In fact, I admire you for it."

Sarah looked at him with puzzled eyes. "I don't understand,

Richard."

"You love children. Didn't you tell me once that you wanted to have a half a dozen kids some day, all sitting around the dinner table, talking and laughing?"

"Yes, I did. I do love children. You know that, Richard. They're my passion, that's why I want to teach grammar school."

"When we went to see Peter Pan last week, it hit me full force. Seeing the joy on your face watching those kids acting up there on the stage, I realized then that you could never be happy if you didn't have children."

"Richard, what does that have to do with anything?"

"Don't you understand what I'm trying to say, Sarah?" he said, flinging out over the water the fistful of stones he'd been squeezing in his hand since they sat down. "I can never give you children!"

Stunned, Sarah turned and wrapped her arms around him. "Oh, Richard, Richard, is that what all this mystery is about? Is that what's been standing between us? Oh, how foolish you are. We can work it out, my darling. I love you. Don't you understand? If we can't have children we can adopt them, as many as we want or can afford."

Richard looked at her with tortured eyes. "It wouldn't be the same, Sarah. You know it."

She leaned back. "Are you telling me what I know? Richard, you don't know what I know. All I know is that I love you and I will love the children we bring into our home and raise as our very own. We'll all grow together as a family, a family as real and loving as any blood-related family."

Richard managed a little smile. "Do you mean it, Sarah? Really mean it? You won't be sorry someday and tell me you made a big mistake?"

"Richard, do you love me?"

"Sarah, you know I do. Madly," he said, pulling her closer.

"And that's the problem I sensed has been bothering you lately?"

"I didn't know whether I should make an excuse and break off our relationship, or— but I couldn't do it. I loved you too much to hurt you. Besides, we promised each other to be honest, didn't we? No matter what the cost? One more thing, Sarah…"

"Yes, Richard?"

"I know what you must be thinking now." He went on without waiting for her to speak. "Other than that, the doctor said it's—"

"It's all right, Richard, it's all right, whatever it is," Sarah said, hugging him. "Being together is the only thing that matters. That's how much I love you."

He stood up and pulled her to her feet. He embraced her. "Sarah, I will love you forever."

"I will love you forever, too, Richard, and the children we'll raise together, forever and ever," she whispered, pressing her eager lips to his.

Chapter 36

When I heard the loud voice, I knew immediately it belonged to Chester Webb in apartment 6.

"What is this!" he shouted, holding out his hand with four shiny coins in his grimy palm.

Chester Junior stood before him, shaking. "Not much business today, Pa. Just slow, that's all."

"Excuses, excuses," he grumped, "all I get from you are excuses." He glared down with contempt at the forty cents in hand.

"I walked all the way down Main Street, Pa, from Utica to Swan Street, but I didn't get no takers. And I didn't use no money for a streetcar, neither. I tried, Pa, honest, I tried. One man even pushed me away when I kept pestering to shine his shoes."

"Well, you didn't try hard enough. How'm I supposed to pay the rent and feed you at the same time if this is all you can bring home, huh? How?" He slapped the coins down on the table. "I should smack you good."

"I'm sorry, Pa. I'll go out earlier tomorrow and maybe beat some of the other shoeshine boys out."

Chester senior hunched over his hairy arms on the kitchen table and stared morosely at the bottle of beer before him. "I feel like an animal caught in a trap."

"I said I'm sorry, Pa."

"Ah, it's not your fault. You can't help it you got that club foot. Cost me a pretty penny for that shoe. If it wasn't for your ma harping on me, you maybe never would've got it." He tapped the bottle. "She could harp; I'll give her that. She sure could harp."

Tears welled in Junior's eyes. "Ma was good to you, Pa. She was good to me, too, before she died. She was always taking care of us and worryin' about us."

"Yeah, yeah, yeah."

"It's true, Pa. You can't say it ain't."

Senior tapped a Camel from the pack, lit it, tossed the match on the floor, took a deep drag and blew an angry plume of smoke into the air. He scowled. "I know, I know."

"All the same, I miss my ma." He wiped his eyes.

Senior looked up with an icy glare. "Cut it out, will you, you're breaking my heart. Go wan now, beat it. I don't need your sorry face to make me feel worse'n I already do." He blew another stream of blue smoke into the air. "If you're hungry, there's some baloney left in the ice box."

Junior clumped away from the table.

"Just make sure you get your ass out of bed early tomorrow. Hit the streets and hustle. You hear what I said?" he growled over his shoulder. "Hustle!"

Two days later I saw Junior climbing slowly up the stairs, his shoeshine box slung over his shoulder. When he stepped into the apartment, I could see the dried blood around his nose and mouth. Senior was stretched out on the couch, staring at the ceiling and smoking a cigarette.

"So how'd you do today, kid? Made some good dough, I hope." When Junior didn't answer, he lifted his head. "What the hell—!" He sat up. "'What happened to *you?* "

"They stole my money, Pa. All of it. Nearly two bucks, Pa."

"Who did? Who stole your dough?"

"They beat me up, Pa. I got down to Allen Street and set up on the corner in front of Dambach's Drug Store. That's when they came along. Three of them. They said it was their corner and I had to get out. When I told them they didn't own it they jumped me, Pa. I tried to fight them off, Pa, but they were too many."

"Goddamned punks." He sprang to his feet. "Come on," he barked, "let's go get them little bastards."

They left the building and went around the corner and half way down Potomac Avenue to where senior's beat up old Hudson stood at the curb.

"Now if this piece of junk starts...." He listened to the starter grind until the engine fired up and blew a puff of black smoke out the tailpipe. "What do you know...Old Faithful does it again," he said, both of them jerking and bouncing in their seats as the car lurched away from the curb and puttered down the street.

That was the last I heard before they disappeared around the corner. It wasn't until later that day when they returned home that I learned what happened.

"Good thing I didn't get my hands on 'em. I'da busted their faces good. Goddamned punks. Nobody's beating up my kid. Only I got that privilege."

"I never saw them, either, before they just showed up and made a circle around me. I didn't mean to upset you, Pa."

"I know, kid, you're okay. Don't pay no attention to me when I get on your case. Sometimes I can't stand myself so I take it out on you," he said, patting his son's back. Senior eased himself down in his chair, groaning. "Goddamned lumbago is killing me. Go get me a beer and a shot of whiskey," he said, lighting up a cigarette.

Junior left to get his father's drink.

"Never should've been lifting them heavy kegs down at the brewery. They ordered me to do it, even though it wasn't my damn job. As soon's I got hurt, they laid me off. Imagine that? Just like that," he said, snapping his fingers. "After all that time working there, loyal as can be. Like I was nothing. I told them my back would be okay in a week or two, but did they care? They didn't give a shit, the lousy bums." He screwed his face up and twisted sideways, rubbing his back.

"I can't be laid up too much longer like this. It's already been over a month. All's I know is I have to get some lighter work. Once I land something, I won't need to be depending on you to keep us going." He took a last drag on his cigarette, snuffed it out in the ash tray and let out a deep sigh.

Junior came back with his drink.

Senior poured the whiskey down his throat and followed it with a long swig of beer. He smacked his lips. "Got it all, huh, those punks? Every last dime?"

Junior lowered his head. "Yes, Pa, after they got me on the ground. But I gave one of them a good sock. I saw blood come out of his nose."

"Good. Too bad you couldn't use that foot of yours to club their heads." He pointed. "There's a bottle of Coke left in the kitchen. Go get it and while you're there, get me another shot," he said, handing him the glass. "Make it a double. And don't forget to get the two cents deposit on your bottle next time you go to the store."

Junior left and came back with the drinks and a book.

"What're you reading there?" he asked, pouring the double shot down his throat and taking a long slug of beer.

"I got it at the library, Pa. It's called 'Huckleberry Finn.' Supposed to be good."

"Yeah, it's that kid saving his nigger slave on a raft in the Mississippi River. They made a movie about it not too long ago."

"Pa, it's Negro, not the other word."

"So what's wrong with the word, huh? My old lady was a Mexican. How many times did I hear her called a Spic. 'Go on back to Mexico, you Spic.' And that lady downstairs who took a boat back to Italy with her kids. I heard somebody say it's good those dagos are gone. Maybe she heard herself called that too many times and couldn't take the name-calling anymore. Who knows?

"Listen, kid, everybody's got a name, so what? Lee, too, with the laundry shop down the street. Everybody calls him a Chink. They're just names, lousy names, sure, but it don't mean nothing. Everybody pins one on everybody else, so everybody's in the same boat. We're all even. Ever hear the words, 'sticks and stones will break my bones, but names will never hurt me'?"

"I know, Pa, but just the same—"

"Get used to it, kid. That's the way the world is, if you're a Kraut, Kike, Pollack or anything else. Just don't say those names to nobody's face unless you want a busted nose." He sagged back and closed his eyes. "My damn back's still murdering me. Get me another shot, will ya?"

Junior called from the kitchen. "The bottle's almost empty, Pa."

"All right, then bring what's left. Might as well polish it off." He took a long swallow of beer and belched.

Junior sat across from his father. "Pa?"

"Yeah?"

"Why don't you like my Ma? She's dead now, so you can tell me."

"How old are you, kid? Ten? Eleven?"

"Thirteen, Pa, going on fourteen next month."

"Maybe you're old enough to understand. Maybe not."

"I think I am, Pa. I hear things." He took a swig of his Coke.

Senior started to slur his words. "Well, kid, it's like this. I didn't love your ma. She was a good woman all right, but I didn't love her, not at first, anyway."

"Then why'd you marry her, Pa?"

"Why did I marry her? Why? Is that what you're asking me? Why?"

"Yes, Pa, why did you marry her?"

"Because of you, that's why."

"Me?"

"I had to marry her. Get it? It's one of them things that happen. You know what I'm talking about?" he asked, his voice husky, his eyes blurry.

"I think I do, Pa."

"So that's the story. Satisfied now?"

"But, Pa, I always remember her being good to you, waiting

on you, hand and foot."

"Yeah, yeah, I ain't faulting her for that. She was a good enough wife, more than I gave her credit for."

"Then what, Pa? What?"

His pa tilted the whiskey bottle up and drained it into his mouth. "Ahhh," he breathed out and smacked his lips. "Truth be known, kid, back then I thought I loved somebody else. A girl named Gladys. But I did what a lot of guys did back then, I cheated. Cheated with your ma. I was seeing her on the side. Of course she didn't know about Gladys, and when your ma told me a couple of months later she was pregnant, what could I do? She had a crazy old man who would've put a shotgun to my head if I didn't get hitched, so I married her. I had to marry her. Get it? *Had* to!"

"And you're sorry about that."

"In the beginning, yeah, I was bitter. I blamed her for my lousy life. I thought I could've been somebody with a different life, a better one with Gladys. Then I found out Gladys was cheating on *me*. How do you like that? Gladys cheating on me, the guy she said she loved! Anyway, your ma found out about Gladys and me, but it didn't make any difference. She was carrying you and I was responsible. Besides, your ma loved me and never cheated on me." He drained the beer bottle, laid it on its side and gave it a spin. "Of course, by then I was done with Gladys, so here we are. You and me, kid. For better or worse, we're stuck with each other. Mostly worse, I think."

"So what do we do now, Pa? You want me to go away?"

Senior scoffed. "You go away? Where to? With what dough? Naw, that won't work. Besides, I need you as much as you need me. Like I said, we're stuck with each other."

"I'm sorry, Pa."

"No sorrier than me, kid," he said, picking up the empty beer bottle, peering with one eye down inside the neck, and standing it up.

"So what're we gonna do, Pa?"

His pa's eyelids drooped. "Maybe we'll get lucky somehow and get a break. I'm way overdue. Anyway, I'll think of something, kid," he muttered hoarsely through a yawn. "Something."

Chapter 37

I mustn't forget to mention one of my favorite tenants, Marjorie Simmons, a long-term tenant who was here longer than almost everyone else. Despite that, she never developed anything more than a casual relationship with anyone in the building. Marjorie was a shapely lady, who wore a blond wig that went well with her blue eyes that flashed whenever she looked at anyone. When she laughed, the deep lines etched in her face multiplied and made her look much older than the probable fifty years she was.

Marjorie greeted everyone she passed with a bright smile and a cheery 'good morning' or 'good afternoon,' whatever the time of the day happened to be. And she'd always say, 'Isn't it a beautiful day to be alive?' There could be a blizzard raging outside and she'd still say, 'Isn't it a beautiful day to be alive?'

At first, newcomers viewed her skeptically, but they soon got used to her pleasantries and responded with broad smiles of their own. She lifted everyone's spirits. Huggs especially loved her because whenever she passed him, she'd always tweak his cheek, brush his unruly hair with her fingertips and quietly purr in his ear, 'And how are you today, you handsome brute?' which turned Huggs's beaming face five shades of red. Whenever he bumped into her in the hall or on the stairs, he'd ask if she needed a favor. On the rare occasion she'd take him up on his offer, he'd do it with such fervor you'd think he won the Irish

Sweepstakes. There was absolutely nothing he wouldn't do for her. I believe Hugs, in his own innocent way, was in love with her, if for no other reason than that she treated him with respect and affection.

Any time Marjorie would see little Rosie sitting on the steps, she never failed to stop and talk to her. Even though Rosie was blind, she knew when Marjorie was near by the smell of a special perfume she always sprayed on herself generously, even if she wasn't going out. The first thing Marjorie would do is ask about Rosie's health and that of her doll, Shirley. She must have realized by Lizzie's cough that she was a sick woman and never mentioned her. Invariably, Marjorie always had a story to tell about a mythological sprite named Pixianna who, like Rosie, couldn't see, and was forever getting into mischief while helping out people. One afternoon I happened to overhear Marjorie talking to Rosie.

"Will you tell me another story about Pixianna, Miss Marjorie? Please?"

"I guess I have a little time, especially for you, Rosie" Marjorie said, tucking her skirt under her and sitting down on the top step beside Rosie. "Let me see…" she said, tapping her cheek with one of her long, red fingernails. "You remember, Rosie, Pixianna had no sight."

"I remember, Miss Marjorie. She was blind like me, I know."

"Good, Rosie…. Well, it was another one of those fine summer days for picking flowers, and you remember how Pixianna loved picking flowers for the house she lived in with her granny."

"Yes, I remember that, too, Miss Marjorie. Please go on."

"All right" she said, patting Rosie's head. "On this particularly sunny day, Pixianna was walking very carefully along a country stream near her house, bending low and delicately feeling with her hands for daisies she would pluck and carry home to her granny because her granny especially loved daisies. Granny would put them in cups and glasses and place them around the room and say, 'Flowers are the way you bring sunshine into the house.'

"Pleasing her granny made Pixianna very happy, and she never hesitated to do it. Being sightless never stopped her from doing what she wanted to do, either, because she never felt sorry for herself."

"Mommy always says happiness is found with our heart, not with our eyes."

Marjorie squeezed Rosie's shoulder. "Your mommy is very wise. Anyway, on this warm sunny day, while Pixianna was collecting her daisies, she heard what sounded like a cry, a cry for help. She listened a moment, then, stooping carefully, she waded through the weeds and wild flowers crowding the bank of the stream, her hands searching for the source of the sound. Suddenly she stopped when her hand rubbed against a very smooth, cool object."

"Get your hand off my face, please, and be careful or you'll knock my crown off." His voice was a soft and sad croaking sound, but Pixianna understood him quite well."

"Who are you," she asked. "And why are you down so close to the ground. Are you a leprechaun?"

"Of course not! Can't you see? I'm a frog. But not really a frog. I drank a potion that turned me into a frog or a toad, I can't be sure which. They all look alike to me. I'm really a prince, Prince Lawrence, but you can call me Prince Larry, if you like."

"Oh, my," Pixianna said, fingering the chain around his neck. "Who put this on you, Prince Larry?"

"The Wicked Master of the Castle. The castle that sits on the tallest hill beyond the stream."

"Why would the Wicked Master of the Castle do that to you, Prince Larry?"

"Jealousy. Just plain, simple jealousy. He loves my beautiful Princess Starla, who he kidnapped and has imprisoned in his castle dungeon."

"That is terrible, Prince Larry. Is there some way I can help you?"

"Yes, you—by the way, what's your name?"

"Pixianna."

"An odd name, but a pretty name for such a pretty girl with eyes as blue as the sky, and hair, golden like the sun."

"Thank you, Prince Larry. But how did this happen? Why are you chained to a rock?"

"I was tricked by the Wicked Master of the Castle, that's how. I received a message saying my princess had lost her way in the forest and was found and safely waiting for me at the castle. Relieved, I immediately set out to get her. At the time I arrived, I didn't know the Master is guarded by three slaves: Snidely, who is really a snake, Ratonio, who is really a rat, and Spidalda, who is really a spider. I found out too late that the Wicked Master of the Castle is really Bullko, a bullfrog."

"I think I understand, Prince Larry. The Wicked Master of the Castle has changed you into what he was, a bullfrog, and he became you, a prince."

"That's right, Pixianna. You are very smart. But he didn't take my crown because he already had a bigger and better one fashioned for himself."

"But how did he change places with you, Prince Larry?

How could he make that happen?"

"It was easy for him. I was thirsty when I arrived to inquire about my beautiful princess and to take her home. The Wicked Master told me to pour a drink for myself while he fetched her."

"But it wasn't water, was it?"

"You're right again, Pixianna. It wasn't water. It was a magic potion that immediately turned me into a bullfrog. He was able to finish the glass by licking it up and it turned him into a real prince— me."

"And you couldn't do anything about it."

"No, because now he had hands and I didn't."

"Well, couldn't you see he was a bullfrog and not a person when you met him?"

"No. You see, Pixianna, anyone who steps into the castle is sprinkled with a powder that falls from a chandelier that hangs above the door. The powder, which looks like gold dust, casts a spell that makes the Wicked Master and his slaves look like real people. That's why he makes you pour your own drink, because he is really a bullfrog without hands or fingers to open bottles. He only looks like a real person."

Pixianna coiled her yellow braid around her finger as she listened to the prince tell his story. "I would love to help you, Prince Larry. I will if you can you tell me how?"

Prince Larry looked around and whispered, "I need the antidote to turn me back to my real self. It is difficult to get the antidote because it's guarded by thousands of jealous bees that sting anyone who dares venture near their hives."

"So it's honey you need?"

"Not just any honey. It's a special honey from the hives of the butterbee, a cross between a butterfly and the giant honey bee. They are very beautiful with large, colorful wings. They're also quite mean, and attack with long stingers when anyone threatens their hives. The honey is not only hard to get; it is scarce, as well. People who are lucky to find and gather it use it for its magical healing powers."

"I know—"

"There are also two other necessary ingredients needed to make it work for me. I can tell you where to get them, too."

Pixianna beamed. "I wouldn't have to find a butterbee hive, Prince Larry, because I know exactly what it is. My granny has a jar with a little of that same honey left in our cupboard. My grampa brought it home a long time ago before he died. Granny uses it sparingly and only when her lumbago hurts too much. I would have to sneak it out. If Granny catches me, she will be very angry and punish me."

"Oh, Pixianna, I wouldn't want you to get punished, but if you only could get it for me, I would be so grateful, and so would my Princess Starla. I must warn you, though, there's one more danger you would face, a danger so great you could—"

A scream and a sudden ruckus drew my attention quickly away to see what was happening on my first floor, where a middle-aged woman ran into the arms of Joe, who came rushing out of his restaurant to investigate.

"He tried to molest me!" she cried, pointing to Huggs, who was shuffling back with his hands raised and shaking his head from side to side. "That monster wrapped his arms around me and tried to drag me away."

"Lady, lady," Joe said, trying to peel her off of him, "it's OK, nothing to…"

And that was it. Another case of Huggs being misunderstood by someone new to the premises. By the time the incident was over, Marjorie and Rosie were both gone.

Like so many others before him, Gustav was taken aback when Marjorie first addressed him by name, but soon he, too, succumbed to her charm and friendliness. After learning Boris, the hurdy-gurdy man, was robbed and living in misery, Marjorie avoided seeing him but made it a point to see that a bag of groceries was anonymously delivered to his apartment every week.

Although she was somewhat aloof, everyone enjoyed seeing her because she was so uplifting and likable whenever she was near. To everyone, she was seen as a 'ray of sunshine' among them. Only Alice Wagman and her sister Agnes had reservations.

"Can you imagine, Agnes, the nerve of that woman turning us down when we invited her to have dinner with us? After all the planning we did. That's the last time I'll take anything for granted or feel sorry for anyone just because they live alone."

"Yes, Alice, and I understand why you feel that way. I do, too, especially after she accepted an invitation from the widow, Lilly. You know, Lilly, the one with the niece from Oregon?"

"You don't have to remind me who she is, Agnes. I'm not senile yet. Of course I know her; after all, she's lived here as long as we have. And I won't forget Lilly standing in the hallway and telling that clown-face she was glad she could join her for dinner."

"Alice, it's not very charitable of us to think badly of… what's-her-name, Marjorie… and I really don't think we should hold a grudge against her, either. She may have had her reasons for being there, like maybe Lilly was repaying her for doing a favor. Anyway, it's not helpful to either of us."

"Perhaps not, Agnes, but to occasionally hold a grudge, right or wrong, simply feels good. And Agnes, for heaven's sake, please, don't ever say, 'like maybe.'"

I never knew any more about Marjorie, either, because she was very private. If I listened carefully, I could hear her radio playing quietly until late at night. She never had visitors and received very little mail. Buried in the fleshy middle finger of her right hand was a ring, which I guessed was originally her wedding ring. The setting was shaped like a small heart encrusted with what I took to be tiny diamonds.

Marjorie was as mysterious as she was cheerful and outgoing. Every Saturday evening after dark, I'd see her quietly close her apartment door, glance around and move quickly away. Even in the semidarkness of the hall, I could see she was dressed rather gaudily with lacy sleeves, garish earrings and high heels. Her makeup looked as if it was troweled on like white frosting on a cake, filling in and smoothing over the deep lines of her face, which was rouged, and accented with a deep, red lipstick. As often as not she wore a hat with a dark veil.

Where she was off to, I could only guess by her condition when she returned home, usually in the early morning hours. She always came in a bit disheveled on wobbly high heels, pausing to take them off and carry them by their straps as she grasped the banister with her other hand and pulled herself up the staircase one step at a time. No doubt she had been drinking. If she happened to pass anyone on her way out or in, she ducked her head, hoping to avoid being recognized. Of course, the next day, unbeknownst to her—or as she may have guessed— speculations over her secretive comings and goings were rampant.

This routine went on for almost a year, during which time I learned Marjorie had once been a dancer at McVan's Night Club on Niagara Street. I often heard her singing quietly in her apartment, so I assume she must have also been a singer, although being a chain- smoker took care of any sweetness her

271

voice might have had. A red scar traveled under her chin and a small one stayed hidden with makeup near her right temple. How she got them I never knew, but I suspected she must have been out with some pretty rough characters in her time.

A week or more passed before my tenants noticed they hadn't seen Marjorie. Little Rosie was the first to sound the alarm. Concerned, Joe called Mrs. Chapman, the landlady, to explain the problem of Marjorie missing, and asked if she'd come and open Marjorie's door. Speculation had it that Marjorie was dead inside her apartment, the way Catherine would have been found dead, if not for Sheila Graham's screams and the quick actions of Huggs, who saved her life in the nick of time. Mrs. Chapman rushed over and opened the door with her master key, only to find the apartment empty. The house was in order, and her bed hadn't been slept in. By then all kinds of rumors were flying and Huggs was beside himself with worrying and pacing the basement floor.

A few days later two detectives visited the premises. They interviewed Joe and a few others in Joe's restaurant. When Mrs. Chapman arrived she identified herself and sat at the table with the two men, who introduced themselves as Detectives Osborne and McClusky.

Osborne held out a heart-shaped ring. "Do you recognize this?"

Mrs. Chapman studied it a moment and shook her head. "No, I don't."

Huggs, who had been standing near the door, leaped forward, his green eyes bulging. "That's Miss Marjorie's ring!" he cried. "I seen it lots of times. Did she lose it someplace?"

Mrs. Chapman spoke up. "Huggs would know," she said. "Is something wrong, detective?"

Osborne cocked his head to his partner. "Tell them,

McClusky."

McClusky, the taller and huskier of the two, spoke in monotone, his voice flat. "Marjorie Simmons is dead."

Osborne bounced the ring in the palm of his hand. "Had a heck of a time getting it off," he said, slipping it into his pocket. "Had to cut the band."

Huggs let out a small moan.

Osborne's small eyes darted from one face the other. "Anybody familiar with any of her friends?"

They shook their heads.

"Anybody know anyone she was associated with, relatives, old boyfriends, anybody at all?"

Again they shook their heads.

"Anybody know of any enemies she might have had?"

They all looked at each other and shook their heads again.

"What happened to her, detective?" Mrs. Chapman asked.

"We fished her out of an eddy in the Niagara; no identification except for the ring. Actually, some bum rummaging in a trash can nearby spotted her body first. Maybe just time, too. She could've drifted out and been washed over the falls. She could've disappeared forever."

Huggs trembled, listening to the conversation.

Joe piped up. "If she didn't have no identification, how'd you know she lived here?"

"She had a swizzle stick in her pocket with the name of one of the gin mills she'd been in. When we investigated, everybody played dumb or didn't know anything, except for one boozy hag who remembered her and called her a flirty barfly. After a couple of drinks loosened her tongue and a few bucks under the table, she tipped us off on where she thought she lived. So now you know how we got here and why."

Joe spoke up. "Did she commit suicide?"

"Only if she could've stuck a knife in her own back. Her underclothes were gone, so it looks like a rape job on top of murder. Apparently the guy wasn't interested in jewelry. More likely he got scared off or found it impossible to get the ring off her finger."

Huggs dropped into a chair at a table, groaning.

McClusky poked his thumb toward Huggs, sobbing quietly. "What is it with him?"

"He was her close friend," Joe said.

McClusky slumped back in his chair. "Must've been a pretty damn close friend."

And that was that. A notice ran in the newspaper for a week asking any relative or friend to come forward with information regarding the deceased, but no one responded. Marjorie died the way she lived, mysteriously and alone. Nothing was found in her room that gave any useful information about her life. It was a sad ending to a deceptively happy woman's life. It seemed to me that, for all her winning ways, Marjorie harbored one grievous fault: she searched for love in all the wrong places.

The city buried her in a cemetery plot for the indigent. A small, flat stone marker was paid for by Mrs. Chapman and placed by a hired man. There was no funeral or church service. The relentless spell of rainy weather and thick, gray fog reflected the somber mood of the event. Under the drumming rain on his black umbrella, a local minister prayed in his sonorous voice over Marjorie's soggy grave. Gathered around him and also protected from the rain spilling like veils of tears over the edges of their noisy umbrellas, stood a small party, including Joe, Lilly, Gustav, and the Wagman sisters, who huddled together under one umbrella and jumped together with every startling clap of thunder.

After the final words and prayers were said, the cluster of black umbrellas separated and the mourners left the reserved corner of Pine Ridge Cemetery quietly with bowed heads and a few sniffles. They returned to Joe's restaurant for a funeral breakfast paid for by Mrs. Chapman and Joe. Only Huggs was absent.

Shortly after noon I saw Huggs come in through the front door, his head and clothes soaked. He stopped to take off his muddy shoes and, carrying them dripping, rushed into the basement, where he flung himself on his cot with his mud-stained pants. I could see his chest heaving and his hollow, crimson-ringed eyes staring up at the ceiling.

As I did with everyone else, I read his thoughts and realized he'd just come back from visiting Marjorie's gravesite. He'd gone by himself later that morning after everyone had left and knelt on the saturated ground beside her flat stone, chiseled with only her name and date of death over the image of a crucifix.

From a wool sack slung from his belt, he took a small statuette of the Virgin Mary with her arms outstretched, palms facing up. He buried her feet in the wet soil at the head of the marker, gathered a few muddy stones and patted them smooth around the base. Glued across the Virgin's hands was a narrow strip of painted wood, with Huggs' words printed in black paint:
REST IN PEASE LOVE HUGGS.

Chapter 38

I turned my attention to Chester Webb's apartment when I heard Junior Webb's club foot echoing off the stairs.

"I'm home, Pa."

"I got ears," senior said, squatting at the kitchen table with a big book opened before him.

"Watcha reading, Pa?"

"Something."

"Like what, Pa, if you don't mind my asking?"

"Like an escape plan."

"I don't getcha."

Senior looked up. "How'd you like to ditch this place?"

"I don't know, Pa. The people here are real nice. I like them. I like them a lot."

"Yeah, we'll there's nice people everyplace, if you're lucky enough to find them."

"But not so much like the lady who lives with her sister. The one everybody calls Miss Alice and who I run errands for sometimes. She's calls me honeybunch almost every time she sees me and always says I should study hard in school. I think she must be a school teacher."

"She ain't no teacher. She's a libary lady."

"How do you know, Pa?"

"'Cause I saw her in the libary a couple of days ago. She helped me find what I was looking for."

"You in the library, Pa? Downtown? What for?"

Senior sat back. "Come here."

Junior came up beside him.

"You got big eyes like your ma, so tell me what you see there?" he asked, pointing to the open book on the table.

"Looks like the kind of maps they show us in school, except this one's got a lot of curvy lines on it."

"Like they show you in school, right. That's why I went to the libary. They look like ordinary school maps, but these are different."

"How do you mean, Pa?" he asked, looking over the page. "I see Phoenix on it, and I know that's the capital of Arizona."

"I guess they do teach you something in school these days."

"Are we moving there? I read it's pretty hot in the summer."

"Naw, this ain't no map for traveling to get there to live or nothing like that."

"Well, it's a geography map with all the cities on it."

"It only looks that way to you 'cause you're a kid and don't know nothing else. Don't you see them swirly lines and the mountains? C'm'ere and sit down next to me."

"Sure, Pa," Junior said, pulling up a chair. He had a worried look on his face. "You ain't going away to live in the mountains by yourself and leave me here alone, are you, Pa?"

Senior lit a cigarette. "Look, kid, I know I've been a skunk of an old man to you, 'specially when I get drunk, but no, I ain't that much of a skunk. And I want you to know I'm changing my life. You notice no beer bottles in the sink?"

Junior glanced around. "You quitting drinking, Pa?"

"That's right, I'm swearing off the stuff. I'm sick of being a shit heel like I been all my life. I was listening to a program on the radio and some guy—a minister, I think—he was talking about how too many people today don't have no self-respect, only he called it by a different word— esteem. That hit home hard, real hard, 'cause everything he said was exactly what my life is like, a rotten mess from top to bottom. It made me think I ain't got no esteem, and like he said, I don't have to keep living like this, like a useless bum laying around sucking up beer and smoking cigarettes while his kid is out there scrounging for pennies."

"Gee whiz, Pa, you ain't so bad as you make it sound."

"Don't counter dict me. I know what I'm talking about. Let's face it, I'm a piece of crap and I been one for a long time." He flicked his ashes on the floor. "Take a good look at this mug, kid," he said, tweaking his cheek, "because you're going to see a different one from now on, a better one, one you won't have to be ashamed of."

"I never been—"

"I said don't counter dict me and listen!"

Junior relaxed. "So what's up, then, Pa? What's different with this map?"

Senior took a long drag on his cigarette. "I'll tell you, kid, while you been in school studying, I been doing a little studying myself."

Junior turned a blank face to his father.

"Surprised you, huh? Me, your old man, studying?"

Junior nodded.

Senior blew out a plume of smoke. "Well, it's like this, I made up my mind. We're scramming out of here in a couple of days, see? After I take care of some last minute business."

"How about school, Pa? It ain't finished yet."

"Don't worry about it. You can start someplace else. I told you we're beating it and we are. Two, three days at most."

"Are we going to Phoenix?"

"I told you it ain't that kind of map."

"Then what, Pa? What kind of map is it?"

"You don't get it yet, huh? For your information, kid, it's a treasure map."

"A treasure map? You mean like a treasure somebody buried? In those mountains you just mentioned?"

"Yeah, but that somebody ain't a pirate or a crook."

"Then what, Pa?"

Senior snuffed out his cigarette in the ashtray. "We're going prospecting."

"Prospecting?" Junior asked excitedly. "You mean it, Pa, prospecting? Like I hear sometimes on the Lone Ranger radio show, when guys go digging for gold and crooks try to take it from them, but then the Lone Ranger comes in with Tonto and saves them?"

"Got your attention, huh?"

"But how we going to do it, Pa? You said we're broke."

"I lied, kid. I got a nest egg, not a big one, for sure, but enough to get us out west and started with a little place to live.

279

A shack's all we can afford and gonna need at first. We gotta stake a claim after I study up a bit and find out how to do it. Must be some spots the big mining companies figure they already picked clean and went elsewhere, but there oughta be enough left over for us to scratch a decent living from. There's gotta be. And it oughta be cheap to get second-hand shovels, a couple of pick axes and pans we're gonna need. If we're lucky, maybe we'll hit a silver vein or if were extra lucky, even a gold one. We're gonna make our fortune, kid. I can feel it in my bones."

"And all this time I thought we were dead broke, Pa?"

"Yeah, we'll you thought wrong. It ain't that bad. I still got some of the dough from your ma's insurance policy and a few bucks more I stashed away for an emergency or a rainy day." He held his palms out, looked up and laughed. "Look, kid, I think it's raining silver dollars already." They both laughed.

About a week later, Chester and his boy packed their meager belongings and headed downstairs to his old Hudson parked outside next to the curb. On the way down they bumped into Alice Wagman and her sister Agnes coming in the front door. Agnes was carrying a bag of groceries in her arm.

"Mr. Webb," Alice exclaimed, pointing to his luggage, "are you and your son going on vacation?"

Senior answered, "No, ma'am, we're moving out, permanent."

"Moving out? Oh, no! Did you hear that, Agnes? They're moving out."

"I did, Alice, I did," she said, shifting the bag of groceries to her other arm.

"Are you moving far?" Alice asked, clasping her hands. "Will we see you again, soon I hope?"

"Afraid not," senior said. "Like somebody said, 'Go west, young man, go west.' We'll, we're taking his advice and we're going west."

Junior piped up, "We'll be prospecting for gold, Miss Alice. Pa says we're going to get rich."

"Don't count your chickens and give us bad luck, kid," senior interrupted, poking Junior's shoulder to move him along.

"Oh, my," Alice said, her face drooping. "So that's why you wanted those special books in the library, Mr. Webb."

"We're starting a new life, the kid and me. And no snow, neither, where we're going. Just warm sunshine."

"Well, honeybunch, you're a very intelligent young man and I truly hope you continue with your schooling," Alice said, touching a corner of her eye and patting Junior's shoulder. "A good education is very important, no matter how rich you are."

"You told me that lots of times, Miss Alice, so I can't never forget it. I'll study hard, I promise."

"And will you please write to me and let me know how you two are doing?" she pleaded, planting a kiss on Junior's forehead.

"Come on, kid, let's get moving. We got to make time."

"I'll write you, Miss Alice," Junior called over his shoulder as senior pushed him out the door, "as soon as I can."

I heard the starter grinding and Chester begging Old Faithful to start before the Hudson backfired a couple of times before finally firing up and jerking away from the curb.

Chapter 39

So, dear reader, here I'll draw a close to my tenant tales, except for a few that were left incomplete, which I will now relate to you. I must jump ahead a few years, just after the end of WWII. Here's the first:

At the end of August 1946, a letter addressed to Miss Alice Wagman, postmarked a small town in Arizona, arrived from Chester Webb, Junior.

"Will you look at this," Alice said, stroking Kitty on her lap while speaking to the photograph of her recently deceased sister on the table beside her. "Finally, after all this time, Agnes,— what, almost two, three years?— another letter from Honeybunch. He and his father weren't faring so well, the last time we heard from him. I hope they're doing better now." She picked up her nail file and sliced open the envelope. "I'm so excited," she said, unfolding the letter and beginning to read aloud:

Dear Miss Alice,

I hope you and your sister still live there and this letter gets to you. I know it has been a long time since I wrote to you and I want to apologize. I guess we didn't get any letters from you in a long while, either, because we had to move around to different places and lost touch. I think I told you in one of my letters that not too long after we got here, Pa staked almost every last penny we had, which wasn't much, to buy up a dozen claims because they were dirt cheap. In fact, they were almost free. That's because everybody and his uncle except us knew the land was petered out and was nothing but worthless dirt no good for gold nor crops nor cattle grazing.

Even though we found that out too late, nothing could discourage Pa, not one bit, especially when he makes his mind up about something. Day after day we did an awful lot of backbreaking digging from one mine to another, and sometimes panning for gold in the Gila River, which ran through the heart of two of our claims. No matter how hard we tried, though, mother nature was stingy and hardly gave us anything at all for our efforts except calluses and sore backs and skin burnt raw from the sun. After a couple of months of sweating and 'bustin' a gut,' as Pa called it, we had to give it up and take jobs on local farms just to keep from starving to death. It was just as hard work plowing land and pitching hay, but at least it gave us a bunkhouse to sleep in and enough vittles to keep us a little more than barely alive. It put some pretty good muscles on my body, too, which is now six feet tall.

In the meantime, Miss Alice, I kept going to school as much as possible and you'll be happy to know that I got good grades all the way through my senior year. One of my teachers told me I was a 'quick study,' although I didn't know what that meant at the time. I guess I should tell you, too, I was elected class president and will give the valedictory speech when I graduate next month when I'm almost eighteen years old. I've already enrolled in college with the hopes of becoming a mining engineer. If it wasn't for you, Miss Alice, always telling me to study hard, it never would have happened, so I thank you very much for your advice and confidence in me. It paid off pretty good.

Before we left Buffalo, Pa said he felt it in his bones we'd be lucky prospecting. Well, things didn't quite work out that way, and at first, as I said, it was rough going for us, but Pa never gave up, although sometimes when he was feeling low, he talked about us heading back to Buffalo and getting a job at Bethlehem Steel. He said at least there in Buffalo, even though he hates winter, in the summer he could get those delicious crabs and clams he used to order at Santasiero's and misses so much. I even remember it myself, how on those warm nights the sweet smell of the clam stands along Niagara Street made you hungry for them. One thing I don't miss, though, are those sand flies swirling around the street lights and landing everywhere.

Anyway, Miss Alice, about the time we were on our last legs and running out of steam working in the fields and cleaning stables and such, Pa got a visit from a couple of bigwigs wearing suits and ties and white Stetson hats, you know, like those ten-gallon cowboy hats you see Hopalong Cassidy and Gene Autry wear in Western movies? Well, they said they needed the land to run their railroad tracks through, and it so happens that the heart of our claims stood right smack in the way. Of course, Pa, being no fool, put up a good front and tried to make the men believe our property was worth a fortune. I don't think he fooled those railroad sharpies much, but still, in the end, they came up with more money than we ever saw in our lives. There's no doubt Pa was lucky all right, but in a way he never expected.

I sure wish you could see me right now sitting on the veranda of our very own country house which sits on 5000 acres of land, which we call the Double 'V' Ranch because that's what the 'W' in our name looks like. Pa leases 2000 acres of it for farming, and keeps 3000 acres for our herd of cattle. We got contracts with the U.S. army for much of our beef, which Pa says has already brought in enough money to keep us afloat for as long as we're alive. Our house is big enough to fit at least twenty people, and we have stables out back, where I keep my very own horse. He's a beautiful palomino with a gold coat and silver mane. I named him King because he holds his head so high and proud.

At this very moment, Pa is sitting in his rocker across from me, looking out over God's country, as he calls it, watching our cowhands work the cattle while he slurps a gallon of lemonade, which our housekeeper, Bonita, makes for him every day. The best news is that Pa never went back to drinking. He quit smoking cigarettes a while back, too, and instead chews tobacco now, which is an improvement, I guess, although I can say it's kind of disgusting seeing him squirting the brown juice out between his lips anywhere he pleases every few minutes. Ever since we shoveled enough dirt on that worthless land of ours to fill Lake Erie, Pa's back and one leg have been giving him more trouble than ever, but he still manages to hobble around as best he can. Because he's still pretty young, he's kind of embarrassed by his limp, so he tells people he got shot while fighting in a range war.

Lined with big cottonwood trees, Cottonwood Creek runs sparkling past our property right down from the mountains and is mighty pretty to see. The sky is always deep blue here with red-tailed hawks circling overhead almost anytime you look up. The air is fresh and clean, too, with the wind carrying the chirping of birds and lowing cattle, and blowing the sweet smells of wild flowers and damp, fresh-plowed earth along between the mountains through the valley and over the land.

As for me, personally, Miss. Alice, I have a girlfriend I'm really happy with. She's half Pima Indian and half Mexican, very smart and cute, too, with her black hair and white teeth. Her only drawback I can see is she hates shoes and always goes barefoot. Her name is Nina and she calls me Puma because she says my eyes are big like the eyes of the puma cats that roam these hills and sometimes take one of our stock. We spend lots of time sitting around campfires at night under the stars, listening to some of the hands strum those sad Mexican songs on their guitars. Nina and me talked about getting engaged next year, but not married until I finish college.

And that's the news up to now, Miss Alice. I would like to add one last thing. If you ever want to take a vacation out west, or ever want to live here permanently, you are always welcome to stay at our ranch. We have tons of room and would love to see you again. Pa said it's OK with him, too. You and your sister will be our honored guests.

Oh, I almost forgot some good news. Six months ago I had an operation on my lower leg. The doctors in Phoenix did something with my leg bones to make them more even. It was an experiment they weren't sure would work, but it did. It was painful and I was laid up a few months, but it was worth every minute of it. I don't have a club foot anymore and I walk almost as normal as anybody else. I won't tell you how much the operation cost.

I think I can say love,

Chester Webb Jr.

P.S. I hope I didn't make too many mistakes in this letter.

Alice caressed the letter a moment, then set it aside. She picked her sister's picture up off the table and said, "You know, Agnes, you and I might just take Honeybunch up on his offer when I retire next year." She set the picture back and massaged her kitten's ears. "I think a change of scenery and climate would do us all good, don't you, Kitty?"

Chapter 40

Grace came straight home after her last class of the day, picked up her mail and hurried upstairs to her apartment. She laid her books on the table and sat down, separating the several letters. She knew the familiar, blue V- mail envelope with the tiny writing was from Michael, another one of many she would store away in a cardboard box she kept in her closet. It always comforted her to hear from him because it let her know he was fine. After several years in the military, he had risen to the rank of technical sergeant. The letter was dated April 26, 1944. She read it aloud.

'Dear Grace

I'm sorry to say I haven't been writing in a while because they got us humping pretty good these days. It seems we just turn in when the darn bugler is blowing reveille for us to get up and shine. It's hard to shine when your bones are aching like a son of a gun. I'm sorry too that this letter will be a short one not like the other ones that were a lot longer. By the time we get through the day with our regular duties and an officer in charge is on your back who don't have no mercy, then shower and eat, well, there ain't much time left over especially when your dead tired. We shoot the bull the other guys and me about what we're gonna do when this damn war is over and I'll tell you, the first thing I'm going to do is sleep in bed for a week without getting up just to try to catch up. Lately they've been driving us pretty hard. We think something pretty big is in the air but nobody's talking so were all left in the dark. Besides, this letter would get censored if I did know something. Whatever it is I hope it gets over fast and we can get back to the good old USA again and pick up where we left off.

Grace I think I'm gonna go into electronics when I get home because I'm in that kind of field right now and I like it a lot and my captain said I'm a natural at it. I'm pretty sure I'll get free schooling with the GI bill they been mentioning, so it won't cost me a red cent. I'm glad to hear your studies are coming along good. I expect someday I'll be calling you Doctor Grace. Wont that be something! You said your not dating because studying takes up most of your time. But remember the old saying about all work and no play makes Johnny a dull boy. In this case though it is Grace not Johnny. I just hope you save some time for me Grace because I'm really looking forward to seeing you and being with you again. I probably shouldn't say this Grace but I think of you all the time and the things we did together and it really helps me get through these crazy days. I look at the picture of you that you gave me before I left and it gives my morale a real lift. I keep it on the wall right behind my bunk. P.S. I think the other guys are jealous.

I guess I have to end it here Grace. It went longer than I thought so I must have enjoyed writing it. The truth is I always do like writing to you and I like it even more when you write to me. As I said we seem to be busier than ever around here so Grace if you don't hear from me in a while don't worry I'll be okay.

Affectionately,

Mike'

Sometime in May of 1944, I overheard one of my newer tenants talking to Joe sweeping the hallway outside his restaurant.

"Hey, Joe, what's going on with what's-her-name, the one always lugging books around? I passed her a little while ago and she acted like she didn't even see me. Usually she gives me a smile going by."

"You mean Grace?"

"Yeah, Grace, that's her. What's her story?"

"She just got a letter?"

"So she got a letter; what's the big deal?"

"From the War Department."

"The War Department? Oh, oh, that's gotta be bad news."

"Yeah, her boyfriend was killed in action."

"Aw, that explains it."

"In Europe someplace, I think."

"Oh, yeah?"

"His name was Mike McGurty. Lived here a while back before you moved in. He was a nasty drunk, always raising hell and driving everybody nuts, but I think Grace reformed him. Never saw him sloshed again after he met her."

"Too bad. Too bad."

It was a year later, not long after Japan surrendered and the war ended, that a soldier dressed in his OD uniform with corporal stripes limped in through the front door and almost got hit in the head with the mop Huggs was swinging back and forth swabbing the floor.

"Oop, I'm sorry, soldier," Huggs said, jerking back and

almost tripping over his soap bucket.

"No harm done, buddy," the soldier said, catching his own balance. "But I wonder, can you tell me if a Miss Pulski still lives here?"

Huggs brightened. "Oh, you mean Grace. Sure, she does. Why do you want to know?"

"Can you give me her apartment number?"

"I don't know if I should. I'm not supposed to give out personal information like that."

"I'd appreciate it a lot if you would."

"Well," he said, staring at the ribbons decorating the soldier's jacket, "I guess it's OK this one time. Right upstairs on the top by your right hand side of the hall."

"Thanks, buddy," he said, starting to climb, his body tilted a little to the left.

Huggs called after him. "You must've seen lots of action to get all them ribbons, huh?"

The soldier threw him back a salute."

Grace answered his knock on her door.

"Yes?"

"Grace Pulski?"

"Yes, what can I do for you?"

"Miss Pulski, my name is Sam Arcuri. Mike McGurty and me were buddies over in England. In Africa and Italy before that. Africa's where we first hooked up."

The surprise was obvious on Grace's face as she opened the door wide. "Won't you come in, Mr. Arcuri?"

"Thank you ma'am, but you can call me Sam."

"And you may call me Grace. Won't you sit, please?" she said. "Can I get you a cup of coffee?"

"No, thanks, Grace." He sat on the edge of the couch across from the chair where she sat down. "I only have a little time before heading back to Central Terminal to catch my train." He looked at his watch. "It's been a long time since I seen my family."

"You're not from Buffalo?"

"No, ma'am. I mean, Grace. I'm from Cleveland. Ohio, you know? I got mustered out two days ago and glad to be back on good old U.S.A. soil. I been gone overseas more than two years."

"That's a long time to be away."

"Sure is. It's at least that long since I first met Mike, too. We both got shipped over to Italy from our campaign in North Africa. You see, Grace, Mike and me hit it off right away and became close friends. They call it camaraderie. We went through a lot together, especially at the battle of Anzio. We got through lucky on that one. Lots of guys didn't.

"Anyway, Grace, that's why I'm here. We made a promise, Mike and me, that if anything happened to either one of us, the other would contact our families after the war. Mike told me he never had a family worth a bag of beans he was ever close to, but he told me a lot about you and gave me your name and address. I almost feel like I know you personally. That's why I'm here... Mind if I smoke?"

"Not at all," Grace said, taking from the end table the saucer Mike always used for an ash tray. She studied Sam as she handed it over. He had a sad and weathered look about him, as if he worked in the sun all day. Short and already partially bald, he had tired eyes, flat and lifeless, as if they had seen too much suffering and wanted to close.

He lit his cigarette and leaned back with the saucer on his lap.

"You see, Grace, after me and Mike saw so much action in Italy, the brass must have figured we deserved a rest, along with a bunch of other dogfaces, of course, so we got shipped to England. We didn't know it then, but the army likes to pull dirty tricks. Instead of getting a rest like they promised, they ran us ragged training for the big invasion of Europe."

"You mean D Day."

"Yeah, but we didn't know that name or exactly where it was then. That came about six months after Anzio. We were kept in the dark— everybody was, actually, except the top brass, naturally. It was late April and colder'n heck yet and about five or six weeks to go before D Day. They worked us till we were in the best shape we were ever in or ever likely to be in. Well, finally, the day come when we had to go out on a practice run, a pretty darn serious one, too, with live ammo. Later they called it a pre-invasion exercise with the name Operation Tiger. All that to prepare us for the big one which, as I'm sure you remember, came about six weeks later exactly on June sixth last year."

He took a drag on his cigarette and blew the smoke off to the side. "Well, long story short, the krauts got wind of our operation ahead of time and were laying for us. We weren't far out in the channel, not really all that far from France, either, where the big invasion was set to be somewhere along the coast, which as I said we didn't know at the time. Then, out of nowhere, there they were, waiting to blow us the hell out of the water. We were sitting ducks caught unawares. Sunk a bunch of our LSTs and killed a whole lot of guys, close to a thousand, I later heard. It was a real bust."

Grace watched his face distort with his words, his eyes dark and far away, as if seeing it all over again.

"Some of them got shot up and killed, others drowned in freezing water. Never had a chance. Nobody saw it coming. Nobody."

Grace felt her heart pounding. She had been informed that Mike was 'killed in action,' but she never knew how he was killed.

"And Mike was one of them?"

"Oh, no," Sam said, as if waking from a bad dream. "Mike never got hit. Never drowned, neither."

Grace looked bewildered. "Then how—"

"No, you see, Grace, or maybe you never knew, but Mike was a great swimmer. Once, I saw him swim across a river in Italy where we set up camp. Must've been a mile to the other side and another mile back. Anyway, once his LST was hit, he swam for his life. I don't know how far it was, but he made it under his own power in the black of night, except for the explosions and boats on fire lighting up the sky. I was lucky; my craft was hit and burning and we lost maybe a dozen guys, but we managed to stay afloat and limp back to shore." He paused to take another drag on his cigarette before snuffing it out in the saucer.

Puzzled, Grace looked at him. "Well, if he made it to—"

Sam raised his hand. "Lots of bodies washed up later, but earlier when I saw somebody laying on the beach I knew right away it was Mike. Nobody else could've made that swim. He was conscious, but barely. You see, Grace, the water in the English Channel is ice cold in April, maybe all year round, for all I know, but it did its job on Mike. Naturally he stripped himself naked so he wouldn't be dragged under by his clothes and gear. When I saw his whole body was turned blue, I knew...well, I knew, that's all."

Sam choked up with his words. "Mike froze to death, Grace, but it took Mother Nature to kill him, not an ambush by a bunch of lousy, sneaking krauts." He snuffled and ran the back of his hand under his nose. "I knelt down next to him and he motioned for a cigarette with his fingers, which could hardly move. I lit one and put it between his lips. Mike didn't have any voice left to talk with. He tried whispering something, but I think he was hallucinating and I could only catch a couple of mumbled words like 'sister' and 'doctor.' I guess he wanted me to call one. I wish I could've heard it all. He smiled, then his eyes closed and the cigarette fell out of his mouth. I said a prayer over him as best I could, not being all that religious myself, and that was it. Nothing more I could do. Nothing more anybody could do."

Grace's eyes flooded with tears.

"Mike loved you, Grace. I think those were the last words he tried to say. In fact, I'd bet my life on it. You were what kept him going. He was a good buddy. Mike didn't have much to leave behind except his shaving stuff, an envelope for you, and your picture he kept pinned on the wall behind his bunk wherever we were stationed." He drew the envelope and photograph out of his pocket and handed it across to her. "You can see all the pin holes in it. It's pretty small picture, too. Mike always said he was going to have it blown up when we got back stateside."

He looked at his watch. "Well, I got to shove off if I want to catch my train." He stood up and moved to the door. "It was a pleasure meeting you, Grace, but I'm sorry it had to be this way. I wish things could've worked out different for you and Mike, I really do. Anyway, good luck."

"Good luck to you, too, Sam," she said, seeing him to the door. "My best to you and your family. I know they're going to be thrilled having you back home after all this time. And thank you so much for coming. You have no idea how much this means to me."

Grace watched him limp down the stairs. When she heard the front door close she went back inside and sat in her chair, the chair Mike first sat in when she and Huggs dragged him in drunk off the stairway so long ago. She put her head back, opened the envelope and removed the letter inside, which began with, 'In case of my death...' It was short and to the point, making her beneficiary to his life insurance. It was signed and dated by Mike and the name of an army captain.

Grace set it aside and picked up her photo, seeing again the pin holes tattooed across the top. She turned it over and saw written in his handwriting, 'My girl Grace,' with a penciled drawing of a heart with an arrow through it.

She fondled the picture in her palm and pressed it against her cheek. "Oh, Mike," she whispered, "Mike."

Chapter 41

Here then is the last chapter of my stories. Again, it was a few months after the end of WWII, when I overheard Bill, one of my tenants, talking to Sal, another tenant. They were having coffee downstairs in Joe's restaurant. Bill had the Courier Express newspaper spread out on the table.

"Hey, Sal, look at this, will you?"

"What's that, Bill?" Sal said, looking over Bill's shoulder.

"Didn't there used to be a colored guy who used to live here a while back? I heard rumors about him having a white wife. Got himself in a lot of trouble somehow."

"Yeah, yeah," Sal said. "I remember. It was a big scandal. I moved in here right about that time. Made a hell of a scene when the cops drug him out of here in cuffs. A whole lot of yelling and screaming going on. It was pure pandemonium, I'll tell you that. I was right there, standing right there by the stairs, almost next to him when one cop bashed him across the head with his billy club. I forgot his name. Something like… like…"

"Says here, former Buffalonian, Jeb Morrison.

"Yeah, that was it, Jeb… Jeb Morrison... yeah, right."

"The way I heard it he was an escaped convict they tracked down here."

"Naw, Bill, that was just a rumor. The fact is he attacked some white woman, and some shyster lawyer helped him beat the rap. At least that's the way I heard it or read it or something."

"Well, here's a picture of him, his wife and their kid. Take a gander," Bill said, raising the newspaper off the table. "The little girl looks white, like the woman."

"Yeah, but she was really black. Or probably a mulatto."

Bill read haltingly: "Says here he was one of ... a...an... elite... group of colored pilots in the war. They called them the...Tus...Tuskegee pilots." He looked up. "Elite. Don't that mean like somebody special or high class? I never heard of no black Tuskegee outfit, myself, but I guess it's true they had one, if the paper says so... Hey, look at the sharp leather jacket he's got on, will you? Says here he won himself a whole bunch of medals, too."

"Lemme get a better look, Bill." Sal bent over closer, nodding, and called over his shoulder. "Hey, Joe, come here and take a look at this, will you?"

Straightening his grease-spotted half-apron, Joe ambled over on his stubby legs. "What'samatter, something wrong with the sandwich?"

"No, Joe, it's this," Sal said, rattling and folding the paper as he took it and raised it up so Joe could see it. "Ain't this a picture of the colored guy who used to live here? Looks a little different from what I remember. His name was Jeb, Jeb Morrison. It says so right here under the picture. It's been what, five, six years ago they drug him out of here in cuffs? That's a long time ago. I barely remember, but I'd bet my life it's him."

Joe took the paper and brought it close to his eyes. "Well, I'll be...that's Jeb, all right. Yep, same guy. Damned if it ain't! That's his wife, too. I recognize her. A real doll. I don't remember nothing about the kid, though, or even if they had one." He shook his head in wonder, almost disbelief.

"It was in all the papers and everybody was talking about it for weeks, maybe months." He slapped the paper. "How do you like that? The guy starts out being a criminal with cops crawling all over the place, and here he ends up a hero, an actual war hero with a bunch of medals. Who could believe it!"

Joe pulled himself up straight. "And he lived right here, right in this building. No joke, I'm telling you, he lived upstairs on the second floor." He poked his finger in the air. "Almost right above this very exact spot where I'm standing now." His chest puffed out. "And I knew him and he knew me personally, actually by our first names. We talked together lots of times about… about stuff." He raised his right hand. "God strike me dead right where I'm standing if I'm lying." He looked up and shook his head in amazement. "Ain't that something? Jeb Morrison, a genu-wine airplane pilot and an honest-to-God war hero. Now ain't that just something!"

One last note: Huggs still has his itching powder waiting for the perfect victim.

About the Authors

James A. Costa is a retired West Seneca, New York, high school English teacher, and the author of a number of novels, including *The Boy Who Made Music; Victim; Portal in Time;* and *Murder on Mulberry Street.*

Frances R. Schmidt is a retired D'Youville University administrator and author of an historical novel: *Fred: Buffalo Building of Dreams; Forever Violet,* and two job search books. In 2021 NYC Big Book award recognized *Fred: Buffalo Building of Dreams* as a Distinguished Favorite for the category of historical fiction. In 2022 the Independent Press award recognized *Fred: Buffalo Building of Dreams* as a Distinguished Favorite in the category historical fiction.

In 2023 the authors collaborated on *Forever Violet,* a novel honoring the life and legacy of Frances' mother, Lillie R. Sharon. In 2024 the novel won a NYC Big Book award as a distinguished favorite in the category of Young Adult Fiction.

In 2024 the authors collaborated on *Accidental Virgin,* a Romance novel, that was published in 2025.

Additional information is available on her website:

https://francesrschmidt.com